THE BONE HILL

A DETECTIVE DEANS MYSTERY

JAMES D MORTAIN

MANVERS PUBLISHING

ALSO BY JAMES D MORTAIN

DETECTIVE DEANS MYSTERIES

1: STORM LOG-0505

2: DEAD BY DESIGN

3: THE BONE HILL

———————

DI CHILCOTT MYSTERIES

1: DEAD RINGER

———————

THE BONE HILL

A DETECTIVE DEANS MYSTERY

by

JAMES D MORTAIN

For my beautiful daughter, Gracie.
Live life to the full and dream big every single day, no matter how
inconceivable it may seem.

PROLOGUE

Archie Rowland drove his trusted twenty-year-old Volvo estate back through the still blackness of the country lanes towards his home, seven miles from the nearest civilised settlement. He had lived with his wife at the ancient land holding for three decades. He loved the unspoilt solace of the moors, but his wife, Jen, had always favoured town life and discussions about moving back to a more vibrant way of living were never far from her lips. It was no doubt different for her; she was at home all day while he was generally at the North Devon Infirmary, or attending pathology meetings with his peers, or with the senior police staff in Exeter. That was a journey he hated and refused to drive. Instead, he would take the excruciatingly slow, but delightfully scenic route between Barnstaple and Exeter by 'snail train', as he called it.

This night, Archie drove with a mechanical vacancy as his troubled thoughts fogged his mind. His gloved fingers fidgeted on the steering wheel as he took the final left hand bend and slowed on approach to his farm entrance. His wife had already illuminated the outside lamps and he quickly checked the clock on the dashboard to ensure that he was still good to his word.

His Volvo clunked and spluttered to a stop and he fumbled with his old leather briefcase and keys. The front door to the house opened for him, and stood in a sheer black gown and glistening jewellery was his beautiful wife of forty-one-years that very day, Jen.

'Thank you, Archie,' she said checking over her shoulder at the antique Grandfather clock ticking precisely in the hallway nearby.

'Yes, well,' Archie said. 'A promise is a promise.'

Jen leaned towards him and gave him an air kiss near both ears. 'Good day, love?' she asked.

Archie's bushy eyebrows twitched, but he smiled for Jen's benefit. 'Yes, yes,' he said, placing his briefcase behind the door next to the Welsh dresser.

'Is fifteen minutes long enough for you?' Jen asked. 'I took the liberty of ordering a taxi, not knowing whether you would make it in time, or not.'

Archie nodded and smiled.

'At least you can have a nice glass of something if some-body else is driving,' Jen said.

'Fifteen minutes. Right, okay.' Archie made his way through the hallway towards the stairs with his wife in his wake informing him a fresh shirt and pressed suit were waiting for him on the bed.

He reached the top of the stairs and paused outside of his youngest daughter's bedroom. His shoulders sank and he looked down at his feet before continuing on to his room, where he quickly freshened up and dressed in the clothes Jen had prepared for him.

The sound of crunching shingle and the flash of headlamps alerted him to the taxi arriving outside. He shook his head, they were never *on time*, probably due to the fact they were so far out of town.

'It's here,' Jen shouted up the stairs.

Tying the knot of his tie as he walked down the stairs, he saw Jen waiting in the hallway.

'When are we going to do away with all these Christmas decorations?' he commented as Jen smoothed down his lapels and ran her thumbs around the back of his collar. 'We only did it for the kids' benefit,' he said.

'Now shush that nonsense,' Jen said. 'We have this every year, and every year you get the same response; Christmas isn't just for the children, it's a celebration, a time for giving, a time for loving—'

'Oh, God, you're not going to sing *that song* again, are you?'

Jen laughed, opened the door and waved across to the taxi driver. 'Come on, Mr Grumpy,' she said. 'Let's go and have a nice meal with our children.'

It was almost midnight by the time they took the return lift home. Their two eldest daughters had met them at the hotel with their respective partners and gone their own way home. Archie's youngest daughter was spending the weekend with her boyfriend, but at least the offer had been there for her to join them. She always distanced herself from the family engagements despite the fact they had done everything they could to make her feel as wanted as their biological children. Archie didn't push, he'd learnt the hard way through her adolescence and knew she was best left well alone.

'You've been unusually quiet tonight, darling,' Jen said taking Archie's hand in hers as the taxi neared their home.

Archie looked down to her hand and twitched his brow.

'Something's bothering you, isn't it?' Jen said, squeezing his hand.

'Oh, it's nothing,' Archie said.

'It must be *something*?' Jen pressed. 'I haven't seen you like this for years.'

Archie coughed behind closed lips and shifted his bottom in the seat. He looked directly at the rear view mirror into the driver's eyes, which focussed on the road ahead, and the muted sound of late-night radio was playing in the front. Archie dropped his head. 'Today's job,' he said softly. 'Well, it was quite... distressing. That's all.' He released Jen's hand and centralised the knot of his tie.

'Would you like to discuss it?' Jen asked.

Archie glanced at the driver's reflection once again. 'Yes. We need to. We *have* to.' He faced his wife with watery eyes. 'But not here.'

Archie paid the driver and gave an extra ten-pound note as a Christmas tip. He walked with his wife to the door and assisted her with her coat.

'Would you like a nightcap, darling,' Jen asked.

'We need to talk about this, Jen,' Archie said.

'Can I get myself a drink first, I am sure it can wait.'

Archie turned Jen to face him. 'Please,' he said. 'I need to tell someone...'

'Okay, okay. Come on, you can tell me anything.'

Archie looked away.

'Arch, what is it?' The volume in Jen's voice increased.

Archie walked into the lounge and stood in the middle of the room. Jen, wide-eyed followed silently behind.

'Sit down,' he said.

Jen did as requested and perched on the lip of the luxurious leather sofa.

Archie blinked quickly several times and swallowed away

4

his anxiety. 'Jen,' he said, 'Do you recall when the children were younger, I taught them suturing. Do you remember?'

'How could I possibly forget, I was forever finding rotting chicken breasts and banana skins lying about the place. Disgusting—'

'That's right,' Archie said softly, 'We practised on chicken breasts and bananas.' He dipped his head, hesitated and then lifted his sombre eyes to meet his wife's. 'I saw something today on a murdered victim that I haven't seen in a long time.'

Jen stared back.

'An unusual suturing technique, seldom, if ever, used in general surgical practice...' He waited to see if his wife was going to say something. She didn't.

'Jen, there's only one person who can replicate that technique – I know that to be a fact, because I invented it.'

Jen didn't speak.

'And the last time somebody else tried it, to my knowledge,' Archie said, 'they were stitching chicken breasts.'

Jen's eyes were unblinking. 'That was over fifteen years ago, Archie. Are you trying to tell me that no one else is capable of copying those stitches?'

Archie nodded.

'Are you certain?'

'It was something I experimented with at Med School,' Archie said. 'I was forever trying new ideas, pushing the limits of my abilities, and I created a method of stitching that was strong, clean, but time consuming and expensive.' He narrowed his eyes and moved over to the sofa sitting down next to his wife, taking her hand in his. 'I've thought about this, Jen. I should inform the police.'

Jen tugged her hand away from his. 'You most certainly will not,' she snapped.

'I must,' Archie said, his voice fractured.

'Can't you get rid of this body? Incinerate it, or something?'

'No,' Archie whispered. 'I'm afraid this is going to be one job that simply won't go away.'

'Why not?' Jen barked.

'Because the victim was the wife of a serving police officer.' He looked deeply into her eyes. 'And she was beheaded…'

Jen recoiled and sat back against the sofa.

'And the sutures I talk of… sealed a surgical wound to her womb and the decapitated body of her unborn son.'

Jen covered her mouth with a hand and dashed out of the room.

Archie didn't try to follow. There was nothing more he could say that would make the problem go away. He knew Jen would return when she was ready, and he didn't have to wait long for that to happen.

She searched his face for answers, but Archie had none. 'What do we do?' she uttered.

Archie rubbed the back of his neck with slow and deliberate passes. 'I need to complete a report,' he said. 'The police will expect one, especially given the nature of the deaths.' He saw Jen squirm and withdraw. 'There are only three people that know about that stitching,' he said reaching out and holding Jen by the rounded tips of her shoulders. 'And that includes you and me.' He gently guided his wife backwards towards the sofa, his hands remaining on her shoulders directing her movement. He gently pushed down and Jen took the seat once again.

'Promise me we won't talk about this again,' he breathed.

Tears welled in her eyes and she shook her head. 'Never,' she whispered.

'Very well,' Archie said. 'Then I will do the *right* thing.'

CHAPTER ONE

Ingrid Andrews loved this time of year. It wasn't for the lack of tourists, or "grockles" as they were colloquially referred to, nor was it for the fact she could park pretty much wherever she wanted. It was because the North Devon coastline in the depths of winter made her feel *alive* with energy. The rumble of the Atlantic Ocean, the flat expanse of the golden-brown sands, the biting nip of the onshore breeze – and it was a haven for dog lovers, like her and her faithful Springer Spaniel, Nelson.

This day was perfect; powder blue skies, a low-slung sun, vast marbled sands and the gentle lap of an incoming tide. Ingrid sloshed through the milky fringe of water, her ruby-red Hunter wellies leaving deep patterned trenches in her wake, only to be licked away with each gradual encroach of the tide. Small beige-coloured shellfish rattled against one another as they rolled back and forth on the leading edge, and tiny waders and sanderlings scampered away as Nelson careered through the shallows as if it was the first time he'd seen the sea. It wasn't. They came every chance Ingrid had, come rain or shine.

'Go on, boy,' Ingrid yelled, hurling another soggy tennis ball through the air with a colour-coordinated ball-launcher to match her wellington boots. Nelson needed no second invitation and sprinted off like a guided missile towards his prize.

Ingrid breathed in the salty freshness of the day. This beat her usual Monday morning slog as a checkout assistant at the local Morrisons superstore. She had pulled all of the busiest shifts over the Christmas period and as a reward for her efforts she had been given a few unexpected days off by her unusually festive boss.

Nelson returned – his liver and white coat matted with Demerara brown sand. He dropped the ball in front of her feet and nudged it closer with his nose.

'Come on, Nelson,' she said dotting the ball with the end of the launcher. 'We need to head back the other way, boy.'

Nelson planted his front feet and prepared to spring back into action. Ingrid giggled. He was like a nine-year-old pup.

'Again?'

She looked briefly at her watch.

'Is nothing going to tire you out today? Okay – one last throw, but we need to head back.' She gave Nelson a hard stare and then tossed the ball into the shallows. Nelson darted off and Ingrid turned to make tracks back to the slipway.

She watched the foamy water lap over her toes and her mind turned to her poor mother, recently diagnosed with Alzheimer's disease. She would have loved the serenity of this place, but she was in Birmingham, in a nursing home. She had tried time and again to convince her to move into one of the local homes, but Mum was as stubborn as they came and refused to leave.

'Nelson,' Ingrid shouted. 'Come on, boy. Time to go home.' She didn't need to turn about, the stiff wind was at her face.

She continued onwards, but strangely, Nelson didn't come back.

'Nelson. Nelson. Come on boy let's go home.' Ingrid stopped and looked back. 'Nelson. Nelson.'

She scanned the beach but Nelson was nowhere in sight. She looked up towards the pebble ridge, but due to the low tide, it was too far away to see anything clearly. Checking her watch again, she doubled back and called out Nelson's name as she went. Then she saw him in the waters beyond the shallows, a hundred metres ahead.

'Nelson, come here,' she shouted sharply. 'Nelson come.' But whatever Nelson was up to, he had no intention of returning on command.

'Come on Nelson, fetch your ball.'

As she got closer, she could see Nelson was out of his depth, his nose barely above the waterline and although the waves were tame by Sandymere Bay's standards, they were still buffeting little Nelson around.

Ingrid stepped deeper into the water, now inches from the top of her boots. An energetic wave came rapidly towards her. She tried to retreat, but water splashed above her knees and slopped into her wellies.

'Bollocks,' she spat. 'Come on, Nelson, that's enough now. I don't care if you can't find your ball. Mummy is wet through.'

She padded back towards the beach, her feet soaked and frozen from the eight-degree waters. Then she saw Nelson's tennis ball washed up on the sand ahead of her.

She bent down with a mumbled expletive and picked it up. 'Here it is, Nelson. Here it is. Come on Nelson. Come and get your sodding ball.'

Nelson had other ideas. The waves were pushing him closer to the shore and Ingrid could sense his determination to retrieve something from within the water. She trudged to the dry sand; her feet absolutely soaked and removed her wellies, one at a time, pouring the seawater out onto the sand. Nelson was now back on his feet, his jaws clamped around a submerged object, his head tugging with single-minded eagerness.

Ingrid could see a much larger wave approaching that would undoubtedly engulf Nelson. She quickly returned her boots to her feet and ran back into the water, but she was too late and water crashed against Nelson and he was lost to sight. Ingrid held her breath and frantically searched the top of the water for her little dog.

'Nelson,' she shouted and started to run deeper into the sea, her legs and feet moving as fast as the thick waters would allow.

'Nelson. Nelson,' she screamed, now wading beyond knee depth. 'Oh my God, Nelson.' Her legs were heavy and weighed down completely by her water-filled wellington boots.

'Nelson.' Her voice was now frantic.

She looked around anxiously for help, but she was still alone.

'Oh, God,' she wept, raking the waters aside with her hands, and then she saw him bob back to the surface.

'Nelson!'

She thrust her legs through the surf, the cold water no longer registering with her brain. Her dog was just feet away.

Ingrid reached out – all she needed was a scruff of fur to hold. He was now tantalizingly close, but each time she lunged forwards, another wave took him away from her desperate grasp.

She took another step, the surf splashed into her chest and face. She timed her reach and caught Nelson by his hind leg.

His weight took her by surprise and pulled her off her feet, face first into the chilly waters.

She thrashed out with her legs and felt the seabed beneath her feet. She still had her dog's leg in her grip and heaved him back, lifting her own head above the water line. Gasping for breath, she planted her feet and got a second hand around her dog. She turned for the shore and heaved him slowly inwards with each laboured step. The briny waters stung her eyes and she struggled to see if Nelson was alive or dead. Either way, his jaws were still connected to the heavy object his jaws were clamped around.

Finding an inner strength, Ingrid dragged Nelson back to knee depth. She reached for his head, lifting his face clear of the water, dislodging the attached object that at first disappeared and then bobbed clear of the waterline into view.

Ingrid took a sudden intake of breath and fell backwards. Water covered her face and gushed into her open mouth. She choked as water went down her throat and she let go of Nelson, her legs kicking wildly in a desperate attempt to get out of the water as quickly as possible. She clawed at the sand and dragged herself clear.

Her eyes fixed wide on a spot in the water. She coughed and at the same time vomited onto the sand beside her, and dragged her body clear of the unpleasant slick.

She composed herself and lifted her body onto her elbows to gain a clearer view of the water. She felt her heart pounding through the saturated and heavy layers of clothing.

The object inched ever closer with each surge of the waves.

Ingrid dragged her legs up to her chest, and rolled onto her hands and knees. Her neck was frozen stiff and wouldn't allow her to look in any direction other than directly ahead, as the object scuffed and slewed against the sandy seabed.

She slowly rose to her feet, her eyes glued to what she

could now clearly see was a human arm floating on the surface.

She stepped hesitantly back into the water and shuffled towards it. The hand on the arm was curled, as if it had once held a honeydew melon. Her breathing accelerated, as she got closer. She bent forwards but then stopped. She inhaled a lung full of chilled air, puffed out her cheeks and grabbed the stiff hand.

The arm was weighty, and as it came towards her, suddenly rolled beneath the water and the connected torso bobbed to the surface.

Ingrid jumped backwards and fell into the water once again, her face stricken with fright. Motionless, she couldn't tear her eyes off the body, now bouncing gently on top of the passing waters. She picked up an object in her peripheral vision and turned her head like it was on a fine-tooth ratchet, though her eyes stayed transfixed to the corpse moving ever closer. The realisation of what was to her side broke the spell of the dead body and she looked away.

There in three inches of water, Nelson lay on his side, his little legs unmoving and stiff.

CHAPTER TWO

Detective Andrew Deans looked himself up and down in the full-length bedroom mirror. He brushed a hand over his shoulder and straightened his black tie. It was less than five weeks since the train crash and he was still tolerating the bulky orthopaedic boot on his leg. Thankfully, he was able to remove the boot and place it over the top of his freshly laundered suit.

He tilted his head, closed his eyes and drew a long slow breath from the sombre air.

'Alexa,' he said to his bedside companion. 'Play me some happy music.' The small round smart-box came to life with a single rotation of lilac light.

"I am sorry," the electronic voice said. "Another device is currently streaming music. Would you like to stream from this device instead?"

Deans looked deeply into the eyes of his own reflection. There was only one *Alexa* device in the house, other than the application on his phone, which was inside his trouser pocket. Unless…

'Yes, Alexa,' Deans said excitedly. 'Repeat the last played song.'

He waited for the music to start and searched his face as the hairs on the back of his neck responded to the opening notes of the song being played through the small speaker. He closed his eyes and dropped his chin to his chest as Jennifer Hudson's voice broke into the introduction of *Golden Slumbers*.

A faint smile ghosted his lips and he remained unmoving, until every note and word of Maria's favourite song had finished. He looked up at the ceiling, tears pooling in his eyes. 'I love you, Maria,' he mouthed.

Detective Sergeant Mick Savage arrived on time with a gentle tap at the door. Some wonders never ceased to amaze Deans.

'Hello, Deano. How are you bearing up, buddy?' Savage asked, shaking Deans' hand and making his way through to the kitchen where he helped himself to the kettle. 'You look very smart, mate. Very smart.'

'Shit the bed, Mick?'

'I know, I know. You probably expected me to be fashionably late, but today I have a duty... to you.' Savage frowned, as he looked closer at Deans' face. 'Are you sure you are all right, Deano?'

Deans wiped moisture from the corner of his eye. 'Yeah. I'm fine, thanks.'

'Great,' Savage said looking at his watch. 'Time for a bacon butty.'

Deans turned away. 'Not for me, thanks.'

Savage hesitated. 'No, you're probably right. I'd only get ketchup down my front or something. How about a brew? Fancy a quick coffee?'

Deans nodded and Savage took two mugs from the kitchen cupboards and rummaged around for the instant coffee.

Deans took himself off to the living room.

'Did you sleep?' Savage asked joining Deans, holding out a coffee mug.

Deans shrugged and took the drink.

'Still having the dreams?'

Deans sipped and nodded.

'Should you see someone about it?'

Deans raised a brow.

'I'm just saying, Deano—'

'Nobody can fix what I've got.'

Savage didn't attempt to answer and they both sat silently finishing their drinks until the transport arrived.

They pulled off the main road and drove between the large pillars of the open-gated entrance. Deans looked directly ahead over the shoulder of the driver. A large crowd was already gathered at the front of the chapel and a smaller clutch of media photographers and TV cameras were camped in a line, two deep, and kept at respectful arm's length by several of Deans' uniformed colleagues. Interest in Deans' *story* had piqued following a mention the week before on Breakfast TV by Piers Morgan, who sent Deans the nation's thoughts and prayers. If it had been just the train crash, the media would have moved on by now and Deans wouldn't have had to become a relative recluse. But Maria's plight along with Deans' lone survival from his wrecked carriage had sent the world's media into a feeding frenzy, and now, everybody wanted a piece of him.

His wife's parents, Graham and Joyce, were sitting alongside him. Deans adjusted the knot of his tie for the fourth time that journey and closed his eyes as the head of the procession slowed to a stop beneath a vine encrusted chapel entrance. The rear doors opened simultaneously and an arm reached towards him with an encouraging hook of the elbow. Cool air invaded the warm confines of the stretch limo. Deans looked towards his mother-in-law, who was being assisted up from her seat by a man wearing a long dark trench coat and sporting an equally long face.

Deans steeled himself with a deep breath. *This is it*. He looked out at the apologetic faces peering back his way. He had decided not to wear dark glasses, even though the sun was blindingly low in the cool blue sky, and now he was beginning to regret that decision.

Deans held his eyes shut for a soothing moment and wished he didn't have to go through with this. He leaned forwards and took the outstretched arm, his heart pounding beneath his suit jacket. He stood as tall as his body would allow and stared straight ahead. As he stepped away from the limo he became aware of the subtle backward movement of bodies in his peripheral vision, like a parting tide, and as he edged forwards, the ocean of guests filed back in behind him. He could see mouths moving, accepted outstretched hands and stood solid to the body hugs, but he was barely aware of what was going on around him.

He locked eyes with Mick Savage, who came forwards and took Deans gently by the elbow. He said nothing, but right then, *nothing* was just what Deans needed and he followed Savage without question. The others filed silently behind into the large acoustic room. The scuff and shuffle of leather clad feet and the occasional sob or blow of a nose was all that could be heard.

The head operative of the funeral procession stood in front of Deans with a knowing, sympathetic smile. He offered Deans a solitary nod and waited for Joyce and Graham Byrne to shuffle in by his side. He caught Graham staring at him – Deans was sure they still blamed him for what happened to Maria. Savage released Deans' arm and left him with a gentle pat on the shoulder.

'Okay?' the funeral director said.

Deans nodded and the funeral director turned his back.

Deans stepped slowly forwards and the sombre notes of a string quartet filled the empty room with Barber's, *Adagio for Strings*. Deans chomped down and blinked tears from his lashes.

They followed the run of deep red carpet, being led at the front by the bald-headed director who walked with stiff purposeful limbs as the music got louder.

The pews were positioned in an L-shape. Deans was shown to the front row pew at the top of the 'L' facing a choir on the other side of the room. He took his seat and Graham sat alongside. Deans fixed his gaze on the stainless steel cradle positioned centrally, several metres directly in front of him, as mourners respectfully took their places. Deans did not try to mask or stifle his grief, and as the music continued, he noticed heads turning towards the entrance.

He tried to turn, but his neck would not allow him, and as the haunting music drew to a close, Maria's wicker coffin was placed gently onto the supporting frame before him.

Reverend Simms addressed the room.

'Dear friends,' he said with outstretched arms. 'We come together at the turn of a new year, on this saddest of days, to pay our final respects to our beloved, Maria Elizabeth Caitlin Deans. Our community and many others have been deeply affected by the sudden and horrific taking of our dear daughter, wife, colleague and friend.'

Deans' blurred eyes grew heavy, but they refused to look

away from the coffin. *If I could swap places, my love, I gladly would.*

Reverend Simms continued speaking, but Deans was taking nothing in, and then in the corner of his eye he saw the fluttering wings of a white butterfly. Deans drew his head back and parted his lips. Others in the chapel began to notice and within thirty seconds, the ripple of whispers had reached the furthest most extremities of the room.

Reverend Simms stopped speaking and watched with seeming wonderment as the creature landed on the head of the cask and brought its graceful wings to a rest.

Maria, Deans mouthed and met the gaze of Reverend Simms, who allowed the congregation a brief instant of comment before continuing with the service. Deans stared at the small creature, which remained at the head of the coffin until the conclusion of the ceremony.

Deans was prompted to his feet, along with his in-laws by the Reverend, and as the choir sang *Ave Maria*, they slowly followed the casket outside through the centre of the mourners. As they reached the outer doors, Deans noticed the bank of media and felt his top lip curl into a snarl.

Savage hurried alongside him. 'Ignore them, Deano,' he said softly in his ear. 'Our boys and girls will keep them at bay, don't worry about that.'

Deans then noticed a man with a handheld video camera standing alone and separate to the others. He didn't appear to have an identity lanyard and there was no urgency to his actions, unlike the mob of photographers and reporters.

Deans stopped walking and squinted to focus. The man appeared to register Deans' attention and slowly lowered the camera from his face, and, motionless, stared back at Deans.

'Come on, Deano,' Savage said, grabbing Deans' arm. 'Come on, mate. Leave them.'

Deans took several steps away with Savage, but kept his eyes on the man with the small video camera.

The chilled air cut through his skin and Deans lifted the collar of his trench coat, tightened the scarf around his neck and turned away. He felt a tug on his arm – it was Denise Moon and she looked at him with a reassuring smile.

'Hello, Denise,' Deans said. 'Sorry… I didn't know you were coming.'

Denise squeezed his hand. 'I'm here for you,' she said. She looked behind. 'I don't know if you would have noticed, but Sergeant Jackson is also here somewhere.'

Deans shook his head. He really hadn't taken in any members of the congregation, if anything, he wanted to avoid eye contact with them.

Up ahead, the coffin bearers came to a halt and Deans saw an opening in the ground and the pea-green surface of artificial turf on either side. Mourners slowly squeezed together in considerate silence, Deans next to Maria's mother and father. He had lost his own parents years ago, and now, Maria's parents were the only family he had. He turned to Joyce, her face was shattered and bereft. He reached for her hand and after a moment's hesitation, she took it.

As the Reverend gave his final blessings, Deans, for the first time, looked around those gathered. DS Jackson was looking right back at him. Jackson was the obtusely difficult skipper of the Major Crime Investigation Team in Devon. They hadn't seen eye-to-eye ever since Deans had been seconded to Devon for the Amy Poole murder investigation, but it had recently become clear to Deans that there was far more to Jackson than the asshole he portrayed.

Jackson extended Deans a nod. Deans reciprocated and then looked back down to the grave as tears once again dropped from his cheeks with each measured lower of Maria's coffin.

Maria's mother and father were the first to approach the graveside. Joyce kissed a rose, dropped it into the pit and fell hysterically into the arms of her husband.

It was Deans' turn to approach the edge of the grave. He felt everyone's eyes bearing down upon him. He wiped his nose with a handkerchief, crouched down, and took a fist full of dry dirt. He ground the granules in his fist and bowed his head. *I won't stop until I've found all of you,* he promised Maria silently. *I know you are still with me.* He drew his hand to his lips, kissed his curled fingers and scattered the soil onto the surface of the casket like small marbles. He closed his eyes for a moment and again spoke silently to Maria; *Love is forever. Vengeance is now.*

CHAPTER THREE

Deans noticed DS Jackson turn away, one hand covering his ear while he attempted to hear the caller on his mobile phone. They were now at the wake in a pub about a mile from the chapel. Deans could count on both hands the number of times he had been to a wake at this particular pub, but never for a second imagined that his wife would one day be the mourned.

He studied Jackson for a moment and then he saw something that made his heart pound; Jackson lifted his head and as he spoke to the caller, he slowly turned and looked Deans straight in the eye with unease. Jackson turned away and made a hasty retreat for an outside door.

Deans apologised to the people surrounding him, placed his half-empty pint glass down on the table and followed Jackson out through the door, into the cold, still air.

Jackson was on the other side of the smoking area with his back to Deans, who closed the door quietly so that Jackson would not know he was there.

'Okay, okay,' Jackson said impatiently. 'I'll give my excuses and leave immediately. Take a statement from the witness and you'd better inform the DCI that we've got another one.'

Jackson ended the call, twisted around and saw Deans facing him. His shoulders tightened and he coughed in an attempt to hide the tail end of the phone conversation.

'Alright, Deans?' he said.

'Another what?' Deans asked.

Jackson's eyes wandered around the patio tiles. 'It's nothing,' he said. 'But I'm afraid I have to go.'

'I heard you,' Deans said.

Jackson rubbed the side of his nose and gave off an insincere smile.

'There's another murder... isn't there?'

Deans noticed the slightest of twitches in Jackson's eye. He was right, there was another.

Jackson chuckled quietly and shook his head as he moved to pass Deans, all teeth and bullshit.

'It's not related,' he said.

'What isn't?'

Jackson stopped beside Deans' shoulder. His steel-blue eyes cutting deep.

'You don't need this, son,' he said. 'It's not your problem.'

'I *need* justice. It *is* my problem.'

'And you will get that. In time.'

'Remember who you are talking to. We both know anything could happen between now and the court case.'

Jackson pinched the bridge of his hooked and slightly off-centred nose.

'Tell me,' Deans said impatiently.

Jackson snorted.

'Tell me,' Deans said again, this time louder.

Jackson jogged his head. 'Okay.' He looked around Deans' face with narrow eyes. 'Another body has been washed up today,' he said. The tendons in his neck tightened and he stared into space beyond Deans' shoulder. 'At Sandymere Bay.'

'I'm coming with you,' Deans said.

'No, you're not.'

Deans gripped Jackson's forearm. 'This isn't over for me, just because I buried my wife today. It's not over by a long stretch.'

Jackson sniffed and looked down at Deans' hand clamped around his forearm.

'I can help you,' Deans said, 'like you can't imagine.'

'I know,' Jackson whispered. 'But—'

'No buts,' Deans interrupted. 'I'm going inside to find Denise and we'll follow you back down to Devon.'

Jackson's lips parted and he gazed at Deans. 'It doesn't sound pleasant,' he said, '…the job.'

Deans released his hand from Jackson's arm. 'I need to do this.'

'Shouldn't you ask your supervisor?'

'No. I'm off work on compassionate grounds.'

Jackson's harsh stare softened. 'Okay,' he said.

'Okay?' Deans repeated.

'I'll wait for you at Torworthy nick. I'll get the lowdown from the guys on the ground, and by the time you arrive, we should know a bit more.'

Jackson held the door wide for Deans to hobble through. Denise Moon was already waiting for them in the narrow corridor. Deans beckoned her over to them.

'We need to go back to Devon, right now,' he said. 'There's another body.'

'What?' Denise said.

'I'll be on my way,' Jackson said. He held out his hand and Deans shook it.

'I'm really sorry,' Jackson said. 'About all of this.' He

squeezed Deans' hand a little tighter. 'But don't come down to my patch if you're going to screw up my investigation.'

Deans let go of Jackson's hand and gave him an uncompromising glare. Jackson walked over to his table, scooped his coat from the back of a chair and left without saying another word to anyone.

Deans moved across to the gathered mourners and stood in the middle of them.

'Listen in everyone,' he said loudly.

Sixty voices dampened to a stifled murmur.

'I'm afraid I have to leave you all.'

The room fell completely still.

'I have to go away for a few days.'

Deans noticed DS Savage forcing his way through the maze of motionless, open mouthed mourners towards him.

'Please stay and enjoy the food, get drunk and remember my beautiful Maria.' He caught a look of utter contempt in Graham's eye.

'We really appreciate all of your support and thank you for coming this morning. I *will* catch up with each of you individually in the coming days. I am sorry, but I really have to leave.'

Savage reached him, just as he stopped talking. The muffled conversations had already begun around the room.

'What are you doing?' Savage whispered. 'You can't leave now. These people have come here today for you.'

Savage looked at Denise Moon and his lips tightened. 'Might have guessed you'd have something to do with this.'

'Hold on right there,' Denise said.

'It was me,' Jackson said, striding in behind Deans. 'I need Detective Deans to help me out with… something.'

'He's not fit to work,' Savage said. 'He's just lost his wife and child—'

'It was my choice,' Deans cut in. 'Sergeant Jackson didn't ask me to go. But I *have* to.'

'For God's sake, Deano,' Savage flared. 'Look around you.' He pointed at the faces staring awkwardly back at them. 'What can be more important than *this*? You need these people. You need them to help you recover. You don't need more stress.'

Deans dropped a heavy hand onto Savage's shoulder. 'I'll be alright, Mick. I am doing this for the right reasons – Maria knows that.'

'No,' Savage said. 'You're not.'

Deans planted his crutches onto the beer-stained carpet, stared at Savage and gave the room one final fleeting look.

eyes that both Jackson and Denise had given him earlier that afternoon in Bath.

'Now that you're both here,' Deans said, putting some distance between himself and Sarah, 'I want to talk about the interview with Paul Ranford.'

The brow of Jackson's bony head ridged like corrugation.

'What's on your mind?' he said.

Deans stared again at Ranford's desk. He walked over to it and sat on the corner of the table. He looked at Sarah and then at Jackson.

'Did it not strike you as surprising that Ranford admitted everything the way he did; Maria's murder; Babbage's; the finer details of Amy Poole's killing?'

Jackson rolled his eyes.

Deans looked at Sarah. Her feelings were less obvious to read, but her wide eyes were fixed upon his.

'No?' Deans asked filling the silence.

Jackson grunted. 'Well, what else could he do?'

Deans rose slowly from the desk.

'He could have given us a right royal run-around. He knows the law as well as any of us – knew how to dodge the bullets, but instead, allowed himself to be stitched with three counts of murder.'

'He had nowhere to hide,' Jackson said, a thin smile returning to his lips. 'You practically caught him in the act of murder.'

Deans shook his head. 'No. That's not the reason.'

Jackson and Gold looked at one another.

'He was protecting someone... or something,' Deans said.

'Like what?' Sarah asked softly.

The corner of Deans' eye trembled as Maria's face came into his thoughts.

'Why cut off someone's head?' he asked. 'Why not simply stab, poison, strangle, or smother them to death?'

Jackson shrugged. 'There are no rules to murder.'

Deans stepped closer to Jackson. 'Establish why the victims are being beheaded and we might find a motive for the killings.'

Jackson sneered. 'Maybe Ranford is just a violent bastard who needed to satisfy his perverse lust for blood and power.'

'Maybe...' Deans said. 'Or perhaps he is taking the hit for someone further up the food chain.'

'Argh! Come on,' Jackson said picking up his bag from the desktop. 'We could talk about *what ifs* all night long. I don't know about you, but I'm keen to see who this latest victim is?'

CHAPTER FIVE

They were let into the mortuary by a young attendant. Judging by her hurried actions and nervous titter, she appeared not to be expecting them.

'Would you let the pathologist know that Detective Sergeant Jackson is here regarding the murder victim, please,' Jackson said with an authoritative arrogance.

'Um...' the young girl hesitated, sweeping straggly dark hair behind an ear. 'He's not here.'

'Bugger,' Jackson spluttered looking at his watch. 'He's usually here until at least seven. How long ago did he leave?'

'No. I mean... he didn't come in today.'

'But it's Tuesday.' Jackson's voice was increasingly barbed. 'He's always here late on a Tuesday.'

'I know,' the young attendant said tugging at her earlobe.

'Have you tried calling him?' Jackson barked.

Deans took a step towards the young attendant. 'It's okay; we know it's not your fault.'

The girl looked at Deans, her eyes glistening as if she had some kind of *connection* with him.

'Yes,' she said, still staring at Deans. 'I've tried to page him.'

'Pager?' Jackson asked with irritation.

'Yes.'

'Well, who has been doing pathology around here today then?' Jackson asked.

The girl shot a glance towards Gold; she appeared to be way out of her depth.

'Nobody,' she finally replied down at her feet.

Deans spoke again. 'We're here for the body that was recovered from the beach this morning.' He positioned himself to partially block Jackson from the attendant's line of sight. 'Do you think we could see it – the body?' he asked.

The girl peered up again at Deans. She didn't blink and held his stare for a long moment.

'Could we?' Jackson asked, nudging Deans off balance.

The attendant nodded and skulked back through heavy-looking double swing doors, similar to the ones you might see in a restaurant service area, minus the peepholes.

Jackson followed first, and then Sarah Gold and she held the door open making it easier for Deans to navigate with his crutches.

'You'll need to wear forensic coveralls,' the girl said, 'until the examination has taken place.'

'Yes, yes,' Jackson muttered, snatching a white paper suit from her hands, ripping away the clear packaging and tossing it into a bin in the corner of the room.

'Has anyone examined the body at all?' Sarah asked.

'Nobody else has seen the corpse since it arrived... other than me,' the attendant said and sneaked a glance in Deans' direction.

Sarah offered a sympathetic smile. 'Thanks for your help. I

know it must be difficult without Mr Rowland around. Does anyone have a clue where he is at the moment?'

The girl shook her head and at the same time pointed over to another set of swing doors. 'Through those doors is the scrubs room,' she said. 'You can get ready in there.'

They followed her directions and dressed in their coveralls and facemasks.

'Check this out,' Jackson said, fiddling with the buttons on an early-looking Technics Compact Disc stacking system, complete with dual tape decks. 'I used to have one like this back in the day.'

'You're not going to break-dance are you?' Deans said in deadpan voice as he looked out through the glass window of the scrub room at the attendant standing motionless in the centre of the examination room, looking right back at him. Deans checked her over – she was wearing a sage-green hospital gown over pale blue trousers rolled up at the bottom of her stumpy legs. Her pigeon-toed white clogs peeped out from beneath the turn-ups.

'Do you think we should wait for the pathologist before we see the body?' Deans asked.

'Nah,' Jackson said from beneath his mask. 'I've done so many of these things now, I know what we should or rather, what we shouldn't be doing.'

Jackson led the way out through the flapping doors, Sarah behind and Deans bringing up the rear. They joined the attendant who took them into another room – a pre-examination area. The air temperature was noticeably cooler than where they had just been and the room was featureless, apart from a stainless steel trolley holding the body of the deceased, shrouded by a pea-green blanket.

They lined up in a row beside the trolley-bed, Deans towards the feet – going by the two pointed objects sticking up from underneath the covers. The smell was uniquely *mortuary*; the pungent sweetness of the rotting dead, mixed with a chemical cocktail of embalming fluid.

Deans looked above his head. The extractor fans were on, but not nearly working hard enough.

'This it?' Jackson asked, speaking from behind his hand. 'The body from the beach?'

The girl nodded and took a half step backwards, which did not go unnoticed by Deans who was standing on the other side to them. She locked eyes with him once more and didn't let go.

Jackson, now at the head end – if the corpse had one – peeled back the covers exposing a tattered fringe of flesh around a small neck stump and naked torso. With only his cold eyes showing between the facemask and paper hood, it was hard to know if he was smiling or grimacing, but Deans gave him the benefit of the doubt.

Jackson lowered the cover around the body's midriff and scratched through the hood of his forehead with a gloved finger.

'Bloody hell,' he said. 'What a mess.'

Deans walked behind Sarah, who hadn't moved an inch since they first walked over. He stood alongside Jackson and stared down at the jagged edges of the wound – there was nothing subtle about this beheading, no cauterised seam, no attempt at making it look "pretty". If anything, the decapitation looked *angry*. He had never seen a fully beheaded corpse before. The severed neck of Babbage was probably the closest he had come. Deans blinked to clear his gritty eyes, but instead of seeing the victim before him, he saw the mutilated body of his wife. His breathing began to race beneath his mask. *What must Maria have gone through?* He gulped air as a nauseas-belch burned the back of his throat. He stumbled sideways and Sarah reached out and grabbed his arm.

'I'm okay,' he said, covering his mouth with the back of his hand. 'I'm okay.'

'Would you rather wait for us outside?' Sarah asked him with pitying eyes.

Deans shook his head, his hand still in position in case of an upsurge from his stomach. He turned back and saw the attendant was watching him with wide, intelligent eyes.

'I think we've seen enough,' Jackson said. He grabbed the sheet material and pulled it back over the stump. 'We need to see Archie before we go any further.'

He turned to DC Gold. 'Have CSI been organised to attend the post mortem examination?'

'Yes,' she said. 'They were notified first thing this morning, but they would normally liaise directly with the pathologist, rather than us.'

'Okay,' Jackson said peeling down his gloves and walking towards the scrubs room. 'Find out from CSI what Archie has planned. I need to speak to the detective chief inspector about this stiff.'

Jackson didn't stick around to chat and was gone with a determined mettle. As Sarah and Deans drove back towards Torworthy along the pitch-black lanes, the horrific image of the decapitated body remained in the forefront of Deans' mind.

'How fresh did that body look to you?' he asked Sarah after a few minutes of silence.

'Very,' she replied.

Deans sucked in his cheeks and pinched a flap of flesh between his molars, biting down to the point that it hurt. He looked ahead with a thousand-yard stare.

'Fresher than if the wounds had been made two weeks ago?' he asked.

'Definitely.'

Deans faced his ghostly reflection in the side window. *It wasn't Ranford.*

'Does it strike you as odd that these bodies are being found so bloody easily?' he asked, after a further pause for thought.

Sarah didn't answer immediately. She kept her eyes on the road ahead.

Deans watched her eyebrows twitching as she appeared to be considering his question.

'Yes,' she eventually replied.

'I mean… all of that ocean. Not to mention the miles of desolate moors right on the doorstep, and yet, all of the innocent victims have been located near to that one beach.'

He whispered and leaned forwards, putting his face in his hands. 'But where are their heads?'

Sarah looked forwards, her hands tight around the steering wheel.

'Why do you suppose that is?' Deans asked

'I don't know,' Sarah muttered, still declining to take her eyes off the road.

'A challenge,' Deans said. 'The killers are provoking a reaction.'

'From who?'

Deans leaned back in the seat and rested his hands in his lap. 'From me,' he said softly. 'They are goading me into a battle.'

He heard the blinking of the indicator, and the car suddenly slewed to the side of the road, onto a small bumpy lay-by and Sarah ground the car to a rapid halt.

'Do you think other killers are still out there?' she asked.

'Yes,' Deans said. 'That body has been dead a day, maybe two at the most. Ranford has been in custody for well over two weeks now, and Babbage has been dead longer still.' Deans stared at Sarah. 'There are others.'

'But why?' Sarah asked.

Deans shrugged.

'I mean… why carry on killing? Why kill that man in there if the "challenge" was intended for you?'

Deans bunched his eyes tight for a moment and tried to remove the face of Maria from the forefront of his mind.

'I guess we'll find that out once we discover who once lived in that body. Ranford was clearly shielding others with his open admissions in interview, knowing that we'd concentrate on him.'

Sarah's mouth was wide.

'We need to work backwards from this murder,' Deans said. 'And our person of interest may just show themselves.'

'But…' Sarah spluttered. 'Where do we start?'

'We start by finding out who is lying on that slab.'

CHAPTER SIX

As Deans and Sarah Gold drove deeper into the North Devon countryside, the lanes appeared to grow narrower and the hedgerows taller. Jackson had given them Archie Rowland's home address and told them to pay him a visit and arrange a meeting at the mortuary. This was different scenery to the one Deans had become accustomed with in North Devon. The air was still with inactivity. They parked in the centre courtyard of three developed barn conversions, each designed to a high specification from the looks of it. Deans had guessed pathologists were good earners – this was the proof. He looked down at the tyre tracks in the shingle driveway. He sniffed and caught Sarah making for one of the stable-doors.

'I suppose this is the main entrance,' she said.

Potted fir trees and curly nut bushes either side of the doorway meant that she was probably correct in her assumption. She knocked on the door and they both waited silently in their own thoughts.

'Do we know what he drives?' Deans asked. 'There's an old Land Rover over there.' He pointed to the end of the side property, to where the nose and front wheels of a silver-coloured Freelander was visible.

'No idea,' Sarah replied. 'I've never met him.'

Just at that moment, the door opened and a woman of retirement age stood in the narrow gap. The smell of baking escaped out into the still, cool air and made Deans feel hungry. His mind wondered and he realised he had not eaten anything since yesterday lunchtime.

'Yes,' the woman said abruptly.

'Hello, sorry to disturb you,' Sarah said. 'Mrs Rowland?'

The woman tightened her grip around the door handle.

'We are looking for your husband, Archie,' Sarah continued. 'Is he here with you at the moment, please? It's very important that we speak with him.'

Mrs Rowland's face dropped. 'No,' she said. 'He's at the mortuary.'

Deans then realised Mrs Rowland was peering at their suits.

'Are you...?' she asked.

'We are detectives from Torworthy CID,' Deans said. 'We were expecting to meet Mr Rowland at the mortuary, but he wasn't there. We were wondering if you knew where he might be instead?'

'Oh!' Mrs Rowland muttered.

Deans studied her stilted movements, her far away eyes and her stiff limbs. 'I'm sorry if our visit has surprised you,' he said.

'Archie didn't come home last night,' Mrs Rowland said. She began mouthing something silently to herself.

'What is it Mrs Rowland?' Sarah asked.

'Well, when I spoke to Annie earlier, she said Archie was at the mortuary.'

Deans leaned forwards on his sticks. 'Annie?'

'Yes, our...' she hesitated over the next words. '...Youngest daughter.'

All of a sudden, Deans' scalp crawled as a bolt of energy shot from the crown of his head and down his spine. He shuddered as the force grounded through his feet. He turned to Sarah – she had not noticed. *Annie*, he thought.

'Do you know what time that was?' he asked.

'Oh... around eleven,' she replied.

Deans looked at his watch. It was almost five-twenty.

Mrs Rowland let go of the door handle for the first time and took a small step towards them. 'Should I be worried about this?' she asked nervously.

'No, no,' Sarah said quickly. 'I'm sure we'll speak to him soon enough. Would you let him know we are keen to catch up with him, when you see him, please?'

'Yes. Yes of course.'

'What about his phone?' Deans asked. 'Surely you can contact him on his mobile?'

Mrs Rowland tittered sarcastically. 'I'm afraid my husband still lives in the past. He does not own a mobile phone. In fact, he refuses to have one. He says they are the cause of modern society's inability to converse correctly.'

'Then how do you get messages to one another?' Deans asked.

'He has a phone at work. And a pager.'

'Have you tried that since you last saw him?'

'No,' she said. 'It's not unusual for Archie to sleep over at the hospital when he is involved with a detailed job. I would rather he rested there, than risk driving home when he's shattered. I sometimes don't hear from him until he walks through this door.'

'Okay,' Deans said. 'Thank you for your time. I'm sure we'll catch up with him sooner or later.'

They crunched back to the car having watched Mrs Rowland return inside the house.

'So what are we going to do now?' Sarah asked.

'Can you drop me off in town? I need some time to think.'

'Do you want some company?'

Deans felt for his wedding band and rolled it around his finger. 'No. Thanks. I just need some time alone.'

'I understand,' Sarah said quietly. 'What about Archie Rowland?'

'Update Jackson and give me a call the moment you hear anything. I'm desperate to speak to Archie Rowland about Maria.'

Sarah looked away.

Deans noticed the sour look on her face.

'What?' he asked.

'Andy... please don't torture yourself with... well, you know.'

Deans did know. But it wasn't torture he was after. Not for him anyhow.

Sarah did as requested and dropped Deans in Torworthy and drove back to the station to update Jackson. Deans made his way to the coffee shop inside the covered market that Sarah had taken him to the time before. It wasn't Nixi's back home, but it was a pretty good substitute and it stayed open until seven in the evening. The same barista was serving as before. Deans nodded to him as he approached the counter.

'Hey, you're the chap who was in here with Sarah?' the barista said.

'Yeah,' Deans said. 'Dan. Right?'

'Yeah,' Dan said. 'Good memory.'

Deans flicked an eyebrow and glanced around the room.

'You work with Sazzy?' Dan asked.

'Sazzy?'

'Oh, sorry… Sarah,' Dan chuckled. 'You must work with Sarah.'

'Must I?'

Dan made a point of looking at the five other sad and lonely faces in the café. He then pointed at Deans' clothing. 'Only people around here who wear suits are estate agents, solicitors, or detectives.'

'I've been to a funeral,' Deans said in a lacklustre voice.

'Oh,' Dan said, turning his back on Deans, dispensing freshly ground coffee from the bean hopper.

'I haven't ordered yet,' Deans said.

Dan looked over his shoulder as he filled the brew head with coffee powder. 'Americano – if I'm not mistaken?'

Deans slanted his head. 'That's right.'

'I'll bring it over,' Dan said. 'Looks like you need both hands for those crutches.' He smiled and turned back to the task in hand.

'Sure,' Deans replied, and took a seat in the corner of the room with his back to the wall.

He needed this *me-time*. He was struggling to rationalize recent events and much of what was happening. He watched Dan making the drink. He was efficient, but *something* was making Deans' radar twitch.

Dan came over with a bowl-like mug. 'One Americano for sir.' He leaned over the table and Deans took a hold of the mug, but Dan hesitated for a second, before releasing his grip.

'Thank you, Dan,' Deans said.

'So,' Dan wavered, 'what did you do to your leg?'

Deans looked sideways at the kid. 'Skiing accident,' he said.

Deans saw a flicker in the corner of Dan's eye and the makings of a knowing smile. 'Oh,' Dan said. 'Nasty.'

Deans noticed someone was waiting beside the counter. He nodded over in that direction and Dan took the hint.

'Oh, okay,' Dan said. 'Enjoy your coffee.'

Deans watched him all the way back to the service area and counted the seconds until Dan next looked his way.

Nine.

Deans creased his brow. That was less than he'd anticipated. He blew the steam from his drink and took the first satisfying slurp of decent tasting coffee in a while.

He continued to study Dan who kept on checking his watch, even though a large shabby-chic wall clock was only feet away from him.

Dan scratched the top of his head and steered another glance in Deans' direction.

Who are you waiting for, Matey, and why so interested in me?

Deans checked his phone. There was nothing from Sarah, but as he placed it back onto the table, his phone pinged. It was DS Savage.

Checking you are okay, Deano? I hope you know that you have friends back home who are concerned about you. Let me know if there is anything I can do. Speak soon. Mick

Deans huffed and drained the remainder of his coffee in three large gulps, placing the mug back down on the table with a solid thump. He rested his head in his hands, stared at the table and sat like that for a number of minutes.

'Have you finished?' Dan asked.

Deans looked up at him with bleared vision.

'Yeah. Sorry.'

He pushed the mug towards the edge of the table and Dan retrieved it, but didn't walk away.

Deans puckered his brow and gazed up at the lad.

'Are you staying here long – in Torworthy, I mean?'

What's it to you, kid?

'How do you know I don't live here?'

Dan chuckled. 'Oh, I think I know pretty much everyone who lives here.'

Deans wiped moisture slowly from his bottom lip with the back of his hand and looked deeper into Dan's eyes. 'How do you know Sarah?' he asked.

Dan scratched the side of his nose with his free hand. 'We used to go out. We *had* a good thing.'

Deans nodded. *Thought so.*

'She's a nice girl,' Deans said.

He noticed Dan munching his jaw, like he was chewing something. He wasn't.

'Something on your mind, Dan?'

'Don't make yourself comfortable here.'

Deans leaned back in his seat and exhaled with a groan.

'Kid, you really don't want to piss me off right now – walking sticks or not.'

A smile spread on Dan's lips. He looked down at Deans' leg and shook his head. He peered back at Deans with an increasing grin. 'You've got no idea – have you?'

CHAPTER SEVEN

Deans met Sarah twenty minutes later at the front of the station. She had driven to meet him. He opened the passenger door and clambered inside, tossing his sticks on the back seat.

'We need to go back to the mortuary,' he said.

'Why?'

'It's time to take control of this *situation*.'

'It'll be closed.'

'Then we'll open it back up again.'

'What are you going to do?'

'What I do best – police work.'

Deans waited a while for Sarah to join the traffic and settle into the half-hour drive ahead before he spoke.

'Just had an interesting chat with an old flame of yours,' he said.

'Who?' Sarah said, quickly swinging around.

'Eyes on the road, please,' Deans said.

Sarah huffed and returned her gaze back onto the road ahead.

'Dan, the coffee man. *Nice* boy.'

Sarah's hands fidgeted on the wheel.

Okay, that hit a nerve.

'And if I'm not mistaken, he was warning me to stay away from you.'

Deans saw her hands grip the wheel so hard, the tight skin of her knuckles turned white.

'You can tell him he's got nothing to be concerned about – obviously,' Deans said.

Sarah's cheeks flushed pink.

'So how long ago did you guys go out?' Deans asked, noticing her quick-fire blinking.

'We didn't,' she said sharply. 'He's just got the wrong idea.'

'It didn't sound that way.'

Deans noticed their speed increasing. They were still within the town-limits, but the engine was working hard under Sarah's irritated right foot. He decided it was best to leave this particular conversation alone and within thirty minutes they were back at the mortuary car park. Sarah had wanted to inform DS Jackson of their return but Deans had stopped her.

He tried the mortuary door. It was locked. He peered at his watch: seven-seventeen in the evening. This time he thumped loudly with the ball of his fist and turned back to Sarah, but she was already walking along the front row of windows trying to look inside the building.

'Is there another way inside?' Deans asked.

'I don't know. Should we try to go inside if there is nobody here?'

'Urgent police work trumps most things,' Deans said joining Sarah at one of the windows.

The mortuary was connected by a narrow glass corridor to another single storey building.

'Let's try in there,' Deans said, making in a determined fashion towards the other entrance.

They were met by an exceedingly tall woman, wearing a long white laboratory jacket and a hospital lanyard dangling in front of her chest.

Deans flashed his police badge. 'We're trying to access the mortuary, but no one seems to be answering the door. Can you help us, please?'

'It's closed.' The technician looked at her watch. 'They left over an hour ago. Who did you want to see?'

'Well, we really need to see the pathologist,' Sarah said.

The technician shook her head. 'I haven't seen Archie all day, I'm afraid. He must be sick.'

'Actually,' Deans interrupted, 'we need to view the corpse again. We were here earlier. Can you grant us access?'

'Not really.'

'This is an ongoing, highly sensitive police investigation,' Deans said. 'Ten minutes is all we need. We won't be touching the body at all, and we will be forensically aware.'

The technician looked down at Deans' walking sticks and scowled. 'Ten minutes?'

'Tops.'

'Okay, just bear with me.'

The technician darted back into the building and returned just as quickly.

'We can go through this way.' She led them through the glass corridor and within moments, Deans and Sarah were again inside the mortuary.

'We know where to go,' Deans said.

The technician gave them both another once over and waited inside the doorway.

'Hello?' Deans called out into the silence. 'Hello?'

The ceiling lamps illuminated automatically the further they moved into the eerily still building.

'Right, let's get garbed up,' Deans said and walked first into the scrubs room.

'Don't go getting us into trouble,' Sarah said in hushed tones.

'Don't fret – don't touch anything and you'll be alright.'

Deans left his sticks and dragged his leg through to the pre-examination room, and saw the body exactly where they had earlier left it. He pulled back the covers, exposing the gruesome carcass once again and dragged the sheet completely away, visually examining the body at close proximity.

'What are you doing?' Sarah asked.

'They've been married a long time. If there are any distinguishing features on this body, then Mrs Rowland should know about them.'

'What?' Sarah gasped. 'Do you think this is Archie Rowland?'

Deans peered up at her, his forehead puckered with surprise at her comment.

'Think about it,' he said.

Sarah stumbled backwards by several steps and looked over to where the head should have been. 'Oh my God!' she said grabbing the sides of her face.

Deans took a pen and sketched the outline of the corpse into his scratch pad, highlighting any distinctive marks; such as birthmarks and surgery scars.

He turned to Sarah whose face had turned putty-grey. 'Right,' he said. 'We can only do the front, but we've got enough to go back to Mrs Rowland.'

Within the hour later and they were back at the Roland farm, standing in the living room that looked like it was straight out of a John Lewis Christmas advert. Deans looked around, there were exposed ceiling beams and a fire place large enough to stand inside.

'Mrs Rowland, when was the last time you saw your husband?' Deans asked. This time, he decided to be more direct with his approach.

Mrs Rowland covered her mouth with a bony hand. Her eyes raked between Deans and Sarah.

'Mrs Rowland,' Sarah said softly. 'This could be important. Can you remember exactly the last time you saw your husband?'

'Around six p.m., yesterday evening,' she spluttered from behind her fingers.

'Where did he say he was going?' Sarah asked.

Deans could tell that Sarah had a better rapport with Mrs Rowland, so he kept quiet... for now.

Mrs Rowland pulled a tight face and shook her head, as if that was a silly question to ask.

Deans could see her building confusion, so he made it easier for her.

'Did he go to the mortuary?' he asked.

Mrs Rowland nodded and her fingertips moved to her lips.

'Because there was a job?' Deans continued.

Mrs Rowland looked at Deans with a fixed stare.

'Go on,' Deans encouraged with an open palm offering Mrs Rowland time to expand.

'Well...' Mrs Rowland faltered. '*You* asked him to go there.'

Deans shot a look at Sarah. 'Who exactly?' he asked quietly. 'Try to remember who in particular asked your husband to return to the mortuary?'

'Well... Annie. She called him on the landline, said the police were requesting he attend for another "big job" like the one he did before.'

Deans looked intensely at Sarah.

'Are you certain it was six p.m. last night – not this morning?' Sarah asked.

Ten seconds of silence followed and was then broken by the fractured voice of Mrs Rowland. 'Where is Archie – where is my husband?'

Deans stepped closer. 'Mrs Rowland,' he said, focussing on the crazy-paved blood veins in the whites of her eyes. 'Is there any chance I could sit down, please? I'm struggling a little with my leg.'

'Oh, yes... yes of course.'

Mrs Rowland fussed with the large cushions on the sofa and offered Deans the seat. He didn't have leg pains, he was trying to find a way of speaking without looming over the top of the frail old woman. Bad news was always best, being broken on the same level.

Mrs Rowland offered Sarah the sofa alongside Deans and she took the armchair closest to him.

Perfect.

'Mrs Rowland, this may sound like an *odd* question, but has your husband ever had surgery?'

She blanched. 'Yes... yes, he has.'

Deans furnished her a pained smile. 'Would you mind telling me where on his body that was, please?'

'Left knee,' she said quickly. 'He had a replacement knee joint on his sixty-second birthday.'

Deans nodded ruefully and turned to Sarah.

'Would you excuse us for just a moment, Mrs Rowland,' Sarah said, standing up from the sofa.

Deans took the invitation and followed Sarah out into the hallway.

'What are you doing?' Sarah asked with stifled tones. 'We don't know who *that* is yet?'

'We do.' Deans did nothing to hide the volume of his voice.

'And we need to take Mrs Rowland back to the mortuary with us to identify her husband.'

Sarah flapped her arms and closed the gap between them. 'And how do you suppose we go about that?' she murmured.

'Follow me.'

Deans walked back into the designer living room. 'Mrs Rowland,' he said assertively. 'I'd like you to come with us, if you wouldn't mind?'

'Go with you where?'

'To the mortuary. We are going to see your husband.'

CHAPTER EIGHT

Sarah had no alternative but to inform DS Jackson of Deans' intentions. Jackson demanded that Deans do nothing with Mrs Rowland until he got to the mortuary himself, and they didn't have to wait long for him to arrive. Jackson pulled nose-in to Sarah's car so that he was immediately alongside – driver door to driver door. His window buzzed downward and he peered into the back of their car. 'Hello Jen,' he said to Mrs Rowland with a deadpan voice.

Deans raised a brow and looked into the back seat at Mrs Rowland.

'Stephen, what's happening – where's Archie?' she replied hurriedly.

'Just wait here a moment, Jen. I'm going to have a word with my colleague. Detective Gold will keep you company.'

Jackson glared over at Deans. 'We won't be long.'

Deans and Jackson walked along the front of the mortuary building and the moment they were around the corner and out of sight of the two cars, Jackson spun Deans by the shoulder and slammed him back against the wall.

'What the fuck are you doing, son?' he snarled.

Deans swiped Jacksons' hand from his shoulder and stood tall. 'First name terms? You know them personally?'

Jackson bore his jagged brown-stained teeth. 'I said, what do you think you are doing?'

'Archie Roland is lying on that slab in there,' Deans said.

Jackson tugged at his earlobe and pulled Deans further away from earshot of the cars.

'What are you talking about?'

'Archie Rowland has been missing since yesterday evening, soon after being called in to work because of *a big police job.* Are you aware of *that* job?'

Jackson's face contorted. 'There was no big job last night.'

Deans tilted his head. 'Well, technically there was… Archie Rowland became the victim of his own job.'

'What?'

'The decapitated body lying on the trolley through there is Archie Rowland. I guarantee it.'

Jackson stepped backwards half a step, his face twitching as the suggestion sank in.

'But now we have an even bigger problem,' Deans said.

Jackson did not answer, still consumed with his own thoughts.

'Archie, or not – there is another killer.'

Jackson turned away and ran a hand over the bald ridges of his pate. He quickly span back around. 'Why do you think somebody else is involved?'

'That's a fresh murder and everyone on our radar is accounted for. Somebody else did this.'

'Jesus!' Jackson hissed. He rubbed the top of his head again as if polishing it would make a genie appear and solve the problem.

'What are you thinking?' he asked Deans.

'Identify Archie. Get another pathologist to forensically examine his remains…' Deans peered at Jackson. 'Get smarter.'

'It's going to take days to identify that body forensically.'

'Wrong. It need only take minutes.'

'And put that poor lady through something like this? We get paid to see this kind of horror. We may not like it, but that's our job.'

'And if we delay, who's to say there won't be another trolley right alongside this one tomorrow?'

'Jesus wept…' Jackson's words tailed away and his hands balled into fists.

Deans stood firm.

'You're crazy,' Jackson said.

'Maybe I am.'

Jackson looked Deans up and down with confliction.

'How is she going to ID her husband when he has no head?'

'Surgical scar. Left knee.'

Jackson squinted with judgemental eyes.

'Confirm this, and we're already a day, maybe two ahead of the game,' Deans said. 'Then we can consider motive. Then we can start looking for suspects.'

Jackson scowled and scratched behind his ear.

'Let me go and talk to Jen,' he said. 'You and Gold get this place opened up.'

Jackson left Deans with a hard stare to mull over, and Sarah joined him moments later.

'God, I hope you're right about this,' Sarah said to Deans. '…For your sake.'

They entered the mortuary via the lab corridor and Deans walked to one of the windows looking out onto the parked cars. He twisted a thin plastic rod of the blinds to open a narrow crack that he could now see through. Jackson was sitting in the back of Sarah's car alongside Mrs Rowland.

Deans leaned back against the cool, smooth wall.

'Now we sit tight and we wait,' he said.

Jackson joined them inside the mortuary with Mrs Rowland linked tightly to the loop of his arm.

'Is Annie here?' Mrs Rowland asked.

Deans cocked his head. *Annie?*

'I'm afraid not, Mrs Rowland,' he said. 'It's just us.'

'Jen,' Jackson said. 'Just come with me for a moment. We won't be in here for long.'

They walked through to the pre-examination room, Mrs Rowland and Jackson bringing up the rear.

Deans stood beside the base of the trolley. Mrs Rowland stumbled as recognition of what she was seeing hit home.

'Now, we are only going to show you the bottom end,' Deans said. 'But I want you to concentrate on what you see, especially around the knees.'

'Why can't I see his face?' Mrs Rowland sobbed into Jackson's arm.

Sarah cringed and glanced at Deans.

'We're just going to show you this for now, Jen,' Jackson said, directing her away from the top end of the body. He looked over to Deans and gestured for him to drag the covers up over the feet.

At first, Mrs Rowland didn't react. Then her eyes rolled into the back of her head and Jackson was left taking her suspended body weight through the crook of his arm.

CHAPTER NINE

Jackson headed back to the office to tie up with the DI, leaving Deans and Sarah to return Mrs Rowland to her home. The journey was stilted, silent and painful. Deans knew what was probably going through her mind, and the last thing she needed was a couple of cops attempting excruciating small talk. Could he have been more subtle in his approach? Yes, of course he could, but there was nothing considerate about the killer, and he wasn't going to catch them by winning popularity contests. Mrs Rowland probably had no idea who *he* was and what he was also going through, but Jackson sure as hell did, and Deans was quietly impressed that the skipper had gone along so readily with his ideas.

'Do you have family you would like us to contact?' Deans asked Mrs Rowland.

'My daughters… Oh… oh, my God!'

'It's okay, Mrs Rowland, we are happy to do that on your behalf. You have already mentioned Annie. Does she live locally?'

'Sandymere Bay,' Mrs Rowland croaked. 'She has a flat. My other daughters live in Exeter.'

'Okay,' Deans said. 'Can you give me the addresses, please? I'll ask our colleagues in Exeter to speak with your other daughters, but we can visit Annie, if you would like us to?'

Mrs Rowland wiped her eyes and gawped at Deans. 'Yes. Yes, please. Annie lives at Seventeen Kingsley Terrace,' she said.

'Seventeen Kingsley Terrace, Sandymere Bay,' Deans repeated as he scribbled the address into his day-book. 'Does she live there alone?'

Mrs Rowland jiggled her head, but did not answer.

'Okay, thank you,' Deans whispered. 'Can you give me her telephone number – just in case she isn't at home?'

Mrs Rowland opened her purse and handed Deans a black-glossed business card with embossed gold writing: *Annie Rowland MBBS*. That meant she was qualified in medicine. Deans ran his finger over the raised letters of her name and instantly heard blood-curdling cries of terror reverberating inside his head. He shot a look at Sarah and then back at Mrs Rowland, they hadn't noticed. Deans coughed into his fist, dropping the card onto his lap.

'Thank you,' he said to Mrs Rowland. He paused and looked deeply into her face. 'Trust me when I say this – I'm not going to stop until I find your husband's killer.'

When they arrived at the farm, Deans walked Mrs Rowland to the front door.

'I'll be okay now,' she murmured keeping Deans at emotional arm's length. She stood at the threshold of the front door, but before going inside she stopped and turned to him. 'You've been very kind and understanding. Thank you.'

Deans removed his wallet from a back pocket and took out his own business card.

'I'm not normally based in Devon,' he said. 'But if you need to talk – at any time – please use this number. I understand what you are going through more than you can imagine.'

Mrs Rowland took the card from Deans' fingertips. A slight flicker of recognition registered in her face and kept sight of Deans as she slithered through the narrow gap in the front door, until she was gone.

Deans stayed put for a moment. *She knows who I am.*

He turned around and rejoined Sarah inside the car. He stared ahead through the windscreen. He couldn't see much, it was dark outside. The loose rattle of the diesel engine provided him with an unusual comfort – a sense of mundane normality – whatever that was, anymore?

'Is this getting too big for us?' Sarah said after half a minute of watching Deans in his fixed position.

'I dunno,' Deans shrugged, still looking ahead at nothing in particular.

'I mean…' Sarah pressed. 'Are we out of our depth?'

Deans dwelled a second. 'I dunno.'

'Are we in… danger?' she asked with fragile tones.

Deans slowly turned her way. She was seeking a reassurance he could not possibly provide, but his answer was simple.

'Probably.'

CHAPTER TEN

Nine-twelve p.m. and Jackson was nowhere to be found back at the station. Sarah Gold located a note from him stuck to her computer screen.

It's been a long day. Get yourselves home. We have another pathologist meeting us at the mortuary tomorrow morning at eleven.

Sarah huffed and placed her bag onto the chair with a loud thud.

'Not being funny, Andy, but can't we ask someone from nights to update the next of kin? I'm knackered.'

'It's fine,' Deans said. 'I'll do it on my own. Just drop me at the address. I'll find my own way back.'

Sarah groaned. 'I can't do that. You are in no fit state to be left on your own. What if something happened, I'd never forgive myself?'

Deans tittered. 'It's a send-to. What's the worst thing that can happen?'

Sarah rocked her head.

'Do you know the way?' he asked.

She lowered her gaze to look at her watch.

'Have you got somewhere else to be?' Deans asked.

'No,' Sarah replied in a quiet voice. 'Come on,' she said.

They spent the ten-minute journey in silence. It didn't matter to Deans, he was in a contemplative state and idle chit-chat wasn't on his menu. They dropped down the hill on approach to Sandymere Bay. In daylight hours this would be the first place he would see the ocean, but tonight all he could see was the amber glow of the village street lamps and the odd passing car. Sarah slowed and turned off the main road onto a steep driveway that doglegged left towards a large white four-story terraced building set back away from the main road. Looking out of his window, Deans noticed a date stone in the centre of the front-facing wall: *1857*. Sarah followed the narrow driveway to a parking area behind the properties and stopped at one end of the terrace, rather than in the middle.

'I wonder where we'll find number seventeen?' Deans asked, already knowing the answer.

'It's just here,' Sarah said.

Deans moistened his lips with the tip of his tongue. 'Been here before?'

'Couple of times,' she said. 'There was a New Year's Eve stabbing in one of these flats a few years ago. I had to sit on the scene all night. I'll never forget it. All my friends were out partying and I was here.'

Deans offered a smile. 'The joys of working uniform.' He waved his hand. 'After you.'

He followed Sarah up an external flight of metal steps towards the fourth floor. It wasn't the easiest of passages with walking sticks.

'Why does it always have to be the top level?' Deans mumbled as he followed some distance behind Sarah.

She stopped outside of number seventeen, but instead of knocking on the door, she took a step backwards.

'What?' Deans said. 'You want me to talk to her?'

Sarah nodded.

Deans rapped his knuckles on the door and waited. He looked over at Sarah. 'Are you feeling okay?' he asked. 'You're very quiet tonight.'

She peered down at her hands. 'I'm fine.'

'You sure?'

'I just don't like death messages. Reminds me of when my dad left.'

Don't worry, Deans thought. *Annie already knows.*

The door eventually opened and standing before them was the person Deans had expected to see: Annie, the mortuary attendant. This time she was wearing red jogging bottoms and a baggy black top. She looked at them both and with a startled expression, nosed out beyond the doorframe and looked back along the walkway. It was sly, but Deans knew exactly what she was doing.

'Yes?' she said, as if Deans was a cold-calling salesperson she had never met before.

'Annie,' Deans smiled. 'We met earlier at the mortuary.'

Annie blinked and scowled.

Crap acting, love.

Deans went along with it and removed his warrant card – as if she really needed reminding of who he was.

'I'm Detective Deans and this is Detective Gold.'

Annie peered at Sarah and held her gaze for longer than was necessary.

'Can we come in, please?' Deans asked.

Annie angled her body sideways, inviting them inside. Deans gave a courteous nod and walked through to the main room of the flat. He walked up to the front-facing bay window and looked out.

'I knew it,' he said, looking beyond the rooftops of the houses below and into the black void where the bay and pebble ridge would be. 'This must have a staggering view by day.'

'It's alright,' Annie said, now standing shoulder-to-shoulder with Sarah in the middle of the room, both facing Deans.

He turned with a grin and looked at them. They both peered back at him with wide staring eyes. Deans cast a cursory glance around the room. The flat was tidy. Clean. He twitched his brows – one might also say, it was spotless. His eyes settled on a piece of red material hanging from the wall. He craned his neck to get a better look. It appeared to be an outline of a black bird in flight, set against a red semi-circular background and framed with a black tasselled boarder on the curved edge.

'Why are you here?' Annie asked, also looking at the decoration.

'Has your mother called you in the last hour? Sarah gently asked.

'No,' Annie said reaching for her mobile phone. She turned it towards Sarah. 'See.'

Deans' questioning eyes caught Sarah's for a second or two. 'Well, that's why we are here,' he said. 'I'm afraid we have some tragic news.'

Annie's face dropped – as it would do, but the following reaction piqued Deans' interest even more.

'Oh no,' Annie said, backing herself towards an armchair. She plopped herself down and stared with wide animated features. 'Oh God!' she said squashing her cheeks between her hands so that her lips were protruding unnaturally. 'When was it?'

Deans stared at her. 'When was what? I haven't said anything yet.'

Sarah kicked out sideways, connecting with Deans' shin.

'Well, you've already said it's tragic news, so obviously it's nothing good, *is it?*'

Deans knit his brow. 'You're quite right. It's not good news at all.'

'Is it Mum?' Annie asked rising to her feet. Her hands clenched together like a pleading child. 'Has something happened to Mum?'

Deans looked around her face for a moment and relaxed the muscles around his eyes. 'No,' he said. 'It's not Mum.'

Annie blinked deliberately several times, her eyes darting between Deans and Sarah. She dropped back to the seat, having first checked where she would be landing. The word, 'Dad,' ghosted from her lips.

'Yep,' Deans said with a huff. He balled his fists into the arch of his back and stretched for a moment. 'Yep, I'm afraid so.'

Sarah bumped Deans off balance on her way towards Annie with outstretched arms. 'I'm so sorry,' Sarah said embracing the young woman.

'How?' Annie asked, her eyes welling with tears.

Deans sniffed and glanced back over to the wall decoration. 'He was murdered.'

Annie stared at him, looking over the top of Sarah's shoulders as they continued to hug.

Deans walked back to the window and rested his hands on the ledge. He leaned his forehead onto the chilled glass, staring out into the blackness.

'His head was cut off,' he said nonchalantly. 'And his body

dumped in the sea.' He tapped his finger loudly on the window pane. 'Just about... there.' He turned and couldn't tell who appeared most shocked – Annie, or Sarah?

Sarah put her arm around Annie's shoulder. 'Come on,' she comforted. 'Is there somewhere I can take you? Maybe back to Mum's?'

'No,' Annie sobbed into her hands. 'I want to be alone. I want you both to leave.'

'Okay,' Deans said.

Sarah lifted her arm away from Annie's shoulder and gave Deans the dirtiest look he had seen for a long while.

Deans was first to make for the door, but not before stopping and looking back at the decoration hanging from the wall. 'Take care,' he said to Annie. 'I'll be in touch.'

Deans was already negotiating the top of the metal stairs with his crutches when Sarah stormed out of the flat.

'What the hell was that?' she said, her voice tense yet restrained.

'What?'

'That poor girl has just lost her father, and you... you have just come across like a completely insensitive prick.'

'Easy,' Deans said putting on a sulky face. 'You can have insensitive, but prick?'

'You know what I mean,' Sarah seethed. 'Is that how you deal with death messages in Bath?'

Deans put a hand to his chin and pretended to think for a beat. 'Nope,' he replied.

Sarah slapped her hands against her thighs. 'So why do it now?'

Deans turned his attention back to walking down the steps. 'You'll see in time,' he said and began negotiating the metal treads with his sticks.

Sarah waited at the top and watched Deans ascend the

steps, until he reached the bottom. She then joined him beside the car.

'Did you notice anything *familiar* inside the flat?' Deans asked her.

Sarah unlocked the doors, tugged the handle on the driver's side and sat inside without saying a word.

Deans looked over the roofline and puffed air from his cheeks, before getting into the car himself.

'Seriously,' he asked as he buckled himself in. 'Did you?'

'No,' Sarah blurted. She dropped her head and took several loud breaths. 'I don't think so?'

'Hmm,' Deans grunted.

Sarah slapped the steering wheel. 'Okay. Okay... should I have noticed something familiar inside the flat?'

'Maybe?'

CHAPTER ELEVEN

An extortionate taxi fare had taken Deans back to Denise's house. Sarah's generosity ended at the police station and now Denise was standing at the front door in her dressing gown.

Deans let himself inside the door before Denise had a chance to say anything.

'Got anything to drink?' he asked.

'Good evening to you too,' Denise said as he wafted by.

'Got any whiskey in the house?'

Denise judged him with her eyes as she closed the front door.

Deans walked on through to the kitchen.

'The best I can offer is wine,' Denise said trailing behind him and re-attaching her robes tightly round her body.

'That'll do,' Deans said. 'Wine will do just fine.'

Denise passed him, removed a single glass from the wall cabinet and pulled out an unopened bottle of red wine from a cupboard. She placed the bottle down on the kitchen table next to the glass and took a backward step.

'What, are you not having one?' Deans asked as he made for the table.

'It's a bit late for me.' Denise gestured towards the bottle. Deans didn't need a second invitation and quickly unscrewed the top, pouring himself a hurried glass.

'How did it go?' Denise asked, keeping her eye on the bottle action.

Deans sank an entire glass in one gulp and topped it back up again. He was aware of Denise looking on, but nailed the second glass with equal determination.

'Want to talk about it?' Denise asked, making a deliberate point of noticing the time on the clock.

Deans pulled out a chair from beneath the table and dropped onto it. Denise looked at the clock again. She smiled reluctantly and took the chair opposite. She watched him for a silent minute, deep in his own thoughts.

'Okay,' Denise said. 'It's almost eleven, I need some sleep. I've got clients booked in from nine-thirty, but I'll be free in the afternoon if you need me for anything.' She scraped the chair legs back, but before she stood up Deans reached out and grabbed the back of her wrist.

'There's something I need to talk to you about. Have you got a pen and paper?' he said.

Denise put her fingers to her lips and watched him for a few seconds, before standing up and leaving the room.

Deans poured himself another glass and Denise returned with a wad of printer paper and a Biro pen.

Deans drew the design of Annie's wall decoration as he gulped from the wine glass.

'Have you ever seen anything like this?' he asked while crudely replicating the flying bird. He pushed the sheets towards Denise.

She placed her specs onto her nose and looked down. She didn't say anything at first, but Deans saw enough from her twitching eyes to know that he was onto something.

'Where did you see this?' she asked. Her smile now replaced by a serious expression.

'At a flat, earlier this evening.'

Denise looked up from the page.

'…And carved into a piece of wood on the deck of Detective Ranford's boat.'

Denise squinted.

'And…' Deans said, '…on a book cover in Ash Babbage's study.'

Denise jerked her head, causing hair to fall across her face. She used a single finger to drag it back and she held Deans' stare. She stood up without saying a word and walked over to the kettle. She filled it at the sink and turned it on.

Deans watched her every movement.

She took out a tall, slender mug and selected herbal tea from one of three glass containers on the worktop. She waited silently as the kettle boiled and then poured the steaming water, clanking the spoon loudly against the inside of the mug. She carefully balanced the tea bag on the spoon and dropped it into a food caddy in the corner of the kitchen. She caught Deans staring and the corners of her mouth upturned for the briefest of moments.

She came back to the table, sat down, placed a coaster in front of her and lowered her mug on top. She swallowed and then looked up at Deans.

'There is a legend,' she said. 'Well… something more like folklore.'

Deans leaned towards her on his elbows.

She lifted her mug with both hands and blew steam from the top before taking a sip.

'North Devon has an ancient history,' she said from behind her mug.

Deans shrugged and shook his head.

'This area in particular, has suggested links to significant events and battles of the Viking Age.'

Deans opened his palm for her to continue and took another drink from his glass.

'Have you heard of Ragnar Lothbrok?' Denise said.

Deans spluttered. 'Yeah, course I have, I love the *Vikings* series on TV.'

Denise grunted behind closed lips. 'This is not a TV series. This is real – real events – real people.'

Deans scratched the nape of his neck and then rested his chin in his hands.

'Ragnar Lothbrok, as you know from watching the TV series, was a famous mythological Viking leader. It is said that one of his son's, Ubba, invaded these shores.'

'Ubba was here – you're kidding?'

Denise looked at Deans in the same way a school teacher might silently reprimand a petulant child.

'Oh, sorry,' Deans said.

'Around the ninth century, Ubba, or Hubba as he was known in these parts, invaded with a heathen army, but they were defeated by Alfred the Great.' She stopped herself and took a sip of the peppermint-smelling brew.

Deans leaned closer still. 'And?'

Denise glanced away and licked her lips.

'And?' Deans repeated.

Denise took another mouthful of tea and gently leaned back in the chair holding Deans' gaze. 'One theory is that Hubba and his entire army of warriors were slaughtered on the ancient meadows of Hemingsford. The defeated army was gathered up and tossed into a mass burial ground. Today, we call this place, Bone Hill.'

'This is a real place?'

'Yes. This is a real place.'

'Where is it?'

Denise drew a deep breath and held Deans' intense stare. She slowly exhaled and narrowed her eyes.

'It's on the headland, hidden by a dense canopy of trees.'

'On the headland?' Deans quickly mirrored.

Denise nodded. 'Not far from Ruby Mansell's house.'

Deans' eyes widened. 'Has it been proven to contain the remains of the Viking warriors?'

Denise shrugged. 'Not to my knowledge.'

Deans' mind raced.

'Another suggestion,' Denise said. 'Is that the invasion happened at a different location entirely and this is all romantic fantasy.' She cleared the back of her throat and shuffled herself in her seat.

'But?' Deans asked impatiently.

Denise blinked heavily. 'But – even though there are a number of hypotheses about Hubba's death, his remains have never been recovered.'

'Suggesting he didn't die here.'

Denise smirked and rubbed the back of her neck. 'Ancient lore has it that a number of invading warriors survived the battle and remained in the area... along with their barbaric, macabre methods.'

'Such as?'

Denise lifted her drink and brought it towards her lips. She held it in front of her mouth like a shield as she spoke. 'There was human sacrifice – females mostly. Young. Nubile. The type of woman who would make a good wife in Valhalla. The most revered of the Norse Warriors to perish on the battle grounds were said to be buried alongside a fresh, young, *living* maiden.'

Deans' thoughts raced to Amy Poole. She had all of those qualities, and had been disfigured and then buried alive on the pebble ridge. He took a mouthful of wine and swallowed it down with a loud gulp.

'And there was ritual sacrifice to appease the Pagan Gods.'

Deans glazed over as Denise continued. 'Savage acts of violence. Brutal murders and… beheadings.'

Deans lowered his glass with a clatter on the table top.

'The natives of that time were also fairly barbaric, compared to today's standards, and didn't need much encouragement to be inspired by their Scandinavian counterparts.'

The skin around Deans' eyes tightened. 'So, what happened?' he asked.

Denise didn't blink. 'It is suspected that a group; a very small group at first, created their own sect of… well… Norse fanatics and disciples of Odin.'

Deans lifted a hand. 'Hold on. Where is all this history stuff heading?'

'You have just drawn me *The Raven Banner*. This was the war symbol of the Norse God, Odin, and a terrifying signal of impending doom to all enemies of the invaders. Hubba was said to have flown The Raven Banner from his flagship.'

'So?'

Denise looked at Deans over the top of her mug. 'Ash Babbage. Detective Ranford. And now this *other* person?'

Seriously? Deans' chin dropped to his chest. 'No,' he said rocking his head. 'What if they were just fans of the TV series, I mean, you must be able to buy this kind of stuff on the internet.'

'Of course, but think about the murder victims. Look what has happened to them.'

Maria's face entered Deans' mind.

'What else do you know?' he asked quickly.

Denise jiggled her head. 'Imagine centuries of coastal erosion. Speculation suggests that the headland of Sandymere

Bay was, as it is now, a rocky outcrop. Manuscripts describe a mythical place – a perfectly flat protuberance of rock where *offerings* were made to the Pagan Gods.' She hesitated. 'I felt *something*,' she said. 'A powerful energy when we were inside Ruby Mansell's house.'

Deans' bottom lip began to quiver uncontrollably. 'I know,' he said. 'I felt it too.'

He stared into Denise's eyes. 'The house, it's on the cliff edge.'

Denise nodded.

'Oh my God!' Deans breathed. *Maria wasn't murdered – she was sacrificed.*

CHAPTER TWELVE

Next morning, Sarah collected Deans from the house. Jackson had arranged to meet them at Torworthy Police Station, but before they got out of the car, Sarah leaned across to Deans and touched his arm.

'I'm sorry about last night,' she said.

'That's okay.'

'No it's not. I forgot how this must be for you. It's understandable that you are reacting differently to the rest of us.'

His eyes flickered. 'Thanks for understanding. Shall we see what Jackson wants?'

Jackson was already waiting for them inside the foyer.

'Bad night?' Jackson said upon seeing Deans. 'You've got bags under your bags.'

'You could say that,' Deans replied and shuffled in through a security door behind Sarah and made his way towards the CID office on the first floor.

'I'm glad you're here,' Jackson said as he followed Deans through the narrow corridor. 'Something we need to talk about.'

'Okay,' Deans replied.

'Come through here,' Jackson said, taking Deans to the small interview room a short distance from the office.

Jackson went inside first and took the seat on the opposite side of the table facing the door, leaving Deans to negotiate himself in the snug gap between the door and the back of his chair.

All right, Deans thought, leaning his sticks against the back of the now closed door. *What is this all about?* He took his seat and watched Jackson, who was licking his thin dry lips and running a thumb and forefinger beneath his jaw line.

'I don't want you here anymore,' Jackson said with a soft firmness. He raised a hand before Deans had a chance to speak. 'It's not that I don't empathize, I truly do.'

'But?'

'*But*, I think that you are a distraction.'

Deans gave Jackson a barbed stare. 'To?'

Jackson leaned on the desk and his cold eyes narrowed to slits. 'DC Gold, for one. To the entire team, for two, *AND*, I think it best if you went home to allow yourself time to recover and let us do what we need to do.'

Deans filled his chest. He held it down for several seconds and then slowly exhaled, so that Jackson would feel his breath on his face. He leaned slightly forwards. 'Trying to get rid of me again are we?'

'It's for your own good. You have a lot to contend with, you don't need any of this on top.'

'No,' Deans said.

'No?'

'No,' Deans repeated. 'I'm not going home.'

'Deans…' Jackson said, flattening his hands on the table. 'Don't force me into a decision I don't necessarily want to make.'

'Then don't make it.'

Jackson's steely eyes cut right through Deans. 'Why do you torment yourself with this?'

'You are a local man, aren't you?' Deans asked.

Jackson fanned a hand. 'I don't *live* here anymore, but yes. I suppose you would say this was my home town.'

'Ever heard of Bone Hill?'

Deans saw a twitch in the corner of Jackson's eye.

'No,' Jackson said. 'Don't believe I have.'

Deans pinched his bottom lip between his teeth and waited for Jackson to respond.

He didn't.

'Aren't you going to ask me?' Deans asked.

Jackson tilted his head and eyeballed Deans. 'Ask you what?'

'*What is* Bone Hill?'

Jackson smirked and scratched the skin between his nose and top lip with a talon-like nail. 'Okay...' he chuckled. 'Go on... *what is* Bone Hill?'

Deans leaned forwards, closing the gap between them. Jackson had nowhere to go – there was a solid wall behind him.

'A mass burial ground of Viking warriors.'

Jackson blinked and forced a smile.

'Maria and my unborn son were sacrificed, as I believe, were others through the ages.'

Jackson covered his mouth with the back of a hand and fixed his gaze at Deans.

'And...' Deans continued. 'Your pathologist friend lying in the mortuary is the latest victim.'

Jackson slammed the palms of his hands onto the table top creating an echo in the small room. 'Stop,' he said. 'There are no sacrifices. We have our killers – Detective Ranford and Ash

Babbage. They were working in tandem and there are no other people involved.'

'Explain Archie Rowland then?'

Jackson breathed heavily through his nostrils, his mouth was clamped tight.

'Couldn't have been Babbage,' Deans said. 'He was already dead. It couldn't have been Ranford. He was locked up.' Deans slid his elbows along the table, until he was nearly up and out of his chair. 'There are others.'

'Why should Archie Rowland be linked to the other deaths, necessarily?'

Seriously?

Deans watched Jackson for a few seconds before answering.

'How many other murders have you dealt with where the victims were decapitated, or their bodies mutilated?' This is North Devon, not Mordor.'

Jackson's eyes dropped to the table.

'You *have* heard of Bone Hill,' Deans said. He saw the tip of Jackson's ears twitch as the skin on his face tightened. 'Your body language gave you away.'

The corner of Jackson's lip curled upwards. 'What am I thinking now, then?'

'You're probably thinking... shit; we've got ourselves a problem.'

Jackson didn't answer.

'And you're also probably thinking – what else does Deans know?' He stared at Jackson and gently bobbed his head in response to the recognition in Jackson's face.

'Well, I know of at least one other person who is involved in some way to this murderous group, but what I don't yet know, is how, or who else may be involved.'

Jackson pushed himself up from the table and chair until he was standing over the top of Deans who remained seated.

Deans could smell Jackson's notoriously bad breath.

Jackson sized him up and down and softly stroked his chin. 'Looks like you're not going anywhere, after all.'

CHAPTER THIRTEEN

They waited for Sarah Gold to return from enquiries and Jackson closed the door behind her as she entered the CID office.

'Take a seat,' he told Gold. Deans was already seated facing Jackson.

Sarah pulled a chair from beneath the desk and dragged it alongside Deans' chair. She gave Deans a fleeting look. Jackson stared at them both with intimidating purpose. Deans could see Jackson's jaw clench as his mind churned over his thoughts.

'We've got a problem,' Jackson at last said.

Deans smiled on the inside.

'We need to keep this tight,' Jackson said. 'Just the three of us.' He turned to the white board behind him and wiped the writing clean. Jackson didn't seem to care about the notes he was destroying. He wrote the names of the four victims across the top of the board in the order in which they had died: *AMY POOLE. MARIA DEANS. ASH BABBAGE* and *ARCHIE ROWLAND*. He used a red pen and in capitals wrote, *RANFORD* in a central position below the names. He connected each of the victims to

Ranford by a straight red line, creating a fan shape on the board. Beneath Ranford's name, he scribbled a large question mark. Jackson faced Deans and Gold. 'There's another killer,' he said.

Deans heaved himself to his feet and approached the board. He tugged the red marker pen from Jackson's grip and added two question marks either side of the one Jackson had scribed. 'Wrong,' Deans said. 'There are multiple killers.'

'Bullshit,' Jackson spat.

Deans glowered at him for a beat and faced the board again. He placed an asterisk beneath the names of Babbage and Ranford and wrote, *ANNIE ROWLAND*.

'We bring Annie Rowland in for questioning and we'll get more answers.'

Jackson grabbed the board wipe. 'This has nothing to do with Annie Rowland?'

'Stop,' Deans said grabbing Jackson's outstretched wrist, inches from the board.

'Something in particular links Babbage to Ranford, and Ranford to Annie Rowland.' He used the marker pen to replicate the image of The Raven Banner he'd seen in Annie's flat. He tapped loudly on the board with the butt of the pen. '*This* links them together.'

'What is it?' Jackson asked.

'The Raven Banner. The battle flag of Odin.'

Jackson and Gold stared silently at Deans.

'*Odin?*' Jackson repeated through gritted teeth.

'It was said to bring glory to the Viking invaders and strike fear into their opponents.'

'*Vikings?*' Jackson barked. 'For fuck's sake,' he laughed loudly.

Deans was already writing on the board again. Beneath Babbage's name he wrote, *Text Book*. Beneath Ranford, he wrote, *Totten Pole*, and beneath Annie Rowland's name, he wrote, *Flag*.

Deans tapped the board again. 'All three had this raven motif in their homes. Have you ever seen it before?' he asked Jackson.

Jackson shook his head.

'Have you?' Deans asked Sarah.

She did enough to shake her head, but didn't speak.

'It's a modern-day cult of an ancient religion. It's the only answer,' Deans said.

'Seriously?' Jackson said, stealing the pen from Deans' hand. 'There are no *cults* in North Devon. Do you not think that I would have heard of it... or Gold for that matter?'

'Actually...' Sarah interrupted.

'Oh, come on! Really? Do you expect me to believe that some ritualistic sect is responsible for these deaths?'

'And others,' Deans said calmly.

'When I was at school, some of the kids spoke of a *Pagan Order*,' Sarah said. 'Do you know what, those kids were never bullied. Never crossed. Even the teachers seemed reluctant to punish them.'

'Nonsense,' Jackson sneered.

Deans hobbled away from the board and sat alongside Sarah.

Jackson faced the white board. 'Well then, tell us what Annie Rowland has to do with it?' he scowled.

'Maybe nothing – possibly everything,' Deans said. 'She has the knowledge and surgical skills, and access to equipment.'

'Granted, she's got the means to do something like this, but Christ, this was her father,' Jackson said jabbing his finger at Archie Rowland's name.

'Human sacrifice was practised at times of war and to pay homage to the Gods,' Deans said. 'I've looked it up.'

'Oh, you've looked it up! 'What? So you are telling me these people have been sacrificed to respect some perverse ancient belief?'

'Not necessarily. To them, this is war; I was closing in on Babbage. You might say I was in their way. Maybe Amy Poole was a sacrifice, maybe she wasn't, but as soon as I became involved, Ranford and Babbage took their vengeance out on Maria.'

'What about Archie Rowland?' Sarah asked.

'Same thing – he was getting answers, exposing the truth. Ring any bells?'

Ice crusted over Jackson's eyes. He took himself to the edge of Ranford's desk and sat down. He had a glazed and far away expression.

'How many others are there?' Sarah asked.

'I don't know,' Deans said.

'And how do you propose we find out?' Jackson asked. 'Put an ad in the *Herald*?'

'We flush them out,' Deans responded blankly.

'Just exactly how do you plan to *flush them out*?'

'We give them what they want.'

CHAPTER FOURTEEN

Jackson's head was buried deep into his hands. 'If you are right,' he said down to his knees, 'this could be massive. Bigger than anything any of us have dealt with. It could become global news.'

Deans nodded.

'It will need serious planning. Resources. Mutual aid.'

'We need just one other person,' Deans said facing the board with his back to Jackson.

'Who?' Jackson asked.

Deans looked back at Jackson and waited a few seconds before answering. 'Denise Moon.'

'You have got to be kidding? I'm not in the game of jeopardising the safety of any of my team, let alone a civilian.'

'She'll keep *us* safe, not the other way around.'

The lines grew deep and wide on Jackson's face. 'Well, how much can you trust her?'

Deans made a point of looking Jackson up and down and then he did the same with Sarah.

'Probably more than the pair of you put together.'

Jackson's shoulders stiffened and his teeth showed between his narrowing lips.

'Denise is fine,' Deans said, preventing Jackson from having an excuse to vent his authority. 'We simply can't do this without her. I'd go as far as to say, she's essential.'

Jackson arched his back and cupped his head in his hands. The damp of his armpits showed through his lavender coloured shirt. It was all of sixteen degrees in the old office. Deans was ready to put another layer on, not the other way round.

'Okay,' Jackson said fixing his stare at Deans. 'Okay. Can you get her to come over now? Time is obviously against us.'

Deans pulled his mobile phone from his trouser pocket and held it in the air. 'Only one way to find out.'

Denise answered on the third ring.

'Hi Denise, it's Andy.'

Hi Andy

'You are on hands-free. Is there any chance you can come and meet me at the station, please?'

Where do you need to go now?

Deans smiled at the others. 'It's actually you that needs to come here.'

Why what's happened. Are you okay?

'I'm fine. It's not me... we need your help.' Deans looked over at Jackson.

We? Denise questioned.

'I'll explain when you come. How quickly can you get here?'

I have an appointment in an hour.

'Cancel it. Cancel the day. You're going to be with us today.'

Us?

'Denise... can you come?'

Well, I suppose so. But what about my appointments? This is my livelihood.

'Tell her we'll compensate her time,' Jackson said.

'Don't worry about your losses, Denise. We'll cover it this end.'

Forty minutes of rearranging appointments and a quick walk along the Quay, and Denise was with them in the CID office.

'So, this is it.' Jackson said. 'Just the four of us.'

'Don't you think we should involve the DCI?' Sarah said.

'How do you know who else we can trust?' Jackson said. 'Look at Ranford. Who is to say others from the station or the wider policing district aren't involved? We don't know how much bigger this thing could be, if at all.'

Jackson stood alongside Deans and studied the white board.

'Where do we begin?' he asked.

'Has to be with Annie Rowland,' Deans said quietly. 'Get her in. Ask her some questions. See what comes out.'

'You think she is going to give it up, just like that?'

'No.'

Jackson turned his feet towards Deans, who reciprocated. Now they were toe to… leg cast.

'We can't arrest her,' Jackson said. 'There is absolutely no evidence. All we have is supposition.'

'We don't need to arrest her. We can pull her in voluntarily. She can leave whenever she wants.'

'And if she doesn't come willingly?'

'Then we use the Ways and Means Act.'

Jackson grimaced and wiped a hand over his face.

'We may not get anything from her, but at least we can

exert some pressure. Become the hunter instead of the hunted,' Deans said.

'But if that doesn't work, we'll need a warrant of entry to bring her in,' Jackson said. 'It's so thin I can't see us getting it.'

'Can we risk not having a go?'

Jackson buried his head in his hands. 'I'll have to involve the DI. I just have to.'

'I know,' Deans said. 'It's inevitable others will need to be brought in at some stage.'

Jackson's eyes skirted around Deans' face.

'We will probably need uniform to help us gain entry,' Deans said. '…If it comes to that.'

'Jesus! This will be impossible to contain,' Jackson spat. 'And what if she is entirely innocent? The poor girl has just lost her father and half a dozen hairy-arsed coppers burst in through the door while she's sobbing into a pillow.' He lowered his head and scuffed his heels against the felt floor tiles, like he was wiping dog mess from the bottom of his shoes.

'Right,' he said addressing the room. 'I need solid information before we do anything else. Gold, I need you to hit that Intel like your job depended on it… it may well.' He pinned back his hunched shoulders and stood tall. 'I want every single aspect covered – no matter how small, how old, how difficult – just get it done. I want to know what time Annie Rowland goes to work, what time she takes a shit, everything. You got me?'

Sarah nodded.

'Deans, you help her; Gold churns it out, you interrogate the material.'

Deans agreed. It sounded like a sound proposition for starters.

Jackson turned to Denise. 'Sorry, but these systems are

confidential and for police eyes only.' He slapped the side of his legs with a thud. 'That's just the way it is.'

'Don't worry about Denise,' Deans said. 'Her help will be required later.'

Denise spoke for the first time. 'What about the archives in North Devon Museum?'

'What about them?' Jackson asked brusquely.

'They may have records dating back. Details of land owners, family names that may still exist. Could be of help?'

'Good call,' Deans said. 'What time do they close?'

Denise shook her head. 'I can make those enquiries.'

'Good,' Jackson said. 'You do that, and if they are open, go across with the other two.'

Deans gave Denise a wink. Jackson smiled at her with insincere eyes.

'And what about you?' Deans asked Jackson.

'Me? Well, somebody has to sell this hair-brained idea to the DI.'

CHAPTER FIFTEEN

By the time Deans and Sarah had exhausted the intelligence databases, the afternoon had all but faded away. The museum manager said he had an interest in local Viking history and despite the closing time of five p.m., he would stay on the premises until they arrived. Deans suspected he was a nosey bugger who wanted to know what was happening, but they tended to be useful in the long run, if they had something of value to contribute.

Sarah began driving them from the station and as they dropped down onto the main road, Deans shot a glance over his shoulder towards the pavement on the opposite side.

'Stop,' he shouted to Sarah. 'Stop the car.'

'I can't just stop in the middle of the road.'

'Pull over,' Deans demanded. 'Pull over now.' Deans was straining to look out of the back window.

'What is it?' Sarah asked – the anxiety in her voice only too clear. She cut in front of the oncoming traffic and dived into one of the available parking bays at the side of the road.

'Sorry,' Deans said still looking backwards. 'But I can't run.'

'Run?'

'See that man?' Deans said, pointing to a man back along the pavement with a video camera. 'I need you to stop him. You have to run after him and detain him until I get there.'

'I can't just—'

Deans flung his door wide open and was already climbing out. Oncoming drivers swerved around him and expressed their displeasure with long blasts of car horns and angry shouted expletives.

Sarah was now also out and chasing behind the man who was quickly moving away. She was a rapid sprinter and soon caught up with him.

Sarah held the man against the handrails at the side of the estuary promenade. Deans could see them both looking his way, as he did his best to catch them up.

The man cowered as Deans came closer. His arms tight in to his body and holding something close to his chest. Sarah was doing what she could to pacify him while still keeping him from escaping.

Breathing heavily, Deans was now just feet away. The man looked desperate. He walked straight up to the man and shoved him backwards firmly in the chest. Instinctively, Sarah straight-armed Deans away.

'What the hell are you doing?' she shouted to him.

'Who are you?' Deans shouted to the man. 'Who are you?'

Deans reached over the top of Sarah's long arm in a vain attempt to have a second strike. The man had nowhere to go; a triple cast iron railing pressed against his lower limbs and was all that separated him from a steep concrete bank and dip in the less than welcoming brown tidal waters.

'Which tabloid do you work for?' Deans shouted.

'I don't,' the man said with fear in his voice. 'I'm not a tabloid reporter—'

'Then why are you following me?' Deans screamed. 'Have some respect.'

'Andy, Andy, please... don't do this,' Sarah pleaded with him, trying to push Deans further backwards.

'This piece of shit filmed me at my wife's funeral,' Deans raged. 'What else do you want from me you fucking parasite?'

'I'm sorry,' the man pleaded, crouching down, his arms now covering his head and face.

Deans could see the camcorder hanging around the man's neck on a long canvas strap. 'Give me that camera,' Deans ordered, lunging over Sarah Gold once again.

'It's not what you think,' the man whimpered from behind his protective arms.

'Then why are you following me?' Deans bellowed.

The man jabbed a hand into his outer coat pocket and produced a fist full of business cards. He held them outstretched in a shaking hand.

Sarah Gold took one of the cards and peered at it. She placed her body directly between the two men, just in case Deans took advantage of her temporary distraction.

She looked at the man, studied the card again and pulled a confused face.

Deans snatched the card from her hand and looked at it. *William E. Palmer – Senior Paranormal Investigator. The British Paranormal Guild.*

'What's this?'

'I'm Billy Palmer. I promise. I'm not a tabloid reporter.'

'But you *are* following me?'

Billy Palmer looked to Sarah for reassurance. She leaned over and helped him to stand up from his defensive squat position.

'It's alright,' she said. 'He won't hurt you.' She glowered at Deans. '*Will you.*'

Deans was still looking down at the rainbow coloured business card.

'Why are you filming me?' Deans asked. 'Wasn't my wife's funeral enough misery for you to witness?'

Billy Palmer ran a hand through his unkempt, bushy beard and once more sought the security of DC Gold.

'Well?' Deans shouted. 'Wasn't it?'

Billy Palmer nodded nervously.

'Give me that,' Deans demanded lunging for the camera.

'You can't,' Sarah said, once more standing in Deans' way. 'You don't have a legal power to seize it.'

'Sod powers. How long have you been following me?'

The man looked left and then right. Deans mirrored his actions.

'There's nowhere to run, sunshine.'

'Since the train crash,' Billy Palmer finally said. 'Since you were the only survivor of your carriage.'

Deans squinted. 'Why?'

'Because...' Billy Palmer hesitated.

'Because?'

'Well, because you should have died.' The man's face dropped on seeing Deans' flaming eyes. 'And because...' he said quickly. 'Because... you are *special*.'

Deans scratched the back of his neck. 'Meaning?' His voice was firm and aggressive.

'This is no ordinary camera,' Billy Palmer said wrapping a protective arm around the boxy casing hanging from his neck. 'It records paranormal activity.'

Sarah's face was screwed up tight.

'How many times have you recorded me?'

Billy Palmer shook his head. 'I can't remember.'

'How did you know where to find me?'

Billy Palmer's mouth widened. 'You are like a beacon to people like me.'

Deans scoffed and waved the back of his hand at the man.

'I want it to stop. Do you understand me? No more filming. No more following. No more anything. You get me?'

'That would be a shame,' Billy Palmer uttered beneath his breath. 'But of course, I understand.'

'Do you?' Deans glared. 'Do you understand?'

'Yes,' Billy Palmer said timidly.

'Good. Now piss off.'

Deans thrust his hand away, turned, and hobbled back towards the car.

Sarah was still talking to Billy Palmer by the time Deans was back inside their vehicle.

'Who was that?' Denise asked.

'No one.'

'You looked annoyed. Are you okay?'

'I'm fine.'

'Are you sure?'

'I'm fine.'

Sarah rejoined them and looked with ferocity at Deans.

'What was that?' she asked sharply.

'Some nut-job.'

'I've probably just sweet-talked that gentleman from placing a complaint of assault against you. What the hell is wrong with you?'

'I thought he was tabloid scum. I got it wrong, but he shouldn't have been filming me.'

'That still doesn't make it right to go around whacking people.'

'I didn't *whack him*. I gave him a little tap and told him to piss off. He got away lightly, if you ask me.'

'Jesus!' Sarah said slapping the steering wheel. 'You are becoming so angry and unpredictable.'

Unpredictable, Deans thought. *Maybe that's not such a bad thing.*

CHAPTER SIXTEEN

The traffic jams in Barnstaple were almost as epic as the ones Deans endured in Bath. True to his word, the proprietor was waiting for them behind an ostentatious locked wooden door. Sarah showed him her warrant badge and he welcomed them inside with willing enthusiasm.

'This is something of a treat,' the proprietor said. 'Someone else with an interest in Viking heritage. We have an extensive display of artefacts, if you'd care to see them?'

'Yes, please,' Deans said catching Denise's eye. 'So they were here?'

'Yes, indeed, and what a fascinating people they were.'

The proprietor took them through to an echo-chamber of a room with glass display cabinets against the walls and a large glass coffin in the middle of the floor containing various decayed items. Deans walked to one of the wall units and studied a misshapen and heavily tarnished battle helmet.

'That was actually one of the Saxon remnants we found on the bloody battle grounds of Hemingsford,' the proprietor said standing alongside Deans.

'You have artefacts from Hemingsford battle ground?' Deans asked.

The man laughed pompously. 'Pretty much everything you see in this room is excavated from those green, undulating pastures. Hard to imagine the horror of that time,' he said looking off distantly.

'Maybe not quite as hard as you'd think,' Deans commented beneath his breath.

'I beg your pardon?'

'How much do you know about the invasion and battles?' Deans said diverting his previous remark.

The proprietor rubbed his hands together and emitted a high-pitched self-satisfied whine. 'I know a fair amount, it must be accepted.'

Sarah had joined Deans. 'Good,' she said. 'We need to understand as much as possible and we don't have long.'

'Oh, well, that's a different story,' the proprietor said pulling himself away from the cabinet and looking to see what Denise was interested in.

'Meaning?' Deans said.

'This is my life's work. You must dedicate yourself to truly understand the intricacies of that extraordinary people and era.'

'We don't have time,' Deans said facing the proprietor. 'What are you doing for the next few days?'

'Working here, of course.'

'Not any more,' Deans said. 'You are now working for the police on a very need-to-know basis.'

'What? I just can't—'

'You can, and you are.'

'Just hold on, young man. Do not assume to know one's business and start throwing your weight around here. I'll have to ask you to leave.'

'I'm really sorry,' Sarah said. 'My friend doesn't mean to be so direct.' She looked daggers at Deans. 'But we really do need someone with extensive local knowledge and advice in your specialist field to help us with a serious and ongoing investigation.'

Deans shook his head and walked over to Denise on the other side of the room. Sarah was proving to be quite the diplomat.

'A serious and ongoing investigation?' the proprietor repeated. 'Related in some way to our Viking heritage – I don't understand?'

'You don't need to,' Deans said from across the room. 'What do you know about the cult following of Hubba The Dane?'

The man chuckled, dipped his head and centred the spectacles on the tip of his nose. 'What do you mean?' he said, looking over the top of his glasses at Deans.

'The modern-day following of Pagan beliefs,' Denise said.

'And their practices,' Deans continued.

Sarah looked confused, but the proprietor moved towards another glass-walled cabinet. He stood silently in front of the display and stared inside.

Deans, Denise and Sarah joined him and all four of them looked inside the spotlessly clear box.

'It is true; there are those who believed the bloodline continued.'

Deans slid his eyes towards Denise.

'But I have never seen evidence of it.'

The proprietor was looking at a metal pendant with three interlinking triangles and leather bound necklace, taking centre stage of the cabinet.

'And what do you believe,' Deans asked, 'being the font of all knowledge on this particular topic?'

Sarah kicked the side of his ankle.

Deans watched the man's reflection in the glass. His focus had shifted from the pendant and he was looking at himself. He noticed Deans staring back at him. 'Oh, I don't think there's anything in it,' he said.

'Really?' Deans asked.

The proprietor turned with a flat smile. 'Really.'

'Okay, thanks for your time,' Deans said. 'We'll be in touch if we have any more questions.'

'Yes. Yes, of course.'

'Oh,' Deans said slapping his forehead. 'Do you have contact details?'

'Yes, hold on.' The proprietor left them in the gallery and walked back towards the museum entrance.

'He knows something,' Deans whispered to Sarah. 'He doesn't believe his own words.'

The proprietor returned and handed Deans a yellow compliment slip. 'Here you are. I'm available most of the time, either here, or on my private number, which I have added at the top of the page.'

'Thanks,' Deans said grasping the small slip of paper.

'I hope you catch them,' the proprietor said.

Deans paused before taking his hand back. 'Most enlightening,' he said. He flapped the paper. 'I'm sure we'll need to talk again.'

CHAPTER SEVENTEEN

The DI was with Jackson. He was talking on the phone. It sounded like there were issues with a prisoner at another station, from what Deans could make out. The DI was young. If ever there was an example of the new fast-track promotion system, this was it. He probably had a good brain on his shoulders and a degree – it seemed any would do to satisfy the human resources recruitment requirements, but he still looked like he needed his mum to get him dressed in the mornings.

The DI ended the call with a slam of the receiver. He noticed DC Gold and a cheesy smile instantly replaced his exasperated expression.

'Okay,' Jackson said. 'Now the others are here we can begin.'

'I'm very busy,' the DI said to Jackson. 'This had better be good.'

The look Jackson gave the DI didn't attempt to hide the disdain he clearly held for the younger man.

'We are dealing with several murders, *sir*. Have you heard about them in the boardroom?'

The DI scoffed and cleared his throat behind his hand. He

glanced over his shoulder to see if DC Gold was looking his way. She was… and so was Deans.

The DI looked at his watch.

'Got something more important than a murder, *sir*?' Jackson remarked.

The DI half-turned, stopping just short of looking at DC Gold again. The silence in the room must have told him that everybody was watching, and listening.

'You know the plight of Detective Ranford, I presume?' Jackson continued.

'Yes. Yes, of course,' the DI replied impatiently. 'Well, he was one of *yours* wasn't he?'

Jackson smiled. 'Not exactly mine, but I see where are you coming from. Anyway, we have to be mindful of who has access to the information we are collating, because we simply don't know if he acted alone or with others.'

The DI appeared confused, the tight youthful skin of his forehead, forming hairline cracks. He had a lot of stress to come his way if he was going to match Jackson's corrugation. His eyes blinked their way to Denise who was standing nearest to the door.

'I need assurances that we have the backing of the bosses, if, and when things get spicy,' Jackson said.

'I can't offer anything of the sort. You will have to follow the legal procedures and protocols like everybody else. You can be rest assured that any material gathered in the course of the investigation will be handled with the utmost confidentiality and respect.'

Deans stood forward. 'People are dying, sir. We know Ranford worked with Ash Babbage, but there's no way either of them murdered Archie Rowland. Another killer is still at large.'

The DI tossed a glance at Jackson who nodded.

'What do we know so far?' the DI asked.

Jackson turned to the board, but before he could speak, Deans cut in. 'It's early days, sir. We just need to know that we can progress this in the most appropriate manner to gain the maximum result.'

The DI smiled a politician's smile. 'I understand that you, more than anyone, have a vested interest in this investigation, Detective Deans.' He looked at each of them in turn. 'But you must realise that none of you are above the law. Forensic Pathologist Rowland's death, tragic as it was, will be investigated in the same manner as every other death in these circumstances. You will not deviate from that. Do you understand?'

Deans stared at the DI.

'I'm sorry, officer. I didn't hear your answer. I said do you understand?'

Deans returned the fake smile and ceremonially bowed his head.

'I don't agree,' Jackson said bluntly.

The DI shot him a look of fury.

'You know what, as detectives we sometimes have to think outside of the box. Those are the skills that got us here in the first place.' Jackson walked an arc in front of the DI as if baiting him. 'I don't know where you worked before becoming the latest DI... the local supermarket for all I care, but this is how *real* detectives work. This is how we get results, and this is how we prevent more deaths. Don't talk to me about procedures and policy. I normally work in Professional Standards. If I can't keep this investigation above board, then nobody can. All we are asking for is anonymity and the authority from you to progress this investigation prudently and expeditiously. I will feed you all the details you need. We will abide by the laws of PACE (Police and Criminal Evidence

Act), but if information seeps, you will be the first to know about it.'

The DI stood planted to the spot.

Deans applauded Jackson in his head. He never thought he would hear himself saying it, but Jackson was starting to grow on him.

The DI turned his back and faced the white board for a moment.

Deans could see his shoulders lift and drop with each deep breath. He waited for the reaction.

The DI began to raise his wristwatch to his face and stopped himself short. 'Right,' he said still looking at the board. 'Right.'

'I want Magistrate's authorisation for a Section Eight PACE search of Annie Rowland's flat and any other buildings she has control of,' Jackson said.

Deans stumbled backwards with surprise.

The DI looked Deans up and down in silence.

'And I want a team of six uniformed officers on standby,' Jackson continued.

'We don't have six PCs to put on standby.'

'Then you'd better find some. People are dying out there and I don't want any of my team to be next.'

The DI looked warily at DC Gold who broke eye contact and her cheeks flushed rouge.

'Can we go somewhere more... private,' the DI asked Jackson.

'I know just the room.' Jackson caught Deans' eye with a wry twinkle.

'Bring all of your supporting material. I'm not authorising anything unless I believe there are solid grounds to suspect involvement with these deaths.'

'Understood entirely,' Jackson said. 'Detective Gold and

Deans have been working tirelessly on that throughout the day – along with Miss Moon.'

The DI cocked his head back towards Denise.

'Good. Good. Good work,' he said addressing Sarah Gold. 'Okay, shall we?'

Jackson looked at Deans and Gold before he left the room. 'Get yourselves home. We won't be implementing any warrants tonight – it'll need thorough planning and risk assessment.' He winked and led the DI out of the room and left Deans and Sarah motionless for a second.

'Can you believe the way he spoke to DI?' Sarah whispered.

'I have to admit,' Deans said. 'He's full of surprises.'

CHAPTER EIGHTEEN

Deans remained in the office with Sarah while Denise made her way back home. There was little point in her staying around while they top and tailed the day's enquiries and prepared themselves for what would no doubt be another onslaught in the morning.

'What are you doing later tonight?' Sarah asked Deans.

'Nothing. Sleeping.'

'Fancy coming over to mine for some pasta?' she asked. 'Nothing fancy, I can knock something up in no time.'

Deans hesitated. This smacked of déjà vu. He raised his eyebrows.

'I won't try to seduce you… I promise,' she said with a mischievous grin.

'Have you got any alcohol?'

'Always.'

'Okay. I'll come.'

Deans phoned Denise to say that he'd be back later. She didn't ask why and he didn't offer a reason.

Deans remembered Sarah's townhouse well, and just as before, he followed her up the steep staircase to the living area.

'Grab a seat,' Sarah said. 'Sauvignon Blanc okay for you?'

'Thanks.'

Deans sat down and was immediately rewarded with a large glass of chilled wine.

Sarah kicked off her shoes and joined him on the sofa. She tucked her legs beneath her and faced him.

'What did you mean when you said you could trust Denise Moon more than me?'

'Oh, it was just a figure of speech, reinforcing my faith in Denise.'

Sarah tipped her head and looked at Deans beneath seductive lids. 'Are you sure?'

'Yes, I'm sure. Jackson needs reining in sometimes, otherwise he gets too excited.'

Sarah offered her glass towards Deans and he tapped it against his own glass.

'So...' she said. 'Here you are again.'

Deans scratched behind his ear and looked away.

'Anyone would think there's something in North Devon that keeps you coming back.'

'There is.'

Sarah smiled.

'My wife's killer.'

The gloss smudged from Sarah's pouting lips and then she said, 'Can I ask you a question?' Her keen eyes searched his face. 'That man, earlier – he said you were, *special*. What exactly did he mean?'

Deans shifted in his seat. 'It doesn't matter.'

'Yes, it does. You *are* special, but I want to know what he meant by it?'

Deans winced and turned the other way.

'Come on, don't be like that.'

Deans sipped his drink creating a few seconds of delay to consider whether to tell her, or not.

He lowered his chin to his chest and bounced his head. 'I should have died on that train.' He closed his eyes and sucked despondently through his nose. 'In some respects, I wish I had.'

'Oh, don't talk that way.'

'I mean it. I don't know why, but I was spared from death and plunged into *this* life.' He gulped wine from his glass, tilted Sarah a look and drank some more.

'You still have some things to live for,' Sarah said quietly.

Deans didn't answer.

'Being a detective, well, we help so many people. What would they do without you?' She pulled her knees up onto the sofa and turned towards him. 'What would I do without you?'

Deans finished his glass and Sarah duly topped it up again. He took another large mouthful and sat bolt upright, spilling wine onto his hand and lap.

'What is it?' Sarah asked looking around the room with sudden alarm.

'Jesus!' Deans cried out launching himself to his feet. 'How bloody short sighted of me.'

'What, what is it?'

'The man from the Paranormal Guild.' Deans was energized.

'What about him?'

'He's been following me. Filming me.'

Sarah shrugged. 'Yes.'

'The killers have been one step ahead of me all this time. The only way they could do that is by knowing my movements.'

Sarah pulled a face.

'His camera,' Deans beamed. 'He might have recorded the killers.'

Their eyes met in wide anticipation.

'Do you still have his card?' Deans quickly asked.

Sarah dug into her front trouser pocket. It was there.

'Call him. Call him now. Let's get him over,' she said.

'You're happy for him to come here?'

'Yes, if it means we are getting closer to the answers.'

'What if he turns out to be a complete loon? He'd have your address.'

'I'm safe, you are with me. He's already petrified of you.'

'Alright, don't make me feel worse than I already am.'

'Give me the card, I'll call him myself.'

Sarah greeted Billy Palmer at the front door less than an hour later. As requested, he brought his camera, along with a second padded shoulder bag. Deans waited for him at the top of the stairs.

'Can we start again, please,' Deans said offering his hand.

Palmer nervously accepted the gesture and Deans welcomed him through to the living room.

'Look, I'm really sorry,' Deans said. 'I overreacted and I really do apologise for my actions.'

Palmer rolled his head – somewhere between a nod and a shake.

'How much footage do you have of me?'

Palmer looked at Sarah who had come alongside him.

'It's okay,' she said. 'Let me explain. You know about Andy's wife, don't you?'

Palmer's timid eyes glanced Deans' way. 'Yeah… yes. I'm aware.'

'The killers are still out there,' Sarah said gesturing with an outstretched arm towards the window. Palmer's head followed her pointing fingers.

'I need the footage,' Deans cut in. 'All of it. You don't realise, but you have been my personal CCTV operator.'

Palmer shook his head. 'I don't understand.'

Deans stepped forward, took Palmer's elbow and walked further into the living room.

'I believe I'm being followed. And in the process of filming me, you may have unwittingly filmed the killers.'

Palmer glanced towards Sarah; he was seeking her constant reassurance. She nodded as such, but Palmer brought the camera closer to his chest.

'It's okay,' Deans said. 'We can view it here with you and if it's obvious nobody else is there, you can have it straight back.'

'It's extremely expensive equipment,' Palmer said turning his body away from Deans. 'It's irreplaceable.'

'We'll take good care of it,' Deans smiled. 'I promise.'

Palmer shuffled his feet further back from Deans.

'Can we have at look at some of it now?' Deans asked.

'We can connect it through the TV,' Sarah suggested, picking a hand controller up from a coffee table at the side of the sofa.

'Do you have cables?' Deans asked.

Palmer looked instinctively at the second padded bag hanging from his neck.

'Great,' Deans said. 'Turn it on, Sarah.'

'It's not a normal video recorder,' Palmer said defensively. 'You… you won't appear *normal*.'

'How do you mean?' Deans asked.

Palmer was hugging his equipment close to his chest.

'Let's just connect it up, shall we,' Deans said keenly.

Sarah took the connecting cable from Palmer's reluctant

grasp and fiddled with the back of the TV until the cable hung down ready to connect to the camera.

'Take a seat,' Sarah said to Palmer, pointing to the armchair.

The TV screen came to life and Deans and Sarah sat down together on the sofa.

'I've got a remote for the camera,' Palmer said giving in to the fact Deans and Sarah were not going to be swayed. 'It'll make it easier to navigate.' He rummaged through the camera bag, removed a small black controller and clicked through a sequence of commands until the screen showed the familiar image of the road beneath Torworthy Police Station.

'This was yesterday?' Deans asked.

'Yes. Before you stopped me.' Palmer "rinsed" his hands in a display of anxiety.

'It's okay,' Deans said to him. 'Relax.'

Palmer scratched the side of his nose and rocked back and forth in his chair.

'Play it,' Deans said.

Palmer caught Sarah's eye, faltered for a beat and then pointed the controller towards the video camera. The image on the television rewound at a fast pace and then began playing with cars driving by in both directions as Palmer panned along the length of the slope leading to the elevated position of Torworthy Police Station. The camera quickly switched back to a car leaving the station grounds. Deans immediately recognised the maroon Ford Focus they had been using that day. He watched as their car drove past the camera position, slowed, and then stopped abruptly as break lights glowed on the screen. Deans saw Sarah exit the car and make her way quickly towards the camera. He leaned in closer to the screen and gave Sarah a sideways glance. She was still looking at the screen with a bewildered expression. Deans turned back to the TV, Sarah had a deep amber glow around her body. His car

door was open and the camera swiftly zoomed in on to Deans'
face, all twisted and determined.

Deans slowly rose from his seat as he watched the large
screen TV. The footage jiggled and blurred, and veered away
ending up at Palmer's own feet as he took evasive action, the
camera still recording.

Deans was motionless. His mouth gaped wide and his
arms dropped to his sides.

Nobody spoke.

Deans lifted a saggy arm and pointed it at the TV. 'What is
that?'

'I told you,' Palmer spluttered. 'It's not a normal video
camera.'

Sarah was gawping at Deans with disbelief etched into her
face.

Deans turned to Palmer. 'Why do we have a kaleidoscope
of colours around us?'

'That is your auric footprint.'

Deans blinked. 'Auric footprint?'

'We all have an aura that denotes our vibrations with the
Universe,' Palmer said.

Deans' eyebrows were reaching for the ceiling.

'Our *spiritual DNA,* if you like.'

'How do you—?' Deans struggled with his question.

'We use a special filter – it's probably the best way to
describe it. Anyone's aura will be displayed in a similar
manner.' Palmer pressed rewind on the remote control and
then froze the image of Deans outside of the vehicle coming
towards him. 'But yours is very exciting.'

Deans turned to the TV again. His head was surrounded by
a hue of indigo, violet and pink light.

Palmer stood up from his seat. 'Up until now, only still
photographs have been available using electrodes on the body.

But this camera brings an aura to life. I have witnessed your spiritual transformation over an extremely short period of time.' He pointed to the TV screen. 'Just two weeks ago, you were something quite different. Something… *almost normal.*'

'Almost normal?' Sarah repeated. 'That's a bit of an insult, isn't it?'

'Have you sensed it?' Palmer asked Deans. 'Are you… *aware*?' His voice was excitable.

'Aware of what?' Sarah asked looking confused at Deans and Palmer in turn.

Palmer was alight with energy. 'Mr Deans is at the very highest level of vibration with the Universe. He is perfectly in tune with the spiritual realms. A conduit of spiritual energy and enlightenment.' He beamed a broad smile.

'What?' Sarah giggled.

Deans shuffled his way to the couch and slowly lowered himself down.

Sarah watched him, her face contorted.

Deans rested his forehead into the palms of his hands and gently rocked back and forth.

'Andy, why aren't you saying something?' Sarah's voice was crackling with stress.

Deans rubbed his face and peered at them both through bloodshot eyes.

Palmer fast-forwarded the footage and paused the screen on a full-frontal image of Deans. They all stared up at the television.

Palmer approached Deans and lowered a soft hand onto his back. 'Look at the aura,' he whispered. 'Look at the colour and shape surrounding your shoulders. It's not a trick of light and it's not a mistake.'

Deans looked deeply into Palmer's eyes.

Palmer nodded. 'They walk among us,' he whispered. '*You*, walk among us.'

Deans and Sarah were alone. Billy Palmer had agreed to leave all of his recordings on the basis that he could spend more time with Deans at a later date. Sarah had opened another bottle of wine and was doing a fine job of seeing it off all by herself.

'This is a joke, right?' she said between rushed sips.

Deans shook his head. 'Afraid not.'

'You *communicate* with the dead?'

'I have done.'

Her eyes bounced around his face with an awkward urgency.

'How exactly?'

'I don't know. It just happens.'

'When? When did you start seeing ghosts and when were you going to let me in on this little secret?'

Deans returned his head to his hands.

'I suppose she knows?'

'Who?' Deans said into his wrists.

'Denise Moon.'

Deans slowly peeled his face from his hands and turned to Sarah.

'I don't want this. I don't understand this and I certainly don't need *this*, but it's real. I'm not sleeping at night because I'm seeing things I don't want to see. I'm scared to close my eyes because of what they show me.'

'What do they show you?' Sarah's tone softened and she bounced closer towards him, her knee resting on top of his leg, her hands wrapped around his.

Deans rocked his head and clenched his teeth. 'Disturbing. Brutal. Tragic. Personal things.'

'Are you seeing crimes being committed?'

He nodded. 'Probably.'

'Any that you... know?'

He bunched his eyes and lowered his chin.

Sarah gripped his hand tightly and pulled herself close in to him. 'Andy,' she softly spoke. 'You're not alone in this. Let me in. I can help you.'

Deans could feel her breath on the side of his face. His heart rate quickened and he breathed in her sweet scent, and held it deep in his chest. He felt a light hand rest on the inside of his thigh. Eyes still closed, he swallowed deeply and turned his head into her breath, and felt the warm moisture of her lips upon his.

CHAPTER NINETEEN

Deans began to cough long before he opened his eyes. He rolled over and pulled a pillow over his face. He knew he had to sleep. Today was going to be a significant day and he needed to be fresh. He'd even refused an alcoholic drink from Denise. He hadn't stayed with Sarah. Her lips were like daggers to his heart. He wrapped his arm over the pillow and pulled it tight to his face, but it was no use. He opened his eyes, his eyelashes brushing the white cotton case as he blinked. His breathing became shallow and his heart pounded loudly against the warm duvet. He tossed the pillow to the base of the bed and eased himself up onto his elbows with a groan, and spluttered as his eyes cut through the sludge of darkness towards the window.

He stared motionless for a disoriented second and then tossed the duvet aside, leaping to his feet with a start as a glow from the window drapes brought flickering light into the room. A bright amber flash of light blinded him, and he stumbled backwards into the dressing table as one of the thin material curtains flared instantly into flames and a cloud of black smoke tumbled its way up to the ceiling and rolled towards him like a large breaking wave.

He ducked down and looked towards the door. It was closed.

'Denise,' Deans shouted. 'Denise. Denise.'

Another explosion of bright flame forced him to shield his face. He quickly looked around. A tall glass of water had been left on the bedside table. He grabbed it and directed it above the flames, careful not to waste any on the wall. The fire erupted as if he'd just thrown petrol and he was forced back by the blast of hot light.

'Denise,' Deans screamed, his voice now as desperate as the situation demanded. He wrapped his neatly folded suit jacket around his knuckles, pulled it tight between his hands and lunged towards the fire in an attempt to starve it of oxygen. He felt the material melting onto his skin and heard the crackle of singeing hair on the backs of his hands. He grimaced in pain and immediately dropped the coat.

'Jesus! Get out, Denise. Get out of here.'

The fire was now well beyond his control, and he then made out a face peering in at him from the outside of the window. It was Sarah Gold.

'Get away, Sarah.' He waved frantically. 'Please, get away from the window.'

A huge rolling ball of flame passed inches above his head and he sank to his knees. He gawped helplessly at the devastation. The door burst open and Denise stepped inside the room and turned on the light.

'Get back,' Deans screamed.

Her calming smile confused him. He shot a look back to the window. The curtains were drawn. There was no fire... and there was no danger.

His chest heaved as he came to terms with his latest night terror.

'Andy, you're okay. You're safe. There's nothing to fear.'

Deans stared between Denise and the window. He struggled for breath, like he'd just sprinted to the room. He was standing beside his bed, just as he had been in the dream.

He gulped air and perched on the edge of the bed.

'You're okay,' Denise comforted and sat down beside him. She took his hand and gave it a squeeze. 'Was it Maria again?'

Deans licked his lips and shook his head. 'No,' he uttered.

Denise smiled. 'It's alright. You're perfectly safe here.'

Deans blinked focus back into his eyes and steadied his breath.

'What was it this time?' Denise asked.

Deans groaned, shook his head and dropped back into bed, pulling the sheets tight beneath his chin.

Denise stood in the doorway. 'Shall I leave the light on in the hallway and half-close the door?'

Deans nodded and within seconds had drifted back to sleep.

Denise was waiting for Deans at the breakfast table. A steaming mug of coffee and two poached eggs on toast were on the place mats opposite.

'Morning,' Deans said and took his seat.

'Morning.' Denise sipped from her cup and smiled at him. 'I've got something for you,' she said and handed Deans a department store carrier bag.

He looked inside and found a twin-pack of pale blue shirts, three pairs of white boxer shorts and three pairs of black socks.

'I forgot to give them to you last night. I thought they would probably make you feel better.'

'Thanks,' Deans said and slurped from his mug.

He removed the shirts, checked the size of the collar and chuckled.

'Did the spirits tell you?' he asked.

'No. I looked at your shirt label when you were showering yesterday morning.'

He lifted a pair of the boxers and checked the tag. 'Thank you. I really appreciate the gesture. How much do I owe you?'

Denise raised a hand and then hid behind her mug, watching Deans.

'Do you want to talk about last night?' she asked after half a minute of silence.

'Thank you for cooking breakfast,' he said evading the question.

Denise smiled with her eyes, but continued to stare at Deans with intensity.

'It was nothing,' Deans eventually answered.

'But it was different to the others?'

Deans glanced at Denise from beneath his lids and started cutting into his breakfast.

'You were calling my name.'

Deans nodded as he chewed his first mouthful of perfectly poached egg.

'So it involved me?'

Deans bobbed a shoulder and took some coffee.

'Andy, it's important.'

Deans placed his knife and fork down onto the plate and interlocked his fingers.

'Do you think it meant something?' he asked.

'I won't know unless you tell me. It might. Your skills are developing all of the time.'

He wiped a finger across his lips and held her gaze. 'There was a fire in my room – from the curtains.'

Denise leaned forwards.

'It was so real; I could feel the heat on my face. I was choking from the gasses. It was really happening.'

'Yes, that's evident from your reaction.'

'I was awake. I could see everything.'

'That is usual in night terrors; as if the dream crosses over with reality.' Denise narrowed her eyes. 'There's something else?' she said.

Deans nodded and lifted his coffee mug from the table.

'I saw Sarah Gold looking in at me from outside the window.'

Denise leaned back slightly in her chair. Deans picked up on the gesture.

'What?' he asked.

Denise shook her head. 'I don't know – what was she doing?'

Deans blinked his heavy lids. 'She was grinning.'

Denise shook her head. 'I can't help you there, other than to say it's okay to be interested in somebody else—'

'I'm not interested in Gold.'

'I see you both together. There's energy.'

Deans shrugged. 'I disagree.'

He finished his breakfast and thanked Denise again.

'Go on...' Denise said. 'There's something else bothering you.'

Deans smiled. Denise was good. He twisted his mug a couple of times to give him some thinking time.

'Ever heard of auric photography?' he asked after taking a measured sip of his drink.

'Yes, of course.'

'Do you believe in it?'

'Absolutely.'

'So, it's real?'

'Completely.'

'Can it show…' he coughed behind his hand. '…if somebody was… different?'

'Different how?'

'Can we use your laptop; I want to show you something?'

'What is it?' she asked, reaching for the laptop charging on the kitchen worktop behind her.

'I'll show you.'

Denise opened the laptop, tapped in a password and turned the screen towards Deans.

He placed a memory stick into the USB and found the sequence Palmer had used in Sarah's home. He found the still image he was hunting for and turned the laptop back towards Denise.

She looked at the image. Deans studied her reaction and she looked over the top of the screen at him, stood up and left the room, returning with a smile and her spectacles on the end of her nose. She sat back down and looked closer at the screen.

She carefully removed her glasses and placed them down on the table between herself and Deans.

'There,' she said. 'It's time to believe.'

Deans looked down at the old oak table and his fingers traced the line of the grain in the wood. 'I know,' he said softly.

'I know you know. So, what's next?'

'I need to go through each of these memory sticks and see if I can find *something*.'

'There must be a dozen sticks. That will take forever.'

'Thirteen. It will take as long as it takes. Welcome to police work.'

'Should I be seeing any of this?'

'Why not, you are part of the team now. On that note, I need you to do me a favour.'

'Of course.'

'There's a briefing at the station with the DI at nine-thirty. That gives us over an hour and a half to get to Ruby Mansell's house.'

'What? Why do you need to go back there?'

'Unfinished business.'

CHAPTER TWENTY

Deans looked at his watch. It was just passing the right side of eight a.m. A black void on the horizon loomed large ahead of them. It was the silhouette of Ruby Mansell's Victorian manor house. The place known locally as the 'haunted house.' The place where unspeakable acts of torture and violence took place in the dim and murky depths of the cellar. The place where Maria undoubtedly took her final breath.

The rising winter sun was unable to penetrate the heavy granite sky. They did not speak. What could they say? Deans knew this house held the secrets to his wife's murder, and possibly that of Amy Poole and Archie Rowland. From the first time he was drawn towards it, he somehow knew that the once home of Ruby Mansell, would define him.

They were now just metres away and Deans was already feeling cold to his core. He looked over at Denise who continued looking ahead as she drove. He was certain she felt the same. After all, *they* were the same.

She pulled slowly to a halt facing the front of the property, now boarded on all windows by half-inch plywood. Police tape gently quivered in the breeze across the entrance to the derelict archway.

'Are we going inside?' Denise asked without looking at Deans or taking her hands from the wheel.

'Yep.'

Deans cut her a look. Denise was blinking fast, still staring ahead through the windscreen. He dug a hand into his go-bag and removed a bunch of keys on a royal blue Devon and Cornwall Police key-fob. He held it up between them and rattled it.

'Where did you get those?' Denise asked, finally looking his way.

'I acquired them from the office.' He winked. 'Shall we?'

'I...' Denise hesitated and gulped air. 'I've got a bad feeling.'

Deans' eyes turned to the house. 'I know. I feel it too.'

'You don't have to do this,' she said. 'You don't have to do *any* of this.'

Deans tipped his head. 'My wife died in that house. I *will* find the killers. You don't have to come with me if you don't want to.'

'It's not that.' Denise looked up at the tall crumbling walls of the house and then at Deans. Her features were strained and alert. 'There's a powerful energy inside,' she said.

Deans could feel his heart beating faster beneath his jacket.

'I'm not saying it's necessarily bad. In fact, spirits aren't inherently evil. They are here to help us, to guide us.' She paused. 'It's just, the energy inside those walls has grown since the last time we were here and I fear it's greater than our combined abilities. If things don't work out as expected, I don't know if I could control it.'

'I hope you can't,' Deans said. 'I need to know what I'm facing.'

Denise fixed her gaze back on the building.

'You can't beat this energy,' she said.

'Denise. I'm not afraid to die, since…' his voice tailed away. '…I'm afraid to exist without living.'

She looked at him again.

'Everything happens for a reason, remember?' Deans said. '*This* is now my reason.'

He tugged on the door handle and the bitter air nibbled at his ankles. He stopped with one leg out of the door. 'And if that means taking a few risks. That's the way it has to be.'

He looked up to the tall, boxy chimney stacks and stood motionless, just as he had done several weeks before, but this time he wasn't fuelled by anticipation; this time, he was filled with revenge. Fingers of super-chilled air penetrated his jacket and tickled his spine. He shivered and shrugged off the unwelcome attention.

'It's here,' Denise said. She was behind him.

'Yes,' Deans breathed.

Denise came alongside his shoulder. 'Are you certain about this?'

'Yes.'

'Have you told anyone else that we are coming… just in case?'

Deans shook his head. 'Nope.' He stepped forward and raised the police tape above head height using his walking stick to gain further leverage. 'After you,' he said to Denise.

She walked below the tape without needing to duck and passed him with a concerned frown on her face.

Deans went to the front door, jiggled with the padlock and unlocked it. The door handle mechanism was removed and been replaced by two heavy steel finger-sized loops for the chunky padlock. He pushed firmly and the door creaked inwards creating a space large enough for them both to walk through. He took a tentative step inside the darkness. The hallway was even blacker than before, on account of the wooden boards shielding all external light. Thick cables criss-crossed the floor ahead of them and ran to a six-foot high tripod with four halogen lamps; leftovers from the forensic search. Deans could hear the throb of a nearby generator. The house had been left without electricity for a decade, since Ruby Mansell had passed away.

'Let's shed some light on this, shall we?' He moved to the lamps and switched them on.

Light carved through the dust-filled air with an incandescent hum, illuminating the hallway with a billion floating particles.

Deans suddenly felt aware and vulnerable, as if the light was screaming, awakening the unthinkable. Denise rushed beyond him and quickly shut them down.

They stood motionless, blinded by the darkness.

'What is it?' Deans whispered, attempting to introduce light from the torch on his mobile phone.

'We're not alone,' Denise uttered.

The hairs on Deans' scalp began to move in an upward motion like iron filings to a strong magnet above his head. He felt the air around his face begin to move and shone the narrow shaft of light at Denise. Her hand was covering her mouth and she turned abruptly and faced him.

Deans grabbed his throat with both hands. Air was locked in his windpipes. His stomach and neck muscles heaved to clear the blockage and free his tubes for a desperate intake of air. He stumbled backwards and his walking stick slammed onto the floorboards with a loud echoing crash. His eyes bulged and he squeezed his neck trying to open the airwaves. There was no sound. Time was frozen. Effort turned to panic as his lungs began to burn. He reached out for Denise, his fingers inches from her face. She rushed at him and shovelled him towards the partially opened front door. Deans fell to the floor on his back, his head outside in the cold sticky dirt of the derelict archway. He felt no air on his face as if his head was bound tightly in plastic sheeting. He could see Denise screaming, but he heard no words. His eyes rolled upward and saw ravens circling above him from the rooftop. There was nothing more to give – nothing more to fight.

I'm coming, Maria.

His body softened, his hands slackened, and Denise's terrified face faded out to blackness.

CHAPTER TWENTY-ONE

He opened his eyes with a start and lashed out wildly with his arms and legs as he tried to back away quickly from the door. He was lying on his back and facing the sky.

'It's okay, it's okay,' Denise said. She was leaning over him. 'Andy, everything's okay.'

He gulped the air. It tasted good. The front of Ruby Mansell's house was just feet away.

'You blacked out,' Denise said placing a warm flat hand onto his forehead. 'My God! You're burning up.'

Dribble trickled down one side of Deans' chin. He sucked oxygen into his lungs and rubbed the skin around his neckline.

'Have I got any marks?' he asked.

Denise leaned in and shook her head.

'I couldn't breathe,' he said.

'I know. You fainted.'

'How long was I out?'

'A few seconds, nothing more.'

Deans brought himself up to a seated position, his legs outstretched. He gawped in through the open front door and regulated his intake of air, until he was breathing normally again.

'They were here,' he said.

'Who were?'

'Not who: The sacrifices… the sacrifices were here.'

Denise gave him a long hard stare. 'Come on,' she said reaching beneath his arms. 'Enough of this talk. We'd better get you checked out at the doctors.'

'No.'

'You need help.'

'I've got all the help I need, from you.'

'Andy, the energy inside that building is powerful and I don't think we should—' she faced away from the house and whispered, as if the walls could hear what she was saying.

'I don't think we should go back inside, and I don't know if I can help you. This is beyond my understanding.'

Deans looked up at the face of the house. The coos and crackled calls from the ravens sounded more like laughter.

'That's exactly why I need to find out who is behind all of this, because I know who will be next.'

Denise took Deans back to her house to clean up before his briefing at Torworthy nick with the DI. He had suffered no lasting effects from his encounter at the old manor house, other than a significant dent to his confidence. They were back in the kitchen, Denise behind her laptop, Deans with a steaming mug of black coffee.

'I already researched Ruby Mansell,' Deans said as he watched Denise type her name into the search bar. 'She died in the house from an unspecified source of asphyxiation.'

Denise peered up over the top of the screen at him.

'I know,' he said. 'Maybe if you hadn't been there with me I would have suffered the same fate.'

He sipped from his drink watching Denise. Her brow furrowed as she absorbed information from the screen.

He rotated his mug back and forth. 'You know…' he said, 'for a moment… just a moment… I was going to give up.' He met Denise's gaze and slowly lifted his mug to his lips. 'But that would only end my pain.'

'That's not the answer,' Denise said.

Deans clenched his teeth.

'I'm going to end this. Not just for Maria, but for all of the victims.'

'How?' Denise asked. 'How can you possibly end it?'

'We give them what they want.'

'Which is?'

'A sacrifice.'

CHAPTER TWENTY-TWO

The DI and Jackson spoke closely in muted tones. Deans sat between Denise and Sarah Gold in front of the white board like eight-year-old school kids on detention.

'Is there a problem?' Sarah asked quietly in Deans' ear.

He shrugged. 'I suppose we are all about to find out.'

Jackson turned away from the DI and locked eyes with Deans. There could be no doubt; they were talking about him.

The DI stepped forward of Jackson and looked at the trio seated before him. 'There will be no investigation into Annie Rowland—'

'What?' Deans spat rising from his seat. 'That's a crazy decision.'

'It is my decision. And it is final, Detective.' The DI glared at Deans until he sat back down in his seat.

'Sergeant Jackson has provided me an investigative update and I do not believe the threshold has been met to arrest Annie Rowland, search her premises, or have reason to suspect that she has any involvement in these crimes.'

Deans looked at Jackson in disbelief. 'What about The

Raven Banner, the means and know how to mutilate the victims, the obvious connections to Ranford and Babbage?'

'You heard the boss, son,' Jackson sneered.

Deans looked to Sarah Gold to give him support. She sat in silence and gripped her knees.

'We won't get another chance to do this,' Deans pleaded.

The DI raised his eyebrows. 'If new evidence comes to light implicating Miss Rowland, then of course I will reconsider—'

Deans snorted sarcastically and shook his head.

'You disagree?' the DI questioned.

You fucking novice.

Deans looked again for Jackson to instil some common sense. Instead, he stood shoulder-to-shoulder with the DI, wearing a smug grin.

'You don't get it. You just don't get it.' Deans stood up and stormed out of the room.

Sarah found him with his head in his hands, sitting at the bottom of the stairs.

'Hey, come on. They're wrong,' she said.

'I can't believe how stupid that DI is. How are we supposed to get results with our hands tied like that?'

'We'll have to find another way.'

'Why didn't Jackson back us up?'

'You know what it's like…'

Deans wiped his face. 'I need a favour.'

'Of me?'

Deans nodded.

'Of course, what is it?'

'Can you drop me off at Hemingsford?'

Sarah's eyes skipped around his face for a moment.

'What are you going to do there?' she asked.

Deans ran a hand through his hair and sighed heavily. 'I'm going to do something I should have done days ago.'

. . .

She dropped Deans on the Quay at Hemingsford, the picturesque North Devon fishing village nestled into the hillside at the mouth of the estuary. He found his bearings and walked up the steep hill to the high-stoned wall that flanked the impressive property that was 'Trade Winds'. A once happy home that was now broken and shattered.

He crunched along the wide shingle pathway and banged on the large ornate wooden door, just as he had done before. To his mind, it seemed like an age ago, but the reality was much, much sooner.

The door opened after a couple of minutes and before Deans stood Mr and Mrs Poole. They looked older than he remembered. They all did. How tragic death could sap the soul from the living.

None of them spoke for an extended moment, and then Mr Poole turned and walked back into the home.

Deans looked deeply into the eyes of Amy's mother. The determination and fight that had burned so brightly, was now just scorched embers.

'Hello, Mrs Poole.'

'Good afternoon, officer,' she softly replied. She noticed his orthopaedic boot. 'What have you done?' she asked.

'A little accident,' Deans replied, surprised that she had not seen the deluge of news reports following the train derailment.

'May I come in, please?' he asked.

Mrs Poole dropped her head and gently nodded.

Deans hobbled through to the large reception room with the spectacular views across the estuary towards the sailing club. But this time, he didn't stand at the bay window and gawp. Instead, he stared at Amy's parents seated together on the sofa.

'How are you both?' he asked.

Neither spoke. Mr Poole faced away with a tight top lip.

'I lost my wife,' Deans said. 'She was murdered not long after Amy.'

Both tracked their hopeless eyes back in his direction.

'The same group who killed your daughter, murdered my wife.'

He saw a tear glistening on Mrs Poole's cheek. He shook his head. 'I'm not here for sympathy.'

She reached out with a clawed hand and he took it. Her skin was cold and dry like paper.

'I'd like, if possible, to see Amy's room again, if I may?'

Mr Poole scowled and turned away again.

'Has it changed?' Deans asked Amy's mother, her hand still clutching his.

She shook her head. 'No.'

'Can I go inside, please?'

Mrs Poole released her grasp and her hand dropped to her lap. 'Do you mind going yourself?' she asked.

No, Deans mouthed and left them in pitiful silence together on the sofa.

He entered Amy's bedroom and took it all in, but this time he was seeing with far more clarity. Mrs Poole was right – nothing had changed – it was still just three months since Amy's murder and Deans wouldn't have expected anything else.

He walked slowly around the outside of the room, his fingertips brushing the oak top of the dresser, his eyes scanning for a sign. He stopped at the entrance to the en-suite and a smile ran away from his lips as he remembered how much Maria had wanted one back at their home in Bath. The photo frame of Amy and Scotty was still on the bedside. He picked it up and looked at their beach-perfect youthful bodies. About to lower the frame, something made him look closer; beyond Scotty's right shoulder, Deans could see Ruby Mansell's house perched on the cliff edge. He had missed that the first time he was in this room, but that was understandable – the house had meant nothing to him then. It meant everything to him now.

He lowered the picture back down and adjusted it so that it was in the same position. He looked over his shoulder and checked the doorway – he was still alone. He pulled the top drawer of the bedside cabinet and sifted through the items. He removed a small metal tin and opened the lid. He lifted a pendant from within and held it aloft in front of his face. The synapses of his brain powered into overdrive.

He snatched the picture frame in his other hand and rushed back downstairs as fast as his broken ankle would allow.

'Do you know what this is?' he asked forcefully holding the dangling jewellery in front of Mrs Poole.

'Yes… it's Amy's pendant.'

'Where did she get it?' Deans asked hurriedly.

Mrs Poole shook her head. 'Scotty gave it to her years ago, when they were still together.'

'Can I take it?'

'Yes, you can take it, if you must?' Mrs Poole answered.

'And this?' Deans showed them the photo frame of Amy and Scotty.'

'Do you have to?' Mr Poole barked. 'We've nothing left of our little girl except…' his voice broke and tailed away.

Mrs Poole grabbed his hand and comforted him.

'Is there any way you can leave that?' she asked Deans.

He nodded. 'I understand. I'll put it back. I'm sorry.'

Mrs Poole gestured a silent apology with her face.

Deans turned the photo to show Mrs Poole. 'Did Amy ever talk about the haunted house; the one in this picture?'

Mrs Poole snorted. 'They were both infatuated with the place. You know what kids are like – scary stories and such.' Her brief moment of fond reflection melted away once again to pain. 'You should speak to Scotty, if you want to know more about it.'

Deans' eyes grew wide. 'Don't worry. I will.'

CHAPTER TWENTY-THREE

Deans found DS Jackson speaking to the DI in the first floor kitchenette.

'Where is Detective Mansfield based while we occupy the CID department?' Deans asked, interrupting them both.

'He's desk hopping downstairs,' Jackson replied. 'Why?'

'I need to see him.'

Jackson thought for beat. 'What about?'

'Doesn't matter what it's about.'

Jackson rubbed a hand over his bald pate. 'Go downstairs behind the Front Office, you will probably find him towards the uniform briefing room.'

Deans followed Jackson's directions and located DC Mansfield in a tiny box room, just about large enough for one desk and one computer. One pissed-off-looking detective was sitting on the chair.

'Hi,' Deans said, rapping a knuckle on the partially opened door.

Mansfield turned and his mouth dropped open. He quickly spun back towards the computer and clicked away from the website on the screen. If Deans wasn't mistaken, Mansfield was booking a skiing holiday.

'Can I speak to you?' Deans asked.

Mansfield glowered. 'Sounds like you are already.'

Deans shuffled in and closed the door. This was even cosier than the bollocking room upstairs.

'Do you remember I made an appointment for Scotty Parsons to give a statement regarding Amy Poole's disappearance?'

Mansfield rocked his head. 'Kinda.'

'Do you remember who was meant to take it after I returned to Bath?'

Mansfield looked down at Deans' leg cast and a curl formed in the corner of his mouth. 'I was.'

'But you didn't take it, somebody else did?'

'He didn't turn up.'

'Didn't you chase him?'

'No.'

'Why not?'

Mansfield poked out his bottom lip. 'I had other things to do, and besides, somebody else was going to take the statement instead.'

'Who?'

'Ranford.'

Deans bobbed his head. 'Do you know Scotty Parsons?' he asked.

Mansfield paused. 'No.' The intonation on the end of the word suggested he was second-guessing Deans' motivation for asking.

'Okay.'

'Meaning?'

'Okay – so, you say you don't know him.'

Mansfield rotated his chair to face the computer again. 'No. I don't know him. Anything else, I'm busy.'

'Did Ranford's involvement in the murders surprise you?'

Deans saw Mansfield's gaze fixate on the computer screen. 'I'm nothing to do with that. Ranford was his own person, just as I am mine. We worked together, that's as far as it went.'

Deans squinted. 'Why do you suppose you're not being involved in the murder enquiry upstairs?'

'Well, someone has to deal with the day-to-day crap, and I suppose that's me.'

'Would you want in?'

Mansfield calculated Deans' face for a second or two before nodding.

'Good,' Deans said. 'I have a little job I want you to help me with.'

'What is it?'

'I need you to spare me half an hour away from your… work,' Deans said.

'Why, what do you need me to do?'

'I need a lift.'

'Where?'

'I need you to drop me at Ruby Mansell's place.'

Mansfield leaned back in his seat and hooked his hands behind his head. He looked Deans up and down. 'What do you want to go back there for?'

'Don't worry about that. Can you take me? Yes, or no?'

A glint came to Mansfield's eye.

'Just so you know,' Deans said. 'I'm going alone. I just need a lift and that's it.'

'What are you going to tell Jackson?'

'Nothing, absolutely nothing – what he doesn't know isn't going to hurt him.'

CHAPTER TWENTY-FOUR

Mansfield dropped Deans close to the manor house and left him there at his request. Deans was taking a gamble, his gut feeling told him Mansfield wasn't involved – he was an arse-hole for sure, but he had an honesty Deans couldn't help but like.

Light was diminishing fast, but Deans had taken one of the dragon lamps from the boot of Mansfield's car "on loan". He walked towards the front of the run-down property and waved as Mansfield drove away. He waited until he was out of sight and then turned his back, facing the steep, tree covered hillside.

There were no directions, no obvious footpaths, but Deans knew that he would find Bone Hill, if he was meant to. He could have brought Denise to help him, but something was telling him he had to do this alone. He looked at the top of the tree canopy and found a raised area no bigger than a couple of tennis courts in circumference that were noticeably higher than those around them. Either they were taller trees, or they were growing on higher ground. It was a good place to start, so he began to trudge up the last piece of road before it ended and turned into uneven vegetation beneath his feet.

Soon, he'd lost the benefit of the outside tree line, but his internal compass was guiding him onward, deeper into the wooded canopy.

He turned on the lamp to counter the fading light. With a full-charge, he had about twenty minutes of light at his disposal, but he had no idea if this lamp had been re-charged before finding its way to the boot of Mansfield's car. The going was tougher than he imagined. His orthopaedic boot was becoming heavy. This was the first time since his surgery that he'd been required to walk for a sustained distance uphill and he was feeling it – especially as he'd decided against using his sticks.

It was a good ten minutes before he found the base of a slope to the higher ground. He sniffed the air, but all he picked up was the pastoral fragrance of foliage disturbed beneath his feet. He stopped at the base. The mound was eight or nine feet higher at the steepest section with thick tree trunks every few steps. This could never be a natural feature. It had to be man-made, but the trees growing on top were mature and well established. The ground was spongy with fallen leaves and debris beneath his feet as he took the first few steps onto the mound. To make it easier for him to approach, Deans walked further up the hillside to where the gradient of the mound was shallower.

A stone structure partially hidden by dense trees caught his attention and he directed the strong beam of light that way and made towards it.

As he neared, he could see a shear stone wall standing at least twelve feet high, yet still hidden beneath the upper branches of the trees. Vegetation had overwhelmed the derelict lower sections of the wall and thick tree trunks growing through the centre of the structure and all around it were probably all that stood between its current state and total collapse.

He edged closer. A bright shaft of light from his dragon lamp bouncing off centuries of decay in the stonework. He reached forward, touched the hard, cold surface and sucked in a deep breath of the petrichor air. Deans found something oddly calming about this place.

He circumnavigated the structure, shining his beam at every feature and came to the conclusion it was an old church or monastery, but why was it here – on this mystical place the ancients called Bone Hill?

He closed his eyes and tilted his head back. 'Maria,' he said quietly. 'If you can hear me, show me the way.'

The sound of cracking twigs nearby snatched his attention and he carved the light of a million candles in that general direction. Fallen leaves whirled into the air and spiralled energetically as if blown by a huge, silent fan below.

Deans strained to focus on the source of the vortex, no more than thirty metres away.

His eyes began to burn, afraid to blink. His heart rate stepped up and his skin became warm and prickly. He trained his eyes on the spot and slowly made his way towards it trying his best not to make unnecessary noise.

As he got closer, the aroma of Maria's perfume overcame his senses and almost instantaneously, the light from his lamp shut down.

He was close.

Show me, Maria. Show me what I need to see.

He shuffled towards the thick base of a tree where just beyond, the leaves had been dancing. His senses were exploding as his vision acclimatised to the darkness. He could hear blood surge past his ears towards his brain. He held his breath and slowly circled the tree until he was standing on the opposite side.

There was nobody there, but the smell of *Maria* was all-encompassing. He took out his phone and used the torch application to scan beyond the next clump of trees. He could hear his heart beating in the deathly silence, and as he moved slowly ahead, his foot became caught on a hidden object. He directed the narrow shaft of light down at his feet.

He didn't know whether to laugh, scream or cry. His foot was trapped beneath a tightly sprung sheet of camouflaged netting, complete with a fresh covering of twigs and leaves. He followed the edge with his foot to the corner and unhooked the net from a sturdy metal peg. He dragged the sheet back and exposed a large patch of "managed" earth. Suddenly, he felt alone and *exposed*, and quickly turned away, and then he saw it; the tree he had been drawn towards had a heart shaped scar and an aged message carved into the trunk. His spine tingled and his skin began to crawl. He glanced between the tree and the cleared patch of soil.

'Jesus Christ!'

CHAPTER TWENTY-FIVE

Deans hurried through the corridors and found Jackson sitting alone in the office.

'Stop!' Jackson shouted and leapt up out of his seat. 'You're getting shit all over the carpets.'

Deans looked down at his feet, caked in clumpy mud. A trail of brown footprints followed behind him.

'Where the hell have you been?' Jackson barked.

'I went to Bone Hill.'

Jackson shot Deans daggers. 'Why have you been there?'

'We have to dig it up.'

'We aren't digging up Bone Hill. Get that hair-brained idea out of your mind, right now.'

'We have to dig it up,' Deans said again.

Jackson scoffed and grumbled something incoherent beneath his breath.

'I walked to the derelict church...'

Deans watched for a reaction. It didn't come.

'I took some photos on my phone of recently cultivated soil.' He handed Jackson his mobile phone.

Jackson looked at the screen for a beat. 'So?'

'We don't have the heads of our victims.'

A twitch in the corner of Jackson's eye gave away his thoughts. He handed Deans back his phone. 'This is bollocks, Andrew – a total waste of your time and energy. Who else went with you?'

Deans held his breath.

Jackson waited for Deans' answer with a keen impatience.

'I went alone,' Deans said.

'Forget all of this shit,' Jackson said. He made a point of looking at his watch. 'Come on, I'll take you home.'

'I don't want to go.'

'Andrew. You have come in here, leaving a trail of crap on the floors for the cleaners to deal with. It's late and I think it's been a long enough day for the both of us.'

'We need to dig it up. We're going to find the missing remains of our victims.'

Jackson winced until a smile crept from his mouth. 'That might look like a piece of unwanted land, but it's still owned by somebody – the council would be my guess, or English Heritage. We aren't going to put a single spade into that soil.'

'Do you want to solve this case?' Deans glared.

Jackson returned the hard stare.

'If you *do* want to solve this, then you have to excavate that land.'

'Deans,' Jackson said, placing a hand on his shoulder. 'That was an old burial ground.'

'I know.'

'No... not the sodding Vikings. That was a Norman church. The ground that surrounds it was a graveyard. If we dig it up, we will find bones, fucking old ones. And we don't have the authority to exhume that land. It's a job for archaeologists, not cops.'

'Then we need to get authority.'

'What don't you understand, son?'

'What don't you understand? That site is still being used as a burial ground. At least get a search team up there to work on the area of recently disturbed ground. I'm not asking for the entire mound to be unearthed.'

'Why do you think it has anything to do with this investigation?'

Deans masked a smile. 'When have I let you down so far?'

Jackson turned away.

'Come on… tell me when I've been wrong.'

Jackson looked back. The creases in the skin around the edge of his eyes had deepened. 'You heard what the DI said.'

'Sod the DI. It's time to involve the detective chief inspector. You tell her… or I will.'

There was no sign of Sarah Gold in the office. Jackson said she was out on enquiries. Deans found a Post-It note on her desk.

Hi Andy

I've gone over to see Mrs Rowland (She called while you were out)

See you later

S x

Deans heaved a deep breath and sank into one of the swivel chairs. He stared into space and slowly gyrated from side to side. There was so much going on in his head that he couldn't figure out where to go next. Maria loved making lists – it was her 'thing'. He would often wake from a night shift to find a list of jobs for him to do before she got home from work. What he would do for one of those notes right now?

Deans logged onto the computer terminal and searched the internet for Pagan and Viking jewellery. He quickly found what he was looking for and dug Amy's pendant out of his pocket. It was the same interlocking triangular design as the one in the museum and was called a *Valknut*. The symbolism related to the knot of the "slain warriors", and was heavily associated to the God Odin and modern-day Heathenry.

This is it, he thought. *This has to connect the others to Bone Hill*. Deans checked his watch. It was getting late and already dark outside.

Jackson breezed into the office. 'I've had a call from Gold,' he said. 'She's had a positive meeting with Mrs Rowland.'

'Go on.'

'It appears Mrs Rowland wasn't so surprised to hear that we are looking for her daughter. She allowed Gold to see Annie's bedroom.' Jackson handed Deans his mobile phone; there was a photograph taken by Sarah. It was another pendant.

Deans dug a hand into his pocket and showed Jackson his pendant.

'Where did you get that?' Jackson asked.

'Amy's bedroom. This piece of jewellery links them. We need to find out what these are and where they are made,' Deans said.

'Gold's already on it.'

Deans locked eyes with Jackson.

'There's a small jewellers at Mullacombe. They make all this kind of stuff, apparently. Gold is paying them a visit as we speak.'

'Good. It would be interesting to see the local sales manifest – discover who else is into these.'

Jackson glared at Deans. 'Like I said, Gold is on it.'

Deans scratched behind his ear. 'We need to go through Ranford and Babbage's belongings again. There will sure to be links to this stuff.'

'Agreed. Perhaps I can leave that with you to liaise with detained property.'

'Of course. Did Sarah say when she would be back?'

'No.'

'Did she say if she was doing anything after visiting the jeweller?' Deans asked.

'Nope.' Jackson glanced at the clock on the wall and then at his watch. 'Don't you have her number?' Jackson asked.

'Yes.'

'Just give her a quick call and see how long she'll be. I don't particularly want to be here all night.'

Deans dialled her number. It went straight to voicemail.

'No signal,' Deans said. 'She must be driving back.'

Jackson came over to Deans' desk. He sat on the edge of the table and loomed large over Deans.

'This is going to be the biggest operation this district has ever seen if we can't resolve it ourselves.'

Deans nodded.

'We would need coordinated warrants at God knows how many addresses? We simply don't have the resources to cope with anything like this, if it gets out of hand. It's down to us to keep a lid on it.' Jackson huffed. 'Andy,' he said softening his tone. 'How sure are you about all of this? I mean, I don't want egg on my face – do you know what I mean?'

'I know it sounds far-fetched, but everything is pointing towards a cult operation.'

Jackson inhaled deeply. 'Yeah.' He checked his watch again. 'Christ, what is she doing?'

'What time did Sarah head to the jeweller?' Deans asked.

'About three, and it's almost seven-fifteen for Christ's sake. I'm going to have to phone my misses. We were heading out tonight. Give her another go on the mobile, will you.'

Deans agreed and Jackson left the office.

Deans attempted three more calls over the ensuing ten minutes – still no signal. In the background, he could hear sirens howling in the police courtyard; first one, then two, and then another, just seconds later.

That's odd. Must be something meaty going down. He hadn't heard a single siren outside the station since he'd been visiting there. He puffed out his cheeks. *Time for a brew.* He sauntered into the kitchen area, dragging his plastic boot behind him and made himself a black coffee with two heaped scoops. He returned to the office. Jackson was still out.

He took a sip from his drink and frowned. He could hear more emergency vehicles passing the station at speed – different sirens. He went to an office with an outward facing window and looked out. He couldn't see anything other than quickly dissipating strobe lights as the emergency vehicles sped on. He hadn't seen the ambulance or fire engines, but assumed they were close by.

He returned to his desk and entered the STORM application on the computer to read details of the ongoing emergency log. This was something most cops did, given half the chance and opportunity.

He looked to the door – Jackson must have been having a bad time of it on the call home. He looked back at the screen and clicked on the 'immediate' list of ongoing calls. There was a list of seven. At the top of the log was a reported fire. He clicked the report to read the comms log of entries and sipped his coffee as the call data filled the screen.

Informant reporting a large house blaze at end of Allen Road.

Fire Brigade aware and attending.

District units dispatched.

Casualties unknown at this time.

Property has been derelict for years.

Deans put his mug down with a splash of hot coffee onto

the back of his hand and he hurriedly scrolled further down the log.

Caller does not know postal address, but states property is known locally as, "The Haunted house".

Deans sprang up from his seat and pulled out his phone. His instinct was to call someone, but who... Jackson?

He rushed out to the hallway and called loudly for Jackson. He shouted again.

Jackson's face appeared around the frame of an office doorway. His phone still attached to his ear.

'We need to go,' Deans shouted urgently ushering Jackson towards him with his hands.

Jackson scowled and dipped back away from view.

Deans ran the best way he could and followed Jackson into the room and tugged his arm. 'We have to go,' Deans said. 'It's urgent.'

'Look, I have to go, sweetness. Something obviously needs my pressing attention.' Jackson's furious eyes were speaking a different type of language to Deans.

'Yeah, you too. Yeah... yeah... see you later. Bye. Bye. Bye... bye.' Jackson ended the call and gave Deans a hard stare.

'We've got to go to Sandymere Bay. Ruby Mansell's house is on fire.'

Jackson shrugged. 'So. Leave it to uniform. If they suspect arson, it'll have to go somewhere else to be investigated.'

'Think about it,' Deans snapped. 'Where's Sarah?'

Deans could see the realisation dawn in Jackson's face. 'Oh shite!'

He ran to the office and quickly scanned through the log on the computer screen and snatched his personal radio from his desk.

'Romeo Hotel Two-zero,' he said – not waiting to see if he

was interrupting radio chatter, which was the usual protocol. 'Romeo Hotel Two-zero, priority.'

Romeo Hotel Two-zero – state your priority, communications replied.

'Have any units arrived at the haunted house, yet?' Jackson asked.

Affirmative, comms replied. *Six-three are at scene and a further three units are en-route, including Charlie Hotel Two-zero* (Duty Inspector) *and Four-zero* (Duty Sergeant).

'Thank you,' Jackson said. 'Be advised, all attending units – do not assume the premises are unoccupied.'

The radio fell silent.

'Romeo Hotel Two-zero, did you copy?' Jackson said anxiously. 'The premises are to be treated as occupied.'

A short pause preceded comms' response. *Roger, Romeo Hotel Two-zero. All units attending the property fire at Allen Road. From Romeo Hotel Two-zero – the premises are to be treated as occupied. First attending units please inform fire brigade and provide an early update, please.*

'Is the FIM monitoring?' Jackson asked impatiently.

Negative, comms replied. *The Force Incident Manager is monitoring another ongoing incident in Plymouth.*

'Make them aware now, please.'

Roger. The comms operator paused. *Am I to allocate you to this job also, Romeo Hotel Two-zero?*

'Yes,' Jackson replied. 'Put me down for that and I will be attending alongside Detective Andrew Deans.'

CHAPTER TWENTY-SIX

The glow in the dark misty sky could be seen long before they arrived at the fire. Strobe lights from the emergency vehicles bounced and glistened off the fine night drizzle, like a million specs of blue and red glitter had been tossed into the air. There was something hypnotic about strobe lights in wet conditions.

Deans climbed out of Jackson's car and peered up at the crackling flames leaping far above the rooftop. Three police cars parked nose-to-tail kept a crowd of onlookers at a safe distance. Deans watched the frantic actions of the fire crew, barely spitting on the rooftop inferno. Although this place housed unspeakable horrors, it was clearly iconic and much loved to the local community.

Jackson and Deans made their way through the police cordon and joined the duty skipper and lead fire officer at the front of the house.

'It's well established,' the lead hand said.

'Has anyone gone inside?' Jackson asked.

'Nobody is going inside there,' the lead hand replied. 'It's an old building, the roof is well ablaze and I'm not risking the safety of my team on an empty property.'

'Didn't you get my radio transmission?' Jackson asked.

Before the late shift skipper could respond Jackson was in the face of the lead hand. 'One of my team might be inside that building and I want you and your team to get her out.'

'Might? Sorry, that's a no go—' The sound of tiles falling and smashing on the ground nearby made them all turn towards the house.

'Deans, how certain are you that—' Jackson stopped talking and did a three-sixty. 'Where's Deans?'

The duty skipper shrugged. 'Is that the guy you arrived with? I didn't see where he went.'

'Jesus, Deans!' Jackson seethed through gritted teeth.

'You need to keep your people out of that building,' the fire officer said with his hand on Jackson's shoulder. 'It's not safe. Lives are at risk.'

Jackson scanned around the numerous police and fire vehicles, the strobes bouncing off his face, but there was no sign of Deans.

'Okay,' Jackson said. 'Keep me updated.' He pulled out his mobile phone and dialled Deans' number. He held the phone tight to his head, but the sound of the pumps and of the roar from the blaze made any attempt to hear, near on impossible.

Deans was outside of the police perimeter. All eyes were on the flames. He sidled to the edge of the ever-swelling crowd of onlookers and ducked below a thick evergreen bush growing next to the perimeter wall of the haunted house. The heat, even from this distance was almost unbearable against the fine chilled drizzle. Using the low wall as a marker, Deans manoeuvred further around to the back of the property. The night was jet black, but flames from the rooftop were sending just enough fingers of amber light for Deans to avoid the cliff edge.

He was now in a cacophony of sound between the growling waves crashing beneath him on the black rocks, and the inferno high above. Stiff branches from overgrown bushes impeded his progress, but he continued onwards despite sharp twigs digging into his sides like hot knives. He was now also contending with the wash from wayward jets of hose-water.

He was perilously close to the edge of the rocks, particularly given his restricted mobility, but he knew he was getting closer. And then he saw it; the small square opening in the footings of the brickwork.

He took out his phone and shone a beam of light around the black void.

'Sarah,' he shouted. 'Sarah?' But there were no cries in response.

The narrow strip of grass that he was currently occupying, ended two feet ahead and dropped away to a jagged rock face.

He used the light to plot a pathway over the slippery obstacle and on to the cellar entrance – an agonizingly close ten feet away. He closed his eyes and inhaled a lung of the acrid smelling air. *I might be with you sooner than I imagined, Maria.*

He reached forwards and gripped the tufts of a plant growing out from beneath the stonework of the low perimeter wall. He tested the integrity of the fixture by tugging at it with both hands. There was give, but he didn't have time to dwell on the potential consequences of it failing to support him.

His heart was pounding beneath his now sodden suit jacket. He dangled his good leg out over the precipice of the cliff edge and took the remainder of his body weight through a bent knee. Suddenly, the narrow grass lip he was occupying crumbled beneath him and his body swung violently to his right side. He peered up at his fists balled tightly around the base of the shrub and blindly prodded out a shoe until he found a solid surface to plant his foot upon. He was now at a diagonal angle, with his right foot connected to a rock, but he needed to let go with his hands to move forwards. A loud crack from above made him look up, as a large section of burning roof toppled in his direction.

He let go of the plant and desperately grasped for something else to take his body weight. He hugged the cliff face and gritted his teeth as smoking clay tiles clattered all about him. A sharp triangle of rock came to his saviour and he steadied himself. The small square entrance was now just beyond arm's length.

'Sarah?' he shouted. 'Sarah, are you in there?' He listened hard, but heard nothing.

He edged along the stone ridge until his good foot was in the mouth of the square entrance. He manoeuvred his body and dropped down, scraping his hands against stone until they were secure once again. Hands bloodied and clothing ruined, he had reached his destination, but what was he going to find inside?

CHAPTER TWENTY-SEVEN

Water dripped through the gaps in the floorboards above his head and down the back of his neck. The room was black, apart from the odd spark of burning debris dropping into the pit around him. Deans used the light of his phone again and pointed it towards the far wall; Sarah was there.

'Sarah,' Deans screamed and scampered across to her.

She was sitting on the floor, back against the wall, her head drooped towards her lap and her left arm suspended out to the side.

Deans gently lifted her head and shone the light around her face.

'Sarah, God! Please no.' He combed hair out of the way of her face and scanned her neckline. She hadn't been cut.

'Sarah, Sarah,' Deans shouted, feeling for an arterial pulse in her neck. She was alive.

Deans quickly inspected the rest of her body; there was no obvious blood, and then his light found her left wrist encased in a thick rusted shackle, chained to the wall.

'Fuck!'

He tugged ferociously at the clasp.

'Fuck, fuck, fuck!'

He shone the light around the edge of the cellar. There was a three step metal ladder, but nothing else he could use to break the seal.

He fumbled with his phone and dialled Jackson's number.

'Ah, Deans where—'

'Shut up and listen,' Deans said over the top of Jackson. 'I'm inside the house with Sarah.'

'What?'

'She's still alive but she's chained to the wall. She needs to be cut free.'

'What?'

'Just sort it out. We're inside the basement cellar at the back of the house.'

'What?'

'Jesus Christ!' Deans screamed. Get an ambulance, she's not responding.'

'But... how... how did you?'

'Just get in here with some cutters.' Deans ended the call.

The heat in the cellar was becoming dangerously hot and increasingly difficult to breath in the choking air. Deans suddenly remembered the hosepipe from the last time he was in this pit. He scrambled across and turned on the tap until it could turn no more. A strong jet of water squirted from the short length of hose and Deans directed it at Sarah spraying her from head to toe. He saw her react to the cold water and then he turned the jet on himself and drenched his head and back. He could hear the sizzle on his skin as water vaporised into steam. He repeated the process and went back over to Sarah scraping bedraggled hair from her face. He felt for a pulse again. It was strong. *Come on Jackson.*

Deans saw a thin strip of bright light illuminate the far

wall. He jumped up and banged on the floor boards above his head.

'In here. In here. Help. Help,' he called out. He slipped off a shoe and banged it repeatedly on the cellar door. Light was flickering from multiple angles and all of a sudden, the trap door sucked upwards and a mask of heat dropped down onto Deans' face. He grimaced through the pain.

'Give me the cutter,' he yelled between splutters and coughs. 'Just give me the damn cutter.'

A hand reached down and Deans snatched a pair of heavy-duty bolt croppers and disappeared back inside the cellar. He returned into view moments later with Sarah's limp body dragging behind him. A pair of well-protected arms reached down and Deans offered Sarah up. He watched until she was free of the hatch and then sank to his knees.

CHAPTER TWENTY-EIGHT

Deans pulled the oxygen mask from his face and spoke to Jackson. 'I'm okay; I don't need all this shit. Just take me to see Sarah.'

Jackson stood up from his chair and moved beside Deans' hospital bed.

'You're going nowhere. You need to clear your lungs.'

'Bollocks to that.' Deans removed the strap from the back of his head and tossed the hissing mask to the side. 'I want to see Sarah. Is she talking?'

'Not yet,' Jackson simpered.

'Where is she?'

'Close by.'

'Is she awake?'

'I believe so. But I haven't seen her yet myself.'

Deans swung his legs off the side of the bed and looked around. There were no nurses in sight to tell him he had to stay.

'Help me down,' he said.

Jackson took a portion of Deans' weight and lowered him until both feet were on the ground.

'They want to x-ray your leg again. They say you may have caused further damage with your heroics.'

Deans pushed Jackson's helping hand away. 'It's fine. I don't need anything.'

'You'll need a new orthopaedic boot if nothing else. That one is unhygienic.'

'That can wait until after I've seen Sarah.'

The corner of Jackson's mouth lifted. 'That was a hell of a thing you did for her.'

'How did the fire officers find us so quickly?' Deans asked.

'I put a suit on and showed them the way to the cellar.'

Deans nodded and turned away. 'Thanks.' He paused. 'I thought it was going to be touch and go for a minute.'

'Sarah is lucky to be alive. You both are.'

Deans looked Jackson square in the face. 'Well, thankfully Sarah did survive, and now, hopefully, she can tell us who put her there.'

Jackson snorted. 'Wouldn't that make life easy for us?' he said.

'Maybe...' Deans squinted. '...For some.'

Jackson walked Deans a short distance through connecting doors and into another open ward.

Jackson approached the nursing bank. 'Sarah Gold,' he said flashing his ID badge.

The nurse gave Deans a once over – he was still in his hospital gown. His suit was destroyed.

'Give us a moment, please,' the nurse said and walked off.

Deans looked around the ward. Most of the beds were occupied and nearly everyone was connected to a bleeping monitor.

'What is this ward?' he asked Jackson.

'Same as yours, only female. Respiratory Unit.'

They waited a few minutes and the nurse returned.

'Okay, you can see her now.'

Deans saw Sarah long before her bed was pointed out to them. She was connected to a drip and a facemask fed her oxygen, the same way his had. She had dressings dotted around her arms and shoulders.

'She has a few minor burns,' the nurse said noticing Deans looking at the bandages. 'But she'll be fine.' The nurse smiled at Sarah and leaned in. 'Okay sweetheart, I'll leave you with these two gentlemen.'

Sarah nodded and the nurse went about her business.

Deans walked to the side of the bed and lifted Sarah's hand into his. 'Hey,' he said.

Her pooling eyes settled on his. 'Hey,' she replied from inside the mask.

'Okay you two,' Jackson said moving to the opposite side of Sarah's bed. 'How are you feeling?'

'I'm okay, thanks.'

'What do you remember?'

Deans frowned.

'Argh,' Sarah groaned. 'Not much I'm afraid.'

Jackson nodded and sneaked a glance at Deans, who was staring back at him.

'Anything at all?' Jackson persisted.

Sarah moaned and Deans felt her fingers tighten around his hand.

'It's alright,' Deans said. 'There's no rush. Your body has had a serious shock. Things may come back to you later.'

'Okay,' Sarah quietly muttered.

'Can I have a moment in private?' Deans asked Jackson.

'There's nothing you can give us?' Jackson asked.

Sarah shook her head.

Jackson peered at Deans for a long second, sniffed loudly and then left the room.

Deans leaned in close to Sarah's face, but checked over his shoulder before speaking.

'How many?'

Sarah rocked her head on the pillow. 'Three. Four maybe.'

Deans nodded.

Sarah looked at Deans' hospital gown. 'Are you okay?'

'Fine. I'm fine. Thank you.'

Sarah reached for her mask and pulled it away from her face.

'They told me what you did,' she said.

Deans shrugged dismissively.

'Come here. Come closer.'

Deans was already in her personal space.

'Closer,' Sarah whispered.

Deans felt his heart clanging like a church bell. He cleared his throat and moved a fraction closer.

Sarah slid her hand from his grasp and reached around the back of his head pulling him near, until their lips were touching.

Deans battled to keep his eyes open, but his instincts were stronger than his will. Her lips were warm, tender and oh so welcoming. He felt her tongue prod the inside of his lips. He pulled back, but she forced his head onto her lips and held him there for way longer than a "thank you" needed to be. Their mouths parted. Deans could feel the race of his breath bouncing back off her face. He straightened up and took a backward step.

'I could never thank you enough,' she said.

You just did.

His tongue lapped moisture from his lips and he ran a

hand through his hair and steadied his breath. 'You'd do the same for me.'

She looked around his face and formed a poignant smile. 'I'd do... *anything* for you, now.'

Deans reached for his tie, but remembered he was in a medical gown, and instead, brushed imaginary lint from his chest. 'Um, tell me about these people. Did you see their faces?'

Sarah slowly blinked. 'They had masks.'

'Masks? Can you describe them?'

Sarah placed a hand to her face. Her eyes suddenly widened. 'Scary,' she breathed, 'Like... like... long black beaks.'

'Birds beaks?'

'Yes... like a bird's face.'

Deans' fingertips crackled through the stubble on his jaw. 'Men, women?' he asked.

Sarah shook her head. 'Nobody spoke to me.'

Deans frowned. 'Nobody spoke the entire time you were with them?'

'I don't know. They put something over my face and I fell asleep. I don't remember anything else and I can't recall any voices.'

'How tall were they? What else were they wearing?'

Sarah shook her head. 'I'm sorry.'

'It's okay,' Deans said running both hands behind his neck and arching his back. 'The main thing is you are still here. Hey, can you do me a favour? If Jackson asks you about anything, anything at all, just say you don't remember, okay?'

Sarah nodded.

'Okay,' Deans repeated.

She reached out for his hand. 'Are you going?'

'Yes, I have to get back to the office.'

Sarah pulled her sheets towards her face. 'I don't want you to go.'

'I have to. I need to finish this.'

Sarah let go of his hand and brought the sheet up over her chin.

Deans turned away.

'Andy?'

He stopped and looked back. Sarah was the picture of vulnerability.

'I owe you everything.'

Deans waved the suggestion aside. 'You owe me nothing.' He smiled, turned and went off to find Jackson.

CHAPTER TWENTY-NINE

Jackson waited while Deans had his leg checked over and his orthopaedic boot replaced. Neither of them spoke as Jackson began the half an hour journey back towards the police station. But the closer they got to Torworthy, the less Jackson seemed able to control his monastic silence.

'You were in there a while – with Gold,' he finally said.

'Yep.'

'What was she saying?'

Deans lifted his brows. 'Nothing. She can't remember anything about her ordeal. She just wanted to thank me.'

'Nothing? Not so much as a description – man – woman – child?'

Deans looked out through his window and saw his reflection as he spoke. 'No. Nothing.'

Jackson drove in silence for five more minutes and then he looked across at Deans. 'You're quiet,' he said.

'Am I?'

'Yeah. Come on, you should be proud of what you did today.'

'I am.' Deans looked back at Jackson for the first time that journey. 'Would you do me a favour and drop me off at Rayon Vert, please?'

'Your friend's shop, is still open?'

'Yeah. She's got some clothes for me there.'

'Sure. Be quick though. The detective chief inspector is holding a briefing at the nick at nine p.m. I'm sure she'll want to see you there.'

'There's a briefing tonight?'

Jackson bobbed his head. 'This job just got political.'

'You go on,' Deans said. 'I'll get a lift.'

He waited for Jackson to drive off and then entered the shop. The door chimes brought Denise out from the back room.

'Andy. What has happened to you now? We can't keep you away from hospitals can we?'

'Did you hear about Ruby Mansell's place?'

'Of course. It's all over social media.' She looked him over from top to toe. 'You were there?'

'Yeah,' Deans muttered. 'I told Jackson that you had some clothes for me. Is there anywhere still open in town?'

'It's your lucky night. Thursdays are late opening in the department store up the road. What do you need?'

'Would you mind? I can't really go out in these.'

'Where did you get those awful trousers? They're half way up your ankle.'

'Custody clothes. Jackson picked them up for me.'

'Well, that's kind of him – he really is turning a corner.'

Deans cocked his head. 'Any chance of a brew?'

'Before or after I get you some appropriate attire?'

'Before, I need to be back in the office for nine.'

'You're going back tonight? You should rest.'

Deans shook his head. 'Crime doesn't rest, neither can I.'

'Is it time to leave this alone?' Denise asked. 'Get back to grieving.'

'Never.'

'Andy, you are in incredible danger. We all are.'

'I know and that's why I can't be seen to walk away from it now. The danger will continue for the rest of you.' He stared ahead into empty space. 'I have to end this for all the victims. For all of the families.' He lowered his head. 'That's what Maria would want me to do.'

'You have far more to offer this world than to avenge those victims... and Maria.'

Deans opened his eyes and lifted his head. He stood tall and slowly filled his chest with air. She was right. Denise was always right. He was feeling increasingly *different* – that was the best he could describe it; neither confident nor fragile, strong or weak. The craziest thing was he was feeling an inner state of completeness. That was the last emotion he should have been experiencing, but he was not able to control it.

'Everything's going to be okay,' he said. 'Whatever comes our way, everything will work out the way it is intended.'

Denise cocked a smile. 'Pleased to hear it,' she said.

He nodded. 'I don't know what I have to do. I just know that it will be done, somehow.'

Denise looked at him with a satisfied grin. 'It's happening,' she said.

'What's happening?'

'Your spiritual graduation.'

I like that, Deans thought. *My spiritual graduation.*

Denise walked off and soon returned with his coffee. 'I'll be quick. Ten minutes tops. Thirty-four waist, regular length and large sized top, yes?'

Deans recoiled. 'How did you know?'

'Seven years' working in a gentleman's retailer when I was young.' Denise winked and left Deans in the shop.

He sipped his drink and walked slowly around the display cabinets. He wasn't really paying attention to the stones and crystals, but he needed something to do to kill time, and then he stopped and peered closer at an item of jewellery; a thick golden coloured ring on the lower display shelf. He clawed at the glass door but it was locked. He removed his phone, took several photographs and zoomed in on the images.

There was a text around the outside of the band – not anything that he could decipher, but it was clearly saying something.

The door opened and in walked Denise with two large department store carrier bags.

'Hope you like them. I'm not going back, unless they don't fit of course.' She gave him a frazzled stare. 'The Boxing Day sales – it's bedlam out there.' She hesitated. 'Are you okay?'

'What's this?' Deans said pointing to the display of golden trinkets and jewellery.

'Gold. It's not just stones that are precious in Rayon Vert, you know.'

'No, I mean what is this.' He bent over and tapped the glass beside the ring.

'Oh, that? Ancient Runes on a twenty-four carat gold ring.'

'Runes?'

'Old language.'

'Viking language?'

'It could have been. It was around even before those times.'

Deans straightened up. 'Can I see it?'

'Of course.'

Denise rummaged behind the counter and came back with a small bunch of keys. She unlocked the cabinet and dropped the ring into Deans' open hand.

'Can I borrow this?' he asked.

'That's worth two hundred and forty pounds.'

'I'll keep it safe. I promise.'

'Okay. Okay.'

'What does it say?' he asked.

'That one? I think it says, *love, friendship, eternity.*'

'That's a nice message.'

'Yes, it's a lovely piece, but it's the only one I have.'

Deans smiled. 'It's okay it'll come back as new.'

'You should change. It's getting close to eight-thirty.'

'And you need to lock up.'

'Why?'

'Because you're coming too.'

CHAPTER THIRTY

Deans and Denise entered the CID department to find the room buzzing with staff. He immediately recognised Detective Chief Inspector Fowler who had an entourage of at least five uniformed officers with varying numbers of pips and stripes on their shoulders. DCI Fowler was Senior Investigating Officer (SIO) for the Amy Poole murder. She was strong and a mightily impressive boss.

'Ah, Detective Deans,' she said clocking Deans as he walked further into the room. She approached and embraced him with a full wrap-around hug. Deans' arms were rigid by his side.

'Detective, you have done an extremely brave duty this evening. My officer is only alive as a result of your extraordinary lack of self-preservation.'

'Ma'am,' Deans replied simply.

She looked down at his hard plastic boot and shook her head. 'Absolutely extraordinary. You know, I'm considering putting you forward for the National Police Bravery Awards.' The DCI then noticed Denise. 'Oh, hello.' She took Denise by the hand. 'You must be the clairvoyant—'

'She's a medium,' Deans said.

The DCI bobbed a shoulder and emitted a low grunt, that if translated would say something like, *Yeah, whatever.*

'We all owe Denise a huge debt of gratitude,' Deans said.

'Yes. I'm sure.'

The DCI and Denise exchanged the same pained smile.

'I haven't had a chance to formally pass you my sincere condolences, Detective Deans. I am truly sorry for your loss.'

'Thank you, Ma'am.'

Deans caught Jackson staring from across the room as the boss continued to speak. Jackson stroked his chin and turned away. Deans was introduced to the entourage in turn, but he kept a watchful eye on Jackson who stood up from his seat and left the room.

'Are you fit enough to re-join us?' a uniformed chief inspector asked.

'Yes, sir, thank you. I'm fine.'

'Are you certain,' the chief inspector probed further.

Deans blinked slowly. His hand was still being shaken enthusiastically by the senior officer.

'Yes,' Deans said. 'I haven't felt better.'

The chief inspector let go of his hand. 'Good to hear it.'

'Just how did you know where to find Detective Gold?' DCI Fowler asked.

Deans thought about his answer for a split-second. 'Instinct, Ma'am.'

She laughed. 'There you go again with that instinct of yours. I don't know. I think we could all use a little of your instinct, it would probably make us all better coppers.'

'It would,' Denise cut in.

They all looked at Denise. Deans saw the surge of fear in her eyes and winked at her.

'Right,' the boss said. 'Let's have some order.'

She stood at the front of the white board and everyone else filed into position – six officers in each of the three rows.

'Apologies for the room size,' the boss said. 'But I'm sure we are all adaptable enough that it won't impair our abilities to listen and think.'

The DCI looked around the room at the seated officers. She paced back and forth. Deans was next to Denise at the end of the front row.

She stopped in the centre of the room.

'Ladies and gentlemen, we are facing a heinous and dangerous foe. These perpetrators have shown an extreme desire to kill in the most inhumane of ways.' She paused. 'They have no boundaries. They have no discretion. I refer to them as our enemy and this is how you must view them. It means nothing to them that you are police officers... we already know that they have been among us and they are willing to take our lives to safeguard their identities.' She looked at Deans. 'We do not know how many of them we are dealing with or how deeply they infiltrate our community, but we do know they have a ruthless lust for murder.' She turned to the whiteboard.

'Look at these names.'

She took a red pen and wrote *DC Sarah Gold* alongside the others. 'You should all by now know that an attempt was made on the life of our own Detective Sarah Gold earlier today and it was only thanks to the timely and considerably brave intervention of Detective Sergeant Jackson and Detective Deans that she is still alive.'

Deans looked along the line of seated officers and saw Jackson peering back at him.

'I've been speaking to the staff in charge of Sarah's care and I'm pleased to report that they envisage her discharge from hospital tomorrow.'

Deans sneaked another glance at Jackson, who was now resting his chin in his hands.

'We have Detective Paul Ranford in custody and I propose we conduct staged interviews of him as the investigation progresses.'

A hand went up from somewhere behind Deans' head.

'Yes,' the boss said.

'I know Paul Ranford,' the officer said. 'He's an experienced investigator. He will know every trick in the book to avoid implication.'

'Well then, it's just as well he's already admitted to the murders of Ash Babbage – his accomplice, and to the murder of Maria Deans and her unborn child.'

The DCI dipped a glance at Deans.

'He is a crucial piece of this increasingly complex puzzle and he is ours to interrogate. That starts tomorrow. We will produce him from prison and bring him to us at the county custody unit. The interview team will be DS Jackson and Detective Deans.' She looked over at Deans. 'Is that okay with you, Detective?'

Deans felt eyes boring into him from all directions. 'Perfect, Ma'am,' he replied.

'Yes,' the DCI said, pointing to another raised hand behind Deans.

'Is that wise, Ma'am? I mean, Detective Deans is heavily *involved* in all of this.'

It was the same officer as before, a uniformed inspector. Deans shifted his body sideways so that he could see the officer and take him all in.

'This line of action is entirely appropriate, Jonathan. From the early stages of the Amy Poole investigation – the murder that started all of this for us, it was Detective Deans getting the results. It was Detective Deans who was driving the investigation forwards, and I want him to do the same again. Ranford may well be a highly trained police interviewer, but he is not Detective Deans.'

Deans locked eyes with the inspector who replied, 'Yes, Ma'am.'

'Good,' the DI said. 'Anything else?'

'I think you'll find Deans has an interesting theory about the murders that everyone should hear,' Jackson said.

'Would you care to share that with us?' the DCI asked Deans.

A dull noise fizzed inside of Deans' head. He looked at Jackson who wrapped one knee over the other and gazed back with a smug expression.

Deans drew a deep breath. 'Ma'am, there is a place that I believe is linked to the murders.'

'How so?' she asked.

Deans sneaked a look at Denise, who prodded the side of his leg.

'Are you aware of the ancient local history, Ma'am?'

The DCI shook her head. 'No. I don't believe I am.'

'I will try to be concise, Ma'am,' Deans said.

Jackson rolled his eyes.

'Sandymere Bay has a Viking history. As you may know, they had particular ways of appeasing their Gods.'

The DCI covered her mouth with a hand and held it in place. This was not a good sign. She wasn't happy with something he was saying.

Deans hesitated. 'There were sacrifices and beheadings.'

The DCI started to walk the room as Deans continued to speak.

'I found a place in Sandymere Bay believed to be the mass burial ground of the Viking Army.' Deans looked over his shoulder. Everyone was looking at him, some with open mouths, but nobody spoke.

'It's called Bone Hill.'

The DCI looked confused with a ridged brow and screwed up eyes.

'I'm sorry; I don't think I understand something here,' she said. 'How is any of this – interesting though it might be, connected to our investigation?'

'Because Ash Babbage, Paul Ranford and Annie Rowland had an interest in the Vikings, or their Pagan beliefs.'

The DCI and Jackson exchanged a look and Jackson conceded with a waft of his hand and a dip of his head.

'Tell me about this burial ground,' the DCI said. 'Where exactly is it?'

'A couple of hundred metres back from the haunted house.'

'Okay,' she said holding out her hand. 'Let's just drop this haunted house stuff shall we.'

'Sorry, Ma'am,' Deans replied.

'What evidence do you have that this location is linked to the investigation?'

Deans saw Jackson smirk behind his hand.

'Give me a shovel and the authority to dig it up and I'll prove it.'

'We've been through this, Deans,' Jackson said slapping his hands loudly on his legs.

'I've already made a decision on this,' the DI's voice came from the back row. 'And it was refused.'

'Thank you,' the DCI said. 'Well, I haven't heard any of this, so please continue, Detective.'

Deans leaned forwards to get a better view of Jackson. 'Who took the statement from Scotty Parsons when Amy Poole's body was discovered on the beach?' Deans asked Jackson directly.

Jackson returned the question with the back of his hand.

'Who took the statement?' Deans repeated.

'I don't believe we ever got one,' Jacksons said.

'Okay,' Deans said. 'Who was tasked to take the statement?'

Jackson rolled his eyes again and was about to speak when the DCI spoke over him.

'Stephen?' she said. 'Who was tasked with the statement?'

Jackson rolled his head and gave Deans a sly smile. 'It was Detective Ranford, Ma'am. Detective Ranford was tasked to take that statement.'

'And did he complete that task?'

'I don't believe so, Ma'am,' Jackson said.

'Why wasn't it chased up?' the DCI asked.

'Subsequent events somewhat overshadowed the enquiry, Ma'am.'

'Why bring this up, Andrew?' the DCI enquired.

'Because at Bone Hill I found a deliberately concealed area of soil that I believe could be a shallow grave.'

'It's probably the local poachers,' the DI called out from the back of the room. 'Just ignore this nonsense.'

The DCI fixed her stare on Deans.

'No, Ma'am, he's wrong,' Deans said.

'And why do you believe that?'

'Because I also found something else.'

The room fell completely silent.

'Close to the disturbed soil, I found a tree carving with a date and two names.'

Deans stood up and walked over to the DCI. Everyone, apart from Jackson, who was now leaning back in his chair with folded arms, were hanging on his next words.

Deans took a pen for the board and leaned towards Jackson.

'Aren't you going to ask me what I found?'

'What did you find?' the DCI asked.

Deans turned his back to the room and drew a large heart shape on the board. Inside, he wrote the exact same words as were seen on the tree. He faced the seated officers and stepped to the side so that all in the room could see it clearly.

Everyone apart from Jackson leaned forwards to read the words: *Scotty loves Amy. 26.10.2008.*

CHAPTER THIRTY-ONE

The DCI paced the room. 'So, let me get this straight – Scotty Parsons was meant to provide a statement to Detective Deans relating to the last time Amy Poole was last seen alive, but didn't turn up at the stated time. The task was then left for Detective Ranford to undertake when Deans returned to Bath, but this never happened.' She glared at Jackson. 'Why was this?'

Jackson scratched the crown of his bald pate. 'I don't know, Ma'am. An oversight?'

'We don't have oversights with murder enquiries, Stephen.'

'No, Ma'am.'

'We then discover that Detective Paul Ranford is sickeningly involved, when he kills Ash Babbage and attempts to frame Detective Deans for the death.'

'Yes, Ma'am,' Jackson agreed.

'Detective Ranford is then remanded into custody as our enquiries continue and Forensic Pathologist Archie Rowland is subsequently murdered in a similar way to poor Maria Deans, whose body he autopsied just a couple of weeks before.'

Deans looked down at his feet. Jackson grunted a noise in accordance.

'On making further enquiries, Detective Deans identifies an obscure object that potentially links Babbage to Ranford and both of them to Annie Rowland, who at this time has not provided an account of any kind.'

'Yes, Ma'am,' Jackson replied.

'Detective Deans then discovers this obscure object has potential links to an ancient Pagan religion and associated sacrificial practices that may or may not influence the reason for the latest string of murders.'

Jackson didn't answer. Deans nodded.

'And now you've been to some *burial site*, where you suspect recent activity through cultivation or a disturbance of the soil, and, you have found a tree carving linking somebody called "Amy" with somebody called "Scotty" to that exact same location on a specific date in two thousand and eight.'

'Yes, Ma'am,' Deans replied.

The DCI glazed over on a spot near the middle of the room. Her eyes flickered and blinked. 'Well then, I suggest we establish if there is any significance with that date and I'd like to know if Amy Poole was aware of the significance of Bone Hill.'

'She was, Ma'am,' Deans said and produced Amy's pendant from his go-bag.'

'What's that?' the DCI asked.

'It's called a Valknut. I found this in Amy's bedside drawer. Scotty Parsons gave it to her.'

'May I?' the DCI asked and took the pendant exhibit from Deans' hand.

Deans looked at Jackson whose cold grey eyes fixed upon his.

'Very well,' the DCI said, handing Deans the exhibit bag. 'I want Annie Rowland and Scotty Parsons located and brought in for questioning.'

'Ma'am?' Jackson queried.

'Trace and interview them, Stephen. It's not rocket science.'

'Are we arresting them based on the evidence of a fantasist?' Jackson said, now out of his chair.

The DCI caught Deans looking at her. She lingered on his face.

'Yes. Let's see what they have to say. Organise a Magistrate's warrant of entry and I think we'd better bring some extra bodies in to help us.'

Deans was studying the white board. He noticed that none of the names had the dates of death alongside them. 'How many unsolved MISPERS do you have?' he asked.

'Missing Persons?' the DCI replied. 'I don't know. Stephen, do you know the answer to that?'

Jackson pinched his top lip between his fingertips and stared at Deans. 'Here specifically, or the district in general?' he asked.

Deans waved a hand. 'Let's start here.'

Jackson looked through a thick wad of intelligence reports on his lap and pulled out a sheet.

'Last count, we had... five.'

'Only five live and ongoing investigations?' the DCI asked. 'Surely we have more than that?'

'Five unsolved.'

'Never found?' Deans asked.

Jackson cocked his head.

'Over what period of time?' the DCI asked Jackson firmly.

Jackson sniffed and looked back down at the report. 'Since Nineteen Eighty-Four.'

'There are five unsolved MISPERS since eighty-four?' the DCI said.

'More than one a decade.' Deans said.

'Haven't they been escalated – reviewed by the Major Crime Team?' the DCI pressed.

Jackson shrugged. 'You'd have to ask them.'

The DCI tutted and snatched the report from Jackson's hand. She read through the document shaking her head. 'How was this never flagged?'

Jackson pouted dispassionately. 'This isn't my district, Ma'am. You're asking the wrong person.'

'I'm asking you now. Find out why these missing person reports have festered, unsolved at this station.'

'Ma'am.'

'Male or female?' Deans asked.

The DCI looked at the report again. 'Female – all of them.'

'Let me guess?' Deans said. 'All went missing in or around October?'

The DCI looked back down at the paper and then frowned at Deans.

'They all went missing within a four week period of one another in their respective years.'

'And no one has identified that before?' Jackson barked. 'What's going on here?'

Deans stood up and made his way over to the board.

'Can I see, please, Ma'am?'

The DCI gave Deans the report and he wrote the names on the board in a column beneath the name of Amy Poole.

Deborah Clarkson – October 15th 2001

Mellissa Derry – November 5th 2006

Sarah Stockdale – October 8th 1992

Angelique Montgomery – October 24th 1987

Tammy O'Shea – October 30th 1985

Deans took the pen and wrote *October 4th* beside Amy's name, and jabbed the board with the butt of the marker pen. 'All of these girls are connected. They have to be.'

'There must be others,' the DCI said coming alongside Deans. 'These are only the ones recorded since PACE (Police and Criminal Evidence Act) came into force.' She kept her eyes on the column of names. 'We haven't got a *problem*,' she mumbled. 'We have an epidemic.'

The room went deathly silent.

'Right,' the DCI said turning to Jackson. 'Find out who owns that land. We are going to dig up Bone Hill.'

CHAPTER THIRTY-TWO

The following morning Torworthy Police Station was crammed with bosses, detectives and additional police officers from out of district. The DCI had organised a briefing for eleven a.m. There were going to be several scenes to manage; the Bone Hill dig, Annie Rowland's flat and Scotty Parson's home. The timings would be coordinated and crucial. Deans wanted to manage each of the scenes, but the DCI had already allocated teams and Deans was going to be a 'floater' due to the fact he was the only officer that had been to each target location already.

Deans received a call on his mobile phone. It was Sarah. She was being discharged from the hospital and was looking for a lift home.

'I'll go with you,' Jackson said.

'Good idea,' the DCI said. 'You can debrief Detective Gold on your way back.'

They met Sarah inside the foyer to the hospital. She said she was fine and wanted to return to the office. They were about to drive off when Sarah's mobile phone went off. It was the ward; she had left a bag of property behind.

'I'll go,' Deans said. 'You stay here and debrief.'

Neither Sarah nor Jackson argued and Deans stepped back out into the cold air.

He was greeted at the nursing desk by the same ward sister who had been in charge of his care.

'I've come to collect my colleague's belongings. She just received a call.'

The ward sister smiled.

'She probably left them behind in her hurry to escape,' Deans laughed.

'I have to be honest; she did seem in quite a rush to leave.'

'I'm sure it's nothing personal. She's probably just keen to return to work.'

They both exchanged the same sarcastic smile.

'Here you go,' she said handing Deans a clear zip lock plastic bag. 'I trust you will return this straight to your colleague.'

Deans placed a hand over his heart. 'Absolutely. She is just in the car outside. I was doing her a little favour.'

'You take care and send our best wishes to Miss Gold.'

'I will, and thank you for everything you've done for us both.'

As Deans left the ward, he lifted the bag and looked inside. She had left a watch, necklace, thin silver ring, and a smaller object stuck in the corner of the plastic bag. He looked closer. It was a small brass key. The scent of perfume he knew so well forced him to a halt. He stared into the bag and leaned against the wall of the corridor. He felt the key through the thin clear plastic.

Maria?

He let go and looked around. The smell of perfume vanished just as quickly as it had come. Eyes wide, his fingers reached out and he touched the key again.

'Maria?' he called out.

Take it, his inner voice told him. *Take the key*. He looked around – there were a few others in the corridor; the walking wounded, the elderly, but none of them paying him any attention.

He bit a small hole in the corner of the bag just big enough to slide the key out, and dropped it into his trouser pocket. He checked around him again before making his way out to meet Jackson and Gold in the car park.

Sarah was in the front seat and both of them were smiling.

'Everything okay?' Jackson asked, as Deans sat down in the rear.

'Perfect.'

'Any problems?'

'Like what?'

'I don't know, maybe they wouldn't give you Sarah's property.'

Deans lifted the bag and shook it in the seat space between them.

'Oh, thanks, Andy. You're a star.'

Deans leaned between the gap in the seat and handed Sarah the bag. He watched her face as she looked inside. He saw a twitch of her brow and a narrowing of her eyes.

'Did I have—'

'Come on, let's get going,' Jackson cut in.

Deans slowly sank back into his seat, his eyes trained on the back of Sarah's head.

'Can you drop me home, please?' she asked Jackson. 'I'm going to have a shower, quick change and I'll be back at the station in time for the briefing.'

'You're not coming back today,' Jackson said.

'I'm fine. They only kept me in for observations.'

'Are you sure?' Deans asked. 'It must have dented your confidence being in that fire.'

'Honestly, I'm okay to come back. I want to come back, especially after what happened to me.'

'Okay,' Jackson said. 'Come back, but make sure you're always around someone in case you take a turn.' He looked back at Deans. 'How about your Guardian Angel here – he always seems to be in the right place at the right time.'

Sarah turned around and smiled at Deans, who looked back with a blank expression.

CHAPTER THIRTY-THREE

Deans was inside one of the unused offices facing out into the car park. He had been there alone for the last ten minutes. He was looking out of the window and finally saw Sarah drive in and take one of the last remaining parking spaces. The yard was crammed with Support Group vehicles, CSI vans and unmarked police cars from the extra staff required to handle an operation of this size. Sarah stepped out of the car and played with her hair. Her long black raincoat was pulled in tight around her waist. Deans dug a hand into his trouser pocket and clutched the tiny key between his fingers. 'Speak to me, Maria,' he uttered. 'Please tell me I'm wrong.'

Deans exited the room and met Sarah in the hallway before she reached the office. 'Hey Sarah,' he said giving her a long firm hug. 'Good to see you back in the fold.'

'Aww,' Sarah answered, squeezing him firmly. 'That feels good. Thank you. And thank you for saving me. I could never pay you back.'

Deans flashed a smile. 'Come on. We'd better join this party.'

. . .

Deans had been involved with murder enquiries in the past but this was on a different scale. It felt almost as if the station was not big enough for the job. The extended team now occupied two floors of the building; the local uniformed cops were ousted and told to parade from the nearest station. Jackson must have hated it – after all, he wanted to keep the operation tight and covert, but the DCI was right to call in assistance from outer districts.

Everyone had moved to the ground floor briefing room, usually occupied by the uniformed teams. It was a bigger room, the biggest in the station.

'I have obtained a Magistrate's warrant for the arrest of Annie Rowland,' the DCI said to the packed and riveted audience. 'You will force entry to the premises if required, and you will arrest Annie Rowland on suspicion of the murder of her father, Archie Rowland, and also with conspiracy to commit murder on Amy Poole and Maria Deans. Seize all electronic recordable devices, mobile phones, cameras – you know the routine. Let's have address books, diaries, calendars, anything and everything that may provide links to these murders.' The DCI paused, cleared her throat and found Deans in the audience. 'I also want anything seized that is suspected to be of Pagan, Heathen, or cult origin.'

'Like what, Ma'am,' the support group skipper asked. 'I don't think I'd know it if I saw it?'

'Then I suggest you and your team familiarise yourselves with Google. That goes for all of you. If anything is there, I am sure it will stand out.'

Sergeant Li, the support group skipper, was a tall and handsome Asian man with muscles on top of his muscles. He looked like he had just come off the set of a *James Bond* movie with his perfectly swept hair and chiselled jaw line. Deans had not seen much in the way of diversity amongst the local officers, but that was not discrimination, as some would like to call it, that was down to the local demographic.

'Sergeant Henshaw,' the DCI said, 'I want your team to tie up with Detective Deans at Bone Hill, where Crime Scene Manager, Mike Riley, and his team will set up station in a mobile control unit. We have another two CSI units coming shortly, one of which will deploy to Annie Rowland's property and the other will remain on standby should this operation get larger than we currently anticipate.' The DCI looked around the room. 'Any questions?'

'What happens if she's not at home?' a voice came from the back of the room.

Annie's long gone, Deans thought.

'Just like any other Section Eight warrant. Force entry. Do the search. Seize and secure all exhibits. Leave the authority somewhere obvious and get out of there. Use the briefing packs being handed around to familiarise your teams with the targets. The Bone Hill team will make their way over as soon as possible with Detective Deans and begin the search and I want Detective Gold co-ordinating events at Annie Rowland's property. You go in at thirteen hundred hours. That gives you well over an hour to prepare. Questions?'

Nobody spoke at first and then a hand went up.

'Yes.'

'Ma'am, it's not personal, but is it wise to have Detective Deans involved with this operation?'

The DCI took a half step backwards. 'What's on your mind?'

'Well, he is obviously deeply affected by the events of this investigation... and...'

'And?' the DCI interrupted.

'Isn't he bringing unnecessary attention with him?'

'Meaning?'

'You must have seen the news on TV and read the internet; what the media are calling him, *"The Angel Detective"*, I mean, it's a bloody joke. This place is already swarming with reporters. He's just going to turn this whole investigation into a pantomime.'

'Finished?'

The officer nodded. The DCI's face had turned a strong shade of red.

'Detective Deans is staying. He is absolutely central to this investigation and I'm not interested in personal opinions of you, or anyone else. If you don't like the fact Detective Deans is here, then I suggest you use the door. We are about to embark on a massive operation. This is a small community. It wouldn't have taken long for the cameras to appear in any event. Put up with it and get on with your job.' She shook her head. 'In fact, see me after the briefing.'

The DCI scratched her head and her eyes sought Deans out in the crowd. She held his stare and breathed deeply.

'One last thing,' she said. 'These murders have been brutal. Look after yourselves and each and every one of your team mates.'

CHAPTER THIRTY-FOUR

Wind whistled through the trees and thick branches creaked and groaned with each solid gust. Deans and Denise Moon were in company with the Police Search Advisor (PolSA), Sergeant Henshaw, and her team of six search specialists. Deans had already briefed them about the terrain and they were in full search apparel: black overalls, baseball caps and search sticks. Two CSI officers were also in attendance with video recording equipment, full recovery kit and a forensic tent stowed in the van... just in case. And of course, the crime scene manager, Mike Riley was calling the forensic shots.

They followed Deans in a long snake using the same route that Deans had previously taken, so as to avoid any footprint cross contamination, until they reached the edge of the mound. One CSI officer was immediately behind Deans, recording their progress as they approached the site. Deans stopped by the tall derelict wall of the old church and gathered his bearings. The area looked much different in daylight. Denise came alongside and gave Deans a knowing look.

'There's a bad energy,' she whispered in his ear.

'I know,' he said and gestured over to the tight group of

trees where he saw the name carving. 'Are you picking anything up?' he asked.

'I don't like it.'

Deans grabbed her hand. 'Maria's here. She's with us now.'

'Are you ready for what might be here?' Denise asked.

Deans drew in a deep lung full of Maria's perfume. 'I'm ready.'

Deans pulled CSM Riley and PolSA Henshaw to one side and pointed over towards the trees.

'It's just beyond that point,' he said.

'Okay,' the PolSA said. 'I will go over with Mike, everyone else stay here for now.'

'I'm coming too,' Deans said.

'The fewer people to disturb the immediate scene, the better,' the PolSA replied.

'I get that,' Deans said. 'But I've been here before. My tread marks are already made.'

'And I'm telling you to stay put.'

Deans walked up to the sergeant and moved her away from Riley.

'Are you married?'

Henshaw glowered. 'I don't think that's an appropriate question. I'm sorry, you aren't my—'

'I am married,' Deans cut in. 'And my wife's decapitated head is probably buried somewhere in that ground. Don't tell me I'm not coming.'

Henshaw stared open mouthed at Deans. 'Nobody told me about this,' she said. 'They commented about your involvement, but...'

'Well, now *I'm* telling you.'

Deans noticed a CSI officer pointing the camera at them. 'Get that out of my face,' Deans shouted.

'Okay,' Henshaw muttered. 'Yes, of course you can come.'

'And Denise Moon,' Deans said.

'Fine – let's just get on with it shall we, before the light fades.'

They walked over to the bed of raised soil and Deans pointed to the tree with the carving. The CSI camera operator filmed the tree.

Deans found the edge of the camouflaged netting and unhooked it. He pulled it back to expose the dark weedless earth.

'Is this it?' Henshaw asked.

'This is it,' Deans replied.

'It's not much.'

Maybe not to you.

'Okay, we'll start at one corner and work our way through.'

Denise tugged Deans' arm and leaned in close to him. 'She's not taking this very seriously.'

'Not yet,' Deans said.

The PolSA called over the six PCs and spread them out in a line, shoulder-to-shoulder, and an arm's length between them.

As they commenced sifting through the cloggy topsoil, Henshaw turned back to Deans. 'We'll start with a surface probe and then go deeper if required.'

'It will be.'

Henshaw smiled and came up closer to Deans. 'Look, I'm sorry about earlier. I didn't realise it was you... I mean, we obviously heard about—'

'How long will this take?' Deans asked.

'How long is a piece of string?'

'I want to stick around as long as I can, but I really want to get across for the warrant on Annie Rowland.'

The PolSA scanned the patch of ground with her eyes. 'I should think no more than twenty minutes for the surface sweep, and then we'll need to mark it out and do a sectioned-dig. That will take some time.'

'No problem. Just make sure you do a thorough search.'

'Don't worry we will.'

CHAPTER THIRTY-FIVE

Deans arrived at the rendezvous point with less than ten minutes to go before the warrant team went in.

'What are you doing here?' Sarah asked.

'I'm coming in too. The dig is going to take ages.'

She looked down at her wristwatch. 'That's enough waiting. Let's muster.'

They were already drawing attention from the locals. A CSI and riot van, two response vehicles and several unmarked cars were never going to blend into the background of this small village. They were in the rear car park of a pub. The landlord had already been out to say that their presence was putting his customers off their beers. The search team van rumbled into life and drove away from the car park towards their target. Sarah, Deans and Denise went in one unmarked car, two other suits from the hastily established investigation team took one car apiece and the district units brought up the rear.

As they neared the flat, Deans saw the support group van parked on the side pavement fifty metres short of the block of flats and officers were scuttling beneath the high wall line towards the main front entrance, attempting to remain out of sight of any onlookers from within the building.

Sarah continued driving to the rear of the premises where they joined the two other detectives and a 'door opening team' from the district officers.

They were all wearing stab vests, including Deans beneath his outer layer. Although, Denise was instructed to remain within the safe confines of the car.

Sarah double-checked her watch. 'Go. Go. Go,' she said through the radio.

The 'door opening team' ran up the rear steps, feet clanking against metal griddles and continued until they were outside of the door. They knew the routine and seamlessly got into position. Deans and the others joined them and Sarah gave the team leader a nod. The three officers were in full protective kit, including NATO helmets and shields. The lead officer tugged at the door handle. It was locked. He banged loudly on the flat door. 'This is the police,' his helmet-muffled-voice shouted. There was no response. 'This is the police we have a warrant to enter these premises. Step away from the door or you may be hurt.'

One of the officers produced a large door ram from a black holdall, known throughout the force as "the big red key" and lined it up against the face of the door.

Deans raised his hand and walked over to them. The officers looked at him with surprised frustration. They were on the fourth floor, what was Annie going to do, jump? Deans lifted the letterbox flap and shouted inside. 'Annie, this is Detective Deans. Please open the door.' He turned his ear to the door, but heard nothing inside the flat.

'Annie,' he called out again. 'We are coming in.' Deans gave the door team a nod and he stepped safely to the side. The officer with the ram dropped his helmet visor and smashed the door with immense force. The door resisted once but then succumbed to the second mighty blow from the sixteen-kilogramme steel Enforcer.

The entry team swarmed into the flat shouting, 'Police Warrant' from the lead officer.

Deans made his way through and stood in the centre of the living room. He looked all around. The Raven Banner had gone. Sarah came alongside him and they both stared at the blank wall.

'She knew we were coming,' Deans said.

'How?' Sarah asked.

'Somebody told her.' He walked to the window and looked out into the bay. 'We turn this place upside down.'

'And if we don't find anything?' Sarah asked.

Deans zeroed in on the pebble ridge in the distance. 'Well, then we go to Plan B.'

'Which is?'

Deans wiped his eyelids with the back of a finger.

'We make sure she comes to us.'

After two hours of searching, the flat had drawn a blank on all fronts, to the point that the support group skipper was questioning the validity of the raid.

DS Jackson was waiting for them back at the station with a sour face.

'Deans with me,' he demanded and headed for the small bollocking room with which Deans was by now becoming very familiar.

'What happened?' Jackson glared. He did not sit down, so neither did Deans.

'She knew we were coming. The place was cleaned out. All she left was a small pile of dirty laundry.'

Jackson dipped his head. The skin on his crown was stretched tight.

'We took up the flooring, emptied the freezer, you name it,' Deans said.

Jackson placed a finger to his lips and looked lost in his thoughts.

'Two scenarios,' Deans said. 'The first visit spooked her and she took flight—'

'Or?' Jackson said.

'Or, this is all part of the next phase of whatever they've planned.'

'They?'

Deans reached for the door handle and pushed it closed. Jackson stood tall with wide staring eyes.

'Something happened to me,' Deans said with dampened tones.

Jackson didn't respond. His features remained stiff.

'This is far bigger than we anticipated,' Deans said.

Jackson blinked.

'The haunted house on the cliff edge…'

Jackson tilted his head back and narrowed his eyes to small slits.

'You were involved – when Ruby Mansell died,' Deans continued.

Jackson slowly brought his head back to the level.

'I saw the *Herald* report on the internet,' Deans said.

'Yes,' Jackson finally said. 'I was involved.'

'Did you attend the body in situ… did you see Ruby Mansell?'

'I did.'

'Was there anything unusual about the strangulation?'

Jackson reached for a chair. He pulled it out from beneath

the table and sat down. He gestured for Deans to do the same and waited until Deans was seated opposite him.

'The official stance was that she was asphyxiated. The implement used was never located. It was as if...'

'As if she strangled herself with her own hands,' Deans said finishing the sentence.

Jackson met Deans' stare. 'How did you know?'

'Because the same thing happened to me.'

'You know, you've been quite the surprise,' Jackson said rising to his feet. He moved slowly behind Deans' chair and placed his heavy hands on Deans' shoulders.

Deans tensed against the downwards pressure.

'At first, I didn't want you around,' Jackson said. 'You were just too bloody... towny. But your mind is...' he hesitated and released the pressure from Deans' shoulders. 'Well, it's on another level.'

Deans tracked him all the way back to his seat.

'How much of this is you, and how much of it is Denise Moon?' Jackson asked wiping the cloth of his suit trousers.

Deans pouted and shook his head.

'What will you do, once all of this is over?' Jackson asked.

'Go back to Bath, I guess. Continue serving my community.'

Jackson beamed a smug grin. 'I'm not the chief; you can cut the political bollocks.'

Deans looked down at the tabletop.

'I don't know,' he said. 'It may never be over for me.'

Jackson smiled as if he was drawing pleasure from Deans' misery. He stood up again and walked to the door. 'Come on,' he said. 'We'd better see what the boss has got lined up for us next.'

CHAPTER THIRTY-SIX

By the time Deans arrived, the woodland was a hive of activity. Three more forensic vans blocked access to the narrow road and inquisitive members of the public were braving the lashing rain to have a nosey. Two uniformed PCs were standing guard at the perimeter of police tape wrapped around every other tree trunk at the leading edge of the wood. Jackson was standing the other side staring at Deans with a deadpan face.

'Let them through,' Jackson ordered the PCs, who lifted the tape allowing Deans and Denise to duck under and join Jackson on the other side.

'We can't tell for sure yet what we have,' Jackson said.

Deans stomped onwards through the broken twigs, barely acknowledging Jackson's presence.

'But I wanted you to know right away,' Jackson said, trying to keep up with Deans, despite his obvious mobility limitations.

Deans didn't speak and continued towards the burial ground. As he got closer, the hairs on the back of his neck tingled and the air deep inside his lungs felt heavy. Up ahead, he saw seven suited forensic officers and two large white forensic tents erected over the ground that Deans had brought them to. A ball of saliva stuck in the back of his throat and he slowed as he began to notice the expressions on the collective faces.

'Let me go first,' Jackson said. 'Wait here a moment.'

Deans was oblivious to the fact that Jackson had been on his shoulder the entire time. Deans stopped walking. His body was limp and heavy. He looked around the now active scene as the rain collected in his hair and trickled down the front of his face. Everyone was moving in slow motion and then he saw Sarah Gold, gaping back at him. She was standing on the periphery of activity, her coat wrapped tightly around her body, her arms hugging herself and her hood up over her head.

Deans approached and joined her at the edge of the dig. She didn't speak, but looked into the open side of the forensic tent. Deans followed her gaze and saw three CSI officers kneeling around the pit in the ground. He edged closer. Jackson intercepted him.

'Let them do what needs to be done. Don't do anything that will harm—'

'Is she there?' Deans asked.

Jackson huffed and groaned.

Deans looked at him. 'Is my wife there?'

Jackson rubbed his nose, partially covering his mouth as he spoke. 'We don't know,' he said.

He was hiding the truth. 'Show me,' Deans said.

'I can't. We mustn't disturb—'

Deans stepped forwards as Jacksons voice tailed away.

One of the CSI officers noticed Deans coming closer. She gestured to one of the other crouched officers who stood up and stopped Deans from entering the tent.

'I can't let you in here,' the CSI officer said from behind his face mask. He looked down at Deans' ID lanyard hanging from his neck and blinked rapidly.

Deans nodded as moisture built in his eyes. 'You've found her head, haven't you?'

The officer scratched through the paper hood and Deans looked around his shoulder and could see into the furthest part of the deep trench. The other officers inside were carefully photographing and videoing something deep within the pit.

'We are about to exhume them, so I must ensure that you remain at a forensically safe distance,' the CSI officer said keeping Deans at bay with an outstretched arm.

Deans felt a tug on his elbow. He swung around. It was Jackson.

'Come on, Deans. Come back with me.'

Deans blinked tears from the wells of his eyes. 'Them?' he said with a broken voice.

The CSI officer gave Deans an apologetic look, released the open flap of the tent, and zipped it closed from the inside.

Jackson walked backwards taking Deans with him.

'Them?' Deans repeated. 'How many?'

'Come on,' Jackson encouraged. 'Let's get in the dry of the van. Let me get you a coffee or something.'

'I don't want a fucking coffee,' Deans shouted. 'I want to see my wife. Can't you understand that?'

Jackson licked heavy drops of rain from his top lip. 'I promise – you will see, once the removal is complete. The CSM will keep us fully briefed, I assure you.'

Deans was escorted to a support group van and handed a thick blanket by a uniformed officer.

'Stay in here,' Jackson said. 'I'm going to get you a brew. You can leave it if you want. It's up to you.' He walked away and Sarah Gold took his place at the open side door.

'Can I come in?' she asked.

Deans shrugged.

'They say this could take hours,' she said.

Deans stared ahead into space through the rapidly misting windscreen.

'Don't stay,' Sarah said. 'They're not going to show us anything. Not yet.'

Deans raked his eyes towards her. 'Have you got a car?'

'Of course.'

'Let's go. I want to show you something.'

CHAPTER THIRTY-SEVEN

They drove less than two hundred metres before Deans told Sarah to stop and turn the engine off.

'Why are we here?' she asked, looking up at the charred exterior of Ruby Mansell's fire-damaged mansion.

'I need to show you something.'

'We can't go inside there, it's dangerous.'

'Just follow me.'

Deans opened his door into the horizontal downpour and began walking around to the far side of the house.

'Where are we going?' Sarah asked, pulling her hood as far over her head as it would go.

Deans ducked beneath the overgrown shrubbery at the cliff edge. The ground was saturated and slippery. He held onto the crumbling dry-stone-wall and inched towards the rocky ledge. The frothing ocean pounded just feet below them.

'Hold on to something firm and follow exactly where I step,' he said.

They made slow progress, but eventually reached the small hole at the back of the cellar and rested on a rocky outcrop before venturing inside.

'Andy, I don't like this.'

'Follow me,' he said.

Deans crawled through the narrow gap and into the blackness of the cellar. A thick sooty sludge coated his hands and knees. The smell of scorched wood and damp masonry transported him back forty-eight hours.

Sarah clambered through the gap and joined him inside.

'Argh, this is disgusting,' she said. 'My clothes are ruined.'

'Have you got a torch?' Deans asked.

'Somewhere. Eww, this is horrible. Why have you brought me back here?'

'Torch,' Deans repeated.

Sarah fumbled inside her pocket and produced a small metal Maglite.

Deans took it and shone the beam around them. He focussed on the floorboards above their heads and pushed against a section that had partially burned away and was left hanging at a steep angle into the cellar.

'We need to be quick,' he said.

'What are we doing here?'

Deans directed the beam into Sarah's face, causing her to flinch. 'Ow,' she complained. 'Watch what you're doing with that.'

Heavy drops of blackened rain fell onto their heads through the gaps in the boards. Deans turned the light towards the shackles attached to the far wall.

'Are you getting anything from being back here?' he asked.

'Just filthy and wet, thank you.'

Deans approached the cast iron restraints and lifted the severed section to look closer. He tracked the light towards the other side – the shackle that hadn't been used to restrain Sarah. It was crusted with age. Deans rattled it.

'Are you sure you're getting no memory from this?'

Sarah didn't respond. Deans could see that she was beginning to shake. He dug deep into trouser pocket and removed the small key that he had been carrying around since the hospital. He wiggled it inside the lock and twisted hard several times until the shackle sprang open with a loud metallic clack. He turned slowly to Sarah. 'Come and have a look at this,' he said.

She took reluctant steps until she was close enough to touch, and Deans then suddenly snatched her wrist and tugged her off her feet.

Sarah screamed and lashed out as Deans dragged her closer to the wall and shut the open clasp around her wrist in one swift movement.

Her screams were deafening in the confined space.

'Call out as much as you like,' Deans said calmly. 'Nobody will hear you.'

Sarah was now hysterical and desperately fighting to release her wrist from the old rusted shackle.

'What are you doing?'Her tears quickly changed to terror. 'Oh, God. What's happening? Help me. Help me,' she screamed.

'You tell me.'

'What are you doing to me?' Sarah's wide eyes flicked between Deans and her imprisoned wrist.

'Nothing you wouldn't do to yourself.'

'What … I don't know what…'

Deans walked towards the hole in the wall leaving Sarah behind. 'Do you think this would reach the water if I threw it from here?'

'Oh, God, no! Please. No. Please don't…'

Deans turned the torch onto her face. Her fear looked genuine, and so it should.

'Aren't you going to ask me how I got the key?' he asked

softly.

'I don… I don't… oh, please, please let me out of this.'

Deans held the key between his fingers so that Sarah could see it more clearly. He brought his hand back as if preparing to toss the key outside.

'No,' Sarah screamed, tugging the chain tight as she attempted to reach out.

'Start talking,' Deans said.

'I don't know what I can say,' Sarah cried.

'You can start by telling me how the key to that shackle made it into your property bag at the hospital.'

A small whimper escaped from her lips. 'Wha—'

Deans looked outside through the hole again. 'I'm fairly certain I can reach the water from here. If not, with those rocks, there is no way anyone is getting this key back. '

'I've never seen it before,' Sarah said breathlessly. 'It couldn't have been in my property.'

'How do you suppose it got there then?' Deans asked calmly.

'I really don't know,' she sobbed. 'You have to believe me.'

'Do I? Do I have to believe you? What makes you think I have to do that?'

Sarah stopped struggling. Her body flopped into submission. 'Why are you doing this?' she snivelled.

Deans approached her, grabbed her other wrist, and squeezed with furious anger.

'Ouch, you're hurting me,' she cried.

'Am I? I'm sorry.' He squeezed harder still.

Sarah screamed and attempted to pull her hand back.

Deans used all his force to keep it where he wanted it. 'Talk,' he snarled.

'Andy…' she cried frantically. 'You are really hurting me.'

'I said talk.'

He felt her resistance ease and released his pressure accordingly.

'What were you going to do... fuck me to death,' he sneered.

'No... No. It's not what you think.'

'Really? How can it possibly *not be* what I think?'

'I really don't know what you're saying,' she wailed.

'Please. Let me go. Please... please.' Her voice wavered, as true fear came up from the pit of her stomach.

'Who else is involved?'

Sarah's constant weeping prevented any answer.

'I said who else is involved?' Deans screamed into her face.

'I don't know,' Sarah screeched back in defiance. 'I don't know how the key got in with my things.'

Deans took a step backwards.

'Is it Jackson?'

Sarah touched her face. 'I don't know,' she blubbed. 'Please...'

'You gave me a bullshit story about being taken.'

'No... it was the truth,' her voice faded away.

'You set me up. You knew that if I couldn't reach you in time, you had the key to let yourself go.'

'No.'

'You are part of the cult.'

'No. No.'

'You were hoping I'd get killed trying to rescue you.'

'No.'

'A slip off the rocks, maybe even burn to death inside the place where my wife was murdered.'

Sarah's despairing eyes met with his for a second.

'You're just as much a part of this as Ranford and Babbage.'

'I'm not.' Dribble trickled down from the corner of her

mouth and her eyes were puffed like a hundred bees had taken their anger out on them.

'Bullshit. How does it feel now all of this *is* real?'

'I'm not part of it. I promise.' Her voice was resigned. Her fight diminished.

'You already knew Annie Rowland. I could tell when we first went to her flat. You even defended her. And all that horse shit about being set up when Amy Poole's exhibits vanished – it was you all along.'

'No,' Sarah wept into her lap.

'Who else is helping you?'

'Andy, I promise—' She was speaking like a punch-drunk boxer.

'Too late for promises, princess. Tell me how you got into the cellar?'

'I can't. I was drugged.'

'Bollocks.'

'It's true. I was making an enquiry...' she stopped talking and rocked her head. 'And then I'm being bundled to the floor. I can't remember anything... until... hospital.'

'Where were you making an enquiry?'

'Sergeant Jackson asked me to check an address.'

'What address?'

'I can't remember.'

'This is a waste of time.' Deans started for the gap in the wall.

'Please,' Sarah pleaded. 'It was an address in Hemingsford.'

'You'll have to do better than that.'

'I can take you to it, but I can't remember what it was called.'

Deans squinted.

'I'm being truthful.'

He looked deeply into her pathetic eyes.

'Somebody planted that key in the bag so that you would find it,' she snivelled.

'Why? Why would they do that?'

Sarah looked up at him. 'For this! To deflect attention from elsewhere. To make you weaker.'

'How does this make me weaker?'

Her helpless eyes beseeched his. 'Because together, we are a strong team.'

Deans looked away. He couldn't deny they had been a good team, but was that because it was all part of the game she was playing.

'I don't remember wearing that jewellery... in the bag,' she said.

'But it is yours?'

'Yes.'

'Then how do you suppose it got there if you weren't wearing it?'

'Someone put it there.'

'Who?'

She shook her head.

Deans licked moisture from his top lip. 'Did anyone visit after me?'

Sarah rubbed her face with her free hand. 'No. Yes.' She gazed at Deans. 'Only Sergeant Jackson.'

Deans lifted his head. 'When?'

'Later that night. He came back.'

'Jackson visited you later that night?'

'Yes.'

'Why?'

'He said it was a welfare check.'

Deans held his mouth and scanned his prisoner for a considered moment.

'Will you take me to the address in Hemingsford?' he asked.

'Yes, yes. Andy, I promise, I am nothing to do with these monsters,' she said desperately.

Deans closed his eyes, tilted his head and quietly said, 'Maria, forgive me if I make the wrong choice.'

He crouched inches from Sarah's head. The torchlight lit both of their faces from below.

'I'm not afraid to die,' he said through gritted teeth. 'In fact, I welcome death. I will do anything... *anything* it takes to avenge my wife.' He leaned forward and took the weight of Sarah's arm from the tight chain. 'I just wanted you to know that.'

He took the key, released her wrist and Sarah folded into his arms.

CHAPTER THIRTY-EIGHT

Jackson peered at his watch as Deans and Sarah came through the door. He looked them up and down and noticed the change of clothing.

'What time do you call this?' he barked. 'We're trying to run a homicide investigation here, not a fucking dating agency.'

'We were following a line of investigation,' Deans said.

Jackson shook his head. 'I am really quite staggered – considering...'

'Any update from the dig?' Deans glared.

'Not yet.' Jackson took a moment to take them both in. 'Have you *followed* everything you needed to *follow*? Do you mind if we try to catch some baddies, or would you like me to put the investigation on hold for a little bit longer?'

Jesus! You are a tortured tosser. Deans looked over at Sarah. 'Nah, I think we've satisfied that one.'

'Right, I've got a job for—'

'We've already made plans for this afternoon,' Deans interrupted.

'What plans?' Jackson scowled.

'We're going back to the address you sent me to before I was attacked,' Sarah said.

Jackson cut her a sharp stare.

'Do you still have the address on the system?' Deans asked him.

Jackson scratched the side of his nose. 'Of course I do. HOLMES (Home Office Large Major Enquiry System) stores every line of enquiry – you know it does.'

'Just checking.' Deans held Jackson's beady glaze. 'Give us the details and we'll be back before you know it.'

'What do you hope to achieve by going to the address, other than putting both of your lives in danger?'

'So you agree it's a significant address?' Deans said.

'Well, if what Gold says is correct; then we must view it as a potentially hostile location.' Jackson hesitated. 'Let me come with you.'

'No,' Sarah quickly replied.

Deans put his hand up to stop Sarah saying anything else. 'Yeah, okay,' he said. 'The more the merrier.'

Sarah turned her back on them and walked out of the room.

'So,' Jackson said, sidling up alongside Deans. 'What are you expecting to find there?'

'I don't know, maybe the answers will find us.'

Deans deliberately sat behind Jackson's driving seat with Sarah in the front passenger side of the car. From this position, he could see Jackson's darting eyes in the mirror and Sarah's reactions to any conversation. The hands-free ring-tone broke the frosty silence and Jackson answered.

'DS Jackson,' he said quickly. 'I'm not alone and you are on hands-free.'

The caller instantly terminated the connection.

Deans twitched a brow and stared out of the side window, trapped in his thoughts.

They rounded a corner onto Hemingsford Quay with its string of festive lights hanging from lamppost to lamppost. If circumstances were different, if Hemingsford didn't leave the bitter taste, this would be a tranquil place to spend Christmas holidays. Deans looked into the rear view mirror. Jackson's eyes were trained back upon him.

They continued beyond the sea front promenade and came to a narrow street of pastel coloured cottages on either side of the road.

'It was near here,' Sarah said. Her voice wavered as she spoke.

'I'll put it in here,' Jackson said, slowing to a stop behind a string of parked cars at the wide mouth of the lane. 'You okay?' he asked, noticing Sarah hugging herself.

'Yes. I'm fine.'

Deans could see that she was not. Her hair was quivering from her trembling head.

They all stepped outside of the car and began down the narrow road that bisected the cottages on either side. It was obvious cars travelled down this road from the grooves worn into the road surface, but it must have been a tight squeeze. The terraced houses were tight and small with doorways Deans would have to duck to get beneath. *Original fisherman's cottages*, Deans thought.

After a few more moments, Sarah stopped and pointed forwards. 'There. It's that one.'

'Alright,' Jackson said. 'You stay here if you like; Deans and I will check it out.'

They approached the house and Deans looked behind; Sarah was leaning against the building at the start of the lane.

'I'll go around the back,' Jackson said. 'You check out what you can on this side.'

Jackson disappeared down a tiny side alley and Deans could see the waters of the estuary just a few feet away. He cupped his hands against the front window and looked inside. He could see straight through to the village on the other side of the estuary. The downstairs looked tidy and inhabited. *Wow. What a place.*

He checked behind. Sarah was no longer there.

They were at a kink in the lane and the colourful cottages continued along and out of sight. Deans wasn't feeling anything untoward about the cottage and walked on. After a short distance, he came to an olde worlde pub by the water's edge. He drew a deep breath and sighed. *In another life.* He turned back and found Jackson back at the front of the cottage.

'Where has Sarah gone?' Deans asked.

Jackson looked all around in a full circle. 'I don't know. Back to the car?'

Deans rubbed his face and groaned. 'What was around the back?'

'Nothing much, apart from stunning views over the estuary.'

'Why did you send Sarah here in the first place?' Deans asked.

'Links to your mate, Scotty. This is his parent's home.'

'Do they still live here?'

'That was what I was sending Sarah here to establish.'

Deans stepped closer into Jackson's personal space. 'Do you believe her account of what happened?' he asked.

'Why wouldn't I? You saw her yourself at Mansell's place.'

Deans' lips parted and he started back towards the car.

'Shall we knock on the door before we go?' Jackson asked.

'No point – you won't get an answer.'

'How can you be so sure?'

'I'm going to find Sarah. Do whatever you like.'

Deans found her inside the car. She had been crying. He tried to open the door but it was locked from the inside. He tapped on the window and she looked at him with startled eyes.

'Are you alright?' Deans asked.

Sarah nodded and blew her nose into a tissue.

'Can you open the door or the window, please?'

She pulled the inside door handle and the latches sprung open.

Deans opened the door a few inches. 'Bit raw for you still?' he said.

She bobbed her head and dabbed a tissue beneath her eyes.

Deans shot around. Jackson was approaching them at speed.

'What is it?' Sarah asked with a stressed voice.

'Nothing,' Deans replied. 'It's nothing.'

'Get in the car,' Jackson said, gesturing wildly with his hand.'

'What is it?' Sarah said again, her tone now panicked.

Jackson jumped into the driver's seat and rushed to put the key in the ignition. 'I've had a call,' he said firing up the car.

'Who from?' Deans asked clicking into his seatbelt.

'The DCI,' Jackson replied as the car lurched backwards.

Deans leaned through the gap between the two front seats. 'Well, what did the DCI say?'

Jackson faced him with an excited grin. 'She's at the mortuary – they've recovered human remains.'

CHAPTER THIRTY-NINE

The DCI was waiting at the front of the mortuary to meet them. Two crime scene vans and three response vehicles were parked alongside her.

Deans was the first to open his door and make his way towards the boss.

'Have they found her?' he said desperately.

The DCI held both palms aloft, like a mime artist pressing against an imaginary plate of glass. 'Let's wait until we go inside,' she said and then noticed DC Gold. 'Are you alright,' she asked.

'Yes thanks, Ma'am,' Gold said, as Jackson crept up alongside her.

'Let's talk inside,' the DCI said.

They funnelled through the doorway and a new mortuary attendant took them into the examination room where a forensic pathologist was waiting to greet them.

'This is forensic pathologist, Camille Cissé. She and her team have kindly come down from Cheltenham to assist us with our investigation, on a short-term basis.'

'Hello,' she said. 'Pleased to meet you all.'

The DCI directed Jackson, Deans and Gold to seats that weren't there the last time Deans was in this room.

'The dig is still progressing,' the DCI said, 'and there have been positive results.' She gave Deans a fleeting look. 'So far, we have exhumed six human skulls and more are believed to be at a lower depth. This has turned into an incident on a major scale and I am deferring command of the investigation to my superiors at Headquarters. A team of detectives will be joining us soon from the Major Crime Investigation Team and I will continue locally as the senior investigating officer.' She took a breath and smiled. 'Okay, that's the formalities out of the way.' The DCI nodded for Dr Cissé to continue.

'As Detective Chief Inspector says, six skulls have so far been recovered. Three of them are recently deceased and three are older. Degradation suggests we are talking by a number of decades.'

'When you say "recent", how recent do you mean?' Deans asked.

The pathologist half glanced at the DCI who closed her eyes with a single nod of the head.

'Is it Detective Deans?' the pathologist asked.

'Yes.'

She held out her hand to shake and Deans shook it. 'We suspect that one of the recovered heads could be that of your wife.'

Deans' brain buzzed like a thousand wasps had just flown in through each ear and collided in the middle. He was suddenly aware of why they were all seated, and it wasn't for the benefit of Jackson and Gold.

'And the others?' Jackson asked.

The pathologist cleared her throat and smoothed her hands down the sides of her white coat. 'I can confirm that one of the exhumed heads is Archie Rowland. I have identified him myself.'

'I am sorry,' Jackson said.

'Thank you.'

'Did you know him well?' Jackson continued.

Deans frowned and stared at Jackson.

'Yes. In fact, Archie Rowland sponsored me when I first came to this country. I even stayed at his family home for a short time until I found my own accommodation.'

Deans waited for Jackson to say something else. He didn't.

'How are we going to do this?' Deans asked. 'I'm not being funny, but I need to know if you have my wife.'

'Of course,' the DCI said. 'As I understand it and correct me if I'm wrong, Dr Cissé, but Andrew will go with you shortly and attempt to make a formal identification?'

'That is correct. I can assure you that the process will be respectfully conducted, but sadly, this is the quickest way of identifying the exhibits.'

'Exhibits?' Deans repeated.

'I'm sorry. That was an insensitive choice of words.'

Deans nodded.

'Shall we get on with this?' Jackson said.

Everyone stared at Jackson.

Deans stood up from the chair. If he was being honest, he was close to vomiting. The DCI took his arm and led him away from the others and into a side room with comfortable seating and a low coffee table.

'We're going to show you some images first, Andrew. If you positively identify your wife from those, we would then offer you the chance to see her in person and in private, for as long as you need.'

'Okay,' he murmured.

Deans' breathing was juddering and his head felt so light he thought it would lift from his shoulders.

'I'll leave you now,' the DCI said. She smiled sincerely and closed the door as she left.

Compassion was oozing from Dr Cissé's glassy-black eyes. She leaned forwards and touched Deans' hand. 'I know how hard this is for you,' she said.

'I'm sorry about your colleague,' Deans replied. 'And I'm sorry you have been caught up in all of this.'

Dr Cissé smiled lightly and opened a laptop on the seat beside her. She typed something into the keyboard and looked up over the top of the screen at Deans. 'Are you ready?' she asked.

Deans blinked and swallowed, even though his mouth was parched dry. He drew a deep shuddering breath. 'Okay.'

The doctor looked back down at the screen. 'I'm going to show you a series of images, and for continuity, I will also show you images of how the heads were located in the grave by the forensic team.'

Deans tried to nod, but his neck was solid.

The doctor turned the laptop around and Deans faced the screen for a long moment without moving. His eyes burned into the image.

'Are you ready for the next one?'

Deans didn't react. His stare was fixed on the laptop.

The doctor turned the computer back to herself, but Deans continued gaping into the space left by the screen. Dr Cissé turned the computer to Deans once again.

He looked at the photograph and finally blinked as tears forced their way out.

'Is this your wife?' Dr Cissé asked quietly.

Deans broke away from the computer and wiped the streams of tears from his cheeks.

'Don't speak if it's hard. Just give me an indication,' Dr Cissé said handing Deans a paper tissue.

He closed his eyes and sank his head. 'Yes,' he muttered. 'That's Maria.'

'There's something I need to tell you about your wife's head.'

Deans slowly looked up.

'Maria's head was… different to the others.'

'Different?'

The pathologist creased her forehead and partially looked away.

'Different how?' Deans asked.

Dr Cissé looked directly at him. 'Her head was bound in plastic wrap – a cling film material.'

Deans grimaced.

'No other heads were preserved the same way.'

'Preserved?' Deans blubbed.

'We suspect the killer wanted to keep her…' she coughed behind her hand. '…fresh.'

Deans scowled.

'Your wife has been dead for what, two months or so?'

Deans nodded.

'Without the preservative layer, she would be unrecognisable today, given the maggots and other creatures that would take her flesh.'

Deans shook his head.

'I'm sorry, this is probably even harder for you.'

Deans bit his lip and dropped his head. 'Can you trace the wrap – fingerprints – DNA?'

'It's possible, but we would anticipate the killer was forensically aware, and this type of PVC cling film can be found in any supermarket, in any corner store.' She stopped talking for a second or two. 'I know this is hard, but I just have a couple more photographs to show you.'

Deans wiped his nose with the back of his hand and mustered all his will to look at the screen. The next image showed a close-up inside the pit; all mud, deep red dirt, and a rounded dome, like a football wrapped for Christmas. Deans spluttered behind his praying hands. He noticed the depth of the trench, surprised at how shallow it was – no deeper than half a metre.

'And this is the last one,' the pathologist said. She repeated the process of finding the photograph on the screen and turned it back to Deans.

This time, he was looking at a wide-angle view of the trench and he could see Maria's bound head once again, but now he could also see two other severed heads, one on top of the other. There could be no doubt, given their *condition*, that they were recently deceased. Deans swallowed hard and leaned closer to the screen.

'The head in the middle is Dr Archie Rowland,' the pathologist said. 'But we are still—'

'I know who it is,' Deans interrupted.

The pathologist picked up her pen and readied her pad.

Deans looked closer again, scrutinising the image a while longer, and then gently bobbed his head. He dropped his chin to his chest and closed his eyes once more.

'Detective?'

Deans looked up at Dr Cissé through broken eyes.

'Are you able to give me a name?'

Deans' chest shuddered as he filled his lungs. He looked back down at the screen.

'It's Archie's daughter – Annie Rowland.'

CHAPTER FORTY

Deans dragged himself out of the examination room after forty minutes alone with *Maria*. Sarah was waiting for him in the hallway. She was teary and immediately hugged him as he came through the door.

'I'm so sorry,' she whispered in his ear and held him tight. Deans finally gave in to his emotions, wrapped his arms around her back, dropped his chin to her shoulder and broke down. They remained like this for several minutes, until Deans pulled away.

'Did you hear who the other was?' he said.

'Yes,' Sarah replied softly. 'Where does that leave us now?'

Deans shook his weary head. 'I don't know, but it's a game changer.'

'Where do you think her body will be?'

'My guess is we'll find it sooner or later on the beach.'

'Why is this happening?' Sarah asked. 'I mean, why so vicious and brutal, and why bury heads and dump the bodies in the sea?'

'It's symbolic.'

'Of what?'

Deans walked to the window, twisted the blind and looked outside through heavy lids. Jackson's car was gone. 'Because… because this is war,' he said.

'Who with?'

Deans rocked on his heels. 'The deadliest adversary I've ever seen.'

The CID office was buzzing like a hive and the queen bee was at the centre of it all.

'Ma'am,' Deans said. 'Can I have a private word, please?'

'Ah, Andrew,' she said taking his hand in hers and turning him to one side. 'I am sorry that this is all so personal for you. Are you okay?'

He thought about it for a second or two. 'Yes, I'm okay. Can we go somewhere else to talk, please?'

'Yes. Just hold on.' The DCI called across to a uniformed inspector and said she needed ten minutes.

Deans took her to the small interview room along the corridor and they sat down. Before speaking, Deans took a measured look around her face. He hoped his gut feeling was correct in placing his trust in her hands. 'I'm wary of Jackson,' he finally said.

'Sergeant Jackson?' she repeated. 'Why?'

'I think he is involved in these murders.'

The DCI pulled a face, something between a smile and a grimace. She tilted her head. 'You'd better tell me what's on your mind.'

Deans planted his palms on the desk. This was it; cards on the table; his deepest concerns exposed, laying himself open and vulnerable.

'Do you trust him?' Deans asked.

'How can you ask me such a thing? Of course I do. He's an

experienced detective. He's done tonnes of good for this community over the years.'

'That's my issue. He is very well established within this community. So wouldn't you expect him to be a little more au fait with its history than he portrays?'

'I'm lost.'

'Ma'am, we are dealing with a cult whose warped teachings and mistaken beliefs result in the deaths of anyone that comes close to identifying them. We are all targets, and the closer we get to exposing the truth, the nearer we all come to death.'

'No. I'm sorry—'

'Think about it. Take it right back to Amy Poole. We focussed on Ash Babbage and there is no doubt Babbage was involved, along with Detective Ranford, but if you remember, when crucial evidence went missing, Sarah Gold was used as a convenient scapegoat. And then Babbage folds in interview and ends up dead when Ranford decides it's time to shut him up. But here's the part I haven't yet worked out – Ranford is captured, thanks to Jackson, and then admits to the murder of my wife and involvement in the Amy Poole murder. We recover forensic evidence from Ruby Mansell's house and the case progresses nicely, until Archie Rowland is murdered. Evidence stacks up against his daughter, we're about to get her in and she turns up dead.'

The DCI did not speak.

'I'm sorry, but all roads lead to Sergeant Jackson. I know he saved me from Ranford, but why was he there in the first place? Don't you think that was rather convenient? He's not usually proactive to the radio – why should he come running when Ranford pressed the emergency button? Just look at how the deaths are linked: Amy Poole – a sacrifice. My wife and unborn child – a sacrifice, and a punishment to me for pursuing the killers. Ash Babbage – murdered before he said too much. Archie Rowland – murdered because he was getting close to the truth. Annie Rowland – murdered because we were about to bring her in. The closer we get to the centre of this *secret society*, the more people are dying. Someone on the inside is calling the shots. They're the centre of it all and my money's on Jackson.'

The DCI didn't take her eyes off Deans as she stood up and silently made her way to the door and peered outside. She closed the door once again and re-took her seat.

'They've found remains of another five victims,' she said, 'and they're still working on the pit.'

'Heads?'

'Yes – well, skulls now.'

'There was something Jackson said to me at the time Ranford was arrested. He said he had come on board when the rate of untraced missing persons had gone up. Young females, he said, over a long period of time. He wasn't here to help, he was attempting to cover this up. We need details of every person reported missing in North Devon,' Deans said. 'Some of them will be our victims, for sure.'

'We would need to involve our cold case department at Headquarters,' the DCI said. 'They have access to data going back decades and obviously knowledge of ongoing investigations.'

'Good,' Deans said. 'How quickly could we get our hands on that information?'

The DCI shrugged. 'I don't know. Just like every specialist team, they have their own pressures. They may be dealing with past lives, but the present demands and politics remain the same.'

A loud knock at the door made them both jump in their seats.

'Yes,' the DCI called out.

The door opened inwards bumping the back of Deans' chair.

'Ma'am, sorry to interrupt.' It was one of the uniformed inspectors. 'The briefing? Everyone's waiting.'

The DCI nodded. 'Yes, yes. Thank you.'

The inspector backed out of the room, leaving Deans with a lingering stare.

'Just before you go,' the DCI called out.

The inspector stopped and poked his head back into the room.

'Is Sergeant Jackson back from enquiries?'

'Yes, Ma'am.'

She glanced at Deans. 'Good. We'll be with you shortly.'

CHAPTER FORTY-ONE

The briefing room was stacked to the rafters with officers. Deans saw Jackson seated at the end of the first row. His arms were folded and his face was a light shade of crimson. Sarah was in the row behind. She had her usual fresh-faced appearance, despite her recent ill adventures.

The DCI engaged the room. 'Apologies for the delayed start everyone.' She looked at Jackson. 'Something important has come up.'

Deans was standing at the back of the room along with several other people, and he saw Jackson trying to seek him out. Deans smiled on the inside. *Got you now, fucker*.

'We have initial results from the examination of Bone Hill,' the DCI said. 'We have three confirmed identities from the recovered heads: Maria Deans – Detective Deans' wife. Archie Rowland who most of you will know, and Annie Rowland – Archie's daughter, who again, some of you will know.'

The room bristled like a gust of stiff wind passing over ears of autumn-ripe corn. The DCI took her time to look at the assembled team, person by person.

'The remains of at least five other victims have also been recovered,' she finally said.

This time, the room swayed.

'Victims, Ma'am?' one of the senior officers asked. 'Wasn't Bone Hill a kosher burial site – a genuine place of rest?'

The DCI gave the officer an indignant look.

'Their heads have been separated from their bodies, Michael. I'd like to think, if this was a genuine place of rest, then these people would also be buried with the rest of their bodies. This site appears to hold symbolic importance for the killers.'

'Killers?' the same inspector challenged.

'Yes. Killers. It is clear that some of these victim's heads have been in situ for decades.'

The room fell quiet for a moment.

'What do you propose, Ma'am?' Jackson asked.

The DCI walked slowly towards the end of the row and stood directly in front of Jackson. Deans could feel the energy between them from the back of the room.

'We are going to find the bastards responsible, and then we are going to throw away the key.'

Jackson rolled his head and smiled. 'With all due respect, Ma'am, that's a rallying cry. But where do we start?'

'We've already started.' She walked back to the centre of the room. 'We have recovered a spade from Bone Hill.' She peered at Jackson. 'It was concealed beneath the same type of netting that hid the mass grave. Our forensic team have examined the exhibit and we should have results soon.'

Jackson scratched the front of his head where his hairline once lived.

'We need to keep the media at bay,' the DCI said. 'Our dig has obviously generated a lot of attention, and speculation is already rife on social media.' She raised her eyebrows. 'Some of it correct, of course.'

'It doesn't help having Detective Deans here, Ma'am,' Inspector "Michael" said. 'No offence, but he was headline news only days ago. How can we keep a low profile when we've got "The Angel Detective" on board?'

Several officers laughed aloud and others scoffed into their hands.

The DCI walked silently up the rows of chairs until she was alongside the seat where the inspector was sitting, three chairs in. Her faced flushed as she loomed over the heads of the two nearest officers. 'See me after briefing,' she said and caught Deans' eye as she walked back to the front.

'I want an interview with Ranford. See if he's willing to speak about the Bone Hill. Any volunteers?'

'I'll do it,' Jackson said without hesitating.

The DCI cocked her head. She considered his offer for a moment before accepting. 'Good,' she said. 'You can go with Detective Deans.'

Deans felt blood rush to his cheeks.

The DCI looked over to him. 'Is that okay with you, Detective?'

'Yes, Ma'am,' Deans replied, and noticed several faces turning behind to peer at him.

'Good. We'll meet again tomorrow, same time, same place.' She glanced at Deans. 'Keep safe everyone.'

Jackson was waiting for Deans in the hallway. The post-briefing-chatter was mostly about the discovery of more heads, and of course, there was the obligatory wisecracking of inappropriate jokes, as was the way of the police at times of great tension.

'I just need fifteen minutes before we get our heads around that interview plan,' Jackson said.

'No problem,' Deans replied. 'Anything I can help with?'

'No.'

Jackson kept Deans in sight as he walked away. 'Stay there,' he called out. 'Start the prep and I'll be back as soon as I can.'

Deans found a quiet corner to settle in while other officers hustled about their business.

The DCI found Deans and quietly confided in his ear. 'It'll be interesting to see what happens next,' she said.

'Yes, Ma'am.'

'I've told the crime scene manager that no persons are to access the exhibit stores alone. We'll do what we can to safeguard the evidence we've captured so far.' She looked around the room. 'Where is Sergeant Jackson?'

'He said he had to go somewhere. He's meeting me back here shortly.'

'Okay, good.' The DCI's focus waned and she stared into space for a moment. 'Good,' she repeated. 'Keep safe.'

CHAPTER FORTY-TWO

Jackson found the detained property clerk in the storeroom sifting through a tabletop covered with brown paper exhibit bags.

'Alright, Sarge?' the property clerk said.

'Yeah. Good, thanks, Rose. How are you?'

'You know.' The clerk gave Jackson a disgruntled smile. 'How can I help?'

'Where are the exhibits from the ongoing job at Sandymere Bay?'

'You mean the mass grave?'

'Yeah,' Jackson said, 'the mass grave.' He showed faked interest in an exhibit label attached to a large brown paper bag of clothing.

'My God, it's scary to think that has happened here, isn't it? I mean there's a serial killer in Sandymere Bay.' The more the clerk spoke, the more animated she became. 'I even heard something about it on the local radio.'

'What did you hear?'

'They were just saying about a large-scale police operation

in the woods. They didn't say much else – they wouldn't know I suppose, I mean, how would they?'

'Do you find this all quite... *exciting*?' Jackson asked.

'Yeah!' The clerk beamed. 'It's amazing.'

'Yes,' Jackson replied. 'It is.'

The clerk stood up from behind her desk. 'What was it you were after, Sarge?'

'The spade. I just need to take a look at it.'

'Oh, um—'

'Problem?'

'I'm not supposed to give any of these exhibits out.'

'Oh, that's okay. I'm not taking it anywhere. I'll look at it right here.'

The clerk hesitated, but then typed something into the computer and went to a separate storage area behind a locked door. She returned with a spade wrapped in a large clear plastic sack and handed it to Jackson.

'Can I use that desk?' Jackson asked pointing to a smaller table behind the clerk.

'Yes, of course.'

Jackson laid the spade flat on the desk and manipulated the plastic, looking closer at the object. He could still see traces of fingerprint dust on the stainless steel shaft.

'Shall I book it out to you, Sarge?' the clerk asked.

'No need for that,' Jackson said. 'You'll have it back in a moment. No need to get bogged down with unnecessary continuity. It's not leaving the store.'

The clerk looked nervously at the computer screen.

Jackson fiddled with the exhibit tag that sealed the top of the bag. He smiled. It was loose and there was *just enough* play. He pulled the bag through the plastic teeth of the seal, being careful not to rip the bag.

The clerk watched him silently.

Jackson removed the seal, opened the mouth of the bag and peered inside.

'Um, shouldn't you…'

Jackson pulled out the spade. It had a shiny green plastic handle and the stainless steel blade was encrusted with dried soil. He held it up in the air, twisting it several times as he gripped the shaft and handle in several different places.

'Um, Sarge?'

'Yes.'

'Shouldn't you be wearing forensic gloves to handle that exhibit?'

'Oh bugger!' Jackson shouted and laid the spade flat on top of the bag. He turned to the clerk with a shocked expression. 'I'm a total knob. I just wasn't thinking. I'd better get this back away before I mess anything else up.'

He slid the spade back into the bag and passed the loose seal back over the top.

'There we go,' he said. 'Good as new. No one will know any different.' He pulled a mischievous face at the clerk. 'Let's hope they don't test this for fingerprints and DNA, or I'm screwed.'

Jackson winked at the clerk. 'Is it okay to leave it with you to put away? I need to prepare an interview.'

The wide-eyed clerk nodded and Jackson left the room whistling a jaunty tune.

CHAPTER FORTY-THREE

'I want Mansfield to join us,' Deans said to Jackson upon his return to the office.

'No way,' Jackson said.

'We need him.'

Jackson peered at Deans. 'No. We don't. He's a prick and he's a liability.'

'Nobody knows Ranford better than Mansfield. He may be able to help us.'

'Or he could fuck this whole thing up.'

'Sarah, what do you think?' Deans asked Gold who was within earshot.

She glanced nervously at Jackson. 'I don't have an opinion.'

'Well, you need one. You are the OIC and carrying this investigation all the way to trial. Would you ask Mansfield to join the team?' Deans pressed.

Sarah grabbed strands of dangling hair and pulled it back behind her ear. She was buying time.

'Sarah?' Deans said.

'I guess so,' she said.

'Hold on, have we all forgotten who the sergeant is here?'

'That can't get in the way,' Deans said. 'It's about making the correct decisions.'

'And I make them,' Jackson glared. His eyes drifted for second or two. 'Very well,' he said. 'Mansfield can come on the team, but the moment he screws up, it's on your head, Deans.'

Jackson phoned down to the box room and ushered Mansfield to join them in the CID office.

Mansfield came in and locked eyes with Deans.

'Detective Mansfield,' Jackson said.

'Sarge.'

'It would appear you have a supporter among our ranks. I'm offering you a chance to be part of our team.'

Mansfield looked at Deans and suppressed a grin.

Jackson tilted his head. 'You, more than anyone, know how sensitive this investigation is, particularly given the current status of your erstwhile colleague.'

Mansfield turned to the white board. Deans watched his reaction as he read all of the names.

'What are we going to do?' Mansfield asked.

'We are taking a little journey,' Deans said. 'We're going to pop in on an old friend.'

The custody sergeant at the charge desk gave Deans a quick once over. 'Are you the cause of all this hassle?'

'Hassle?' Deans repeated.

'The reason we've had to ship our prisoners off to outlying stations, so that you can have the custody area to yourself.'

Somebody had obviously decided it was safer to have Ranford as the sole prisoner in the unit – less chance of escape, mishap, or collusion.

'Nothing to do with me,' Deans said.

'Is Detective Ranford here?' Jackson asked.

'You know, I'm not very comfortable with this,' the desk sergeant said. 'This should be happening somewhere else.'

'Well, it's not,' Jackson said. 'Just point us to the interview room.'

The sergeant opened his arms out wide. 'Take your pick, there's nobody else here – just you, me, a couple of DOs, and Torworthy CID detective, Paul Ranford.'

'Can you get him out, we're ready to roll,' Jackson said passing the sergeant.

Deans entered the same interview room he used to grill Ash Babbage and placed his go-bag on the stainless steel chair, directly opposite the 'hot seat'.

'Are the bosses coming to listen remotely?' Deans asked Jackson who was fiddling with the recording equipment.

'Don't know. But we'll have the disks to play back if needs be.'

Deans looked over at Mansfield who was hovering near the door. A waft of perfume assaulted Deans' senses. *Maria.* The sound of chatter further down the corridor made Deans' heart race. He heard laughter and a voice that he recognised: Detective Paul Ranford.

The desk sergeant appeared at the open door and Ranford stepped into the room.

'Manny,' he said noticing Mansfield. 'What are you doing here?'

Mansfield shifted uncomfortably from foot to foot.

Deans stared at Ranford and their eyes met. Ranford gave him a nod and a smile. Deans did all he could to restrain his wrath as Ranford walked towards the opposing seat.

'Sit down,' Jackson said.

Ranford winked at the desk sergeant who closed the door on his way out.

'This interview is being visually recorded,' Jackson said. 'Oh, you know the score, being the trained police interrogator that you are. Do you want a solicitor?'

Ranford shook his head and hooked one leg over the other in a display of unflustered ease. He clutched his bent knee, drew a long disinterested breath and licked the corner of his mouth as he peered back at Deans, Jackson and Mansfield in turn.

'When they told me I had visitors, I have to be honest, I wasn't expecting you, Andrew. So what's all this about?' Ranford asked. 'I was rather enjoying my prison suite. These cells are rather basic, you know.' He peered directly at Deans. 'It's actually not that bad in the clink…' he smiled. 'So long as they keep the scrotes away from me.' He lifted the flap of his top lip and displayed a broken tooth.

'Sarah Gold is dead,' Deans said.

Jackson swung around, his eyes burrowing into the side of Deans' face.

Deans saw a flicker in the corner of Ranford's eye and the slightest twitch of his brow.

Interesting. 'Does that surprise you?' Deans asked.

Ranford blinked and looked at Jackson. 'I'm not the prophet here.'

Jackson leaned forwards, his moist palms squeaking as they slid across the stainless steel desk, but before he could intervene, Deans continued. 'She was burned alive.'

'Why are you telling me this? It obviously wasn't me.'

'No,' Deans repeated. 'Obviously not.' He noticed Ranford looking at his left ring finger. *Good. Keep it coming.* Deans made a point of lifting his hand and spinning the ring between his fingers – the ring he had borrowed from Denise. 'Like it, do you?' he said looking at the ring himself.

Ranford dipped his head lopsidedly and shot another glance the way of Jackson.

'I think we should start this again,' Jackson said in a commanding voice. 'Sarah Gold is not dead.'

'What?' Ranford said and scowled at Deans.

'There was an attempt on her life, but she survived,' Jackson continued.

'Why would you say that?' Ranford asked Deans.

'I was seeing if you already knew.'

Ranford looked beyond Deans' shoulder at Mansfield who was still standing close to the door.

'Well, I obviously didn't. Is this right, Manny?'

'Yes.'

'What happened?'

'She was chained to the cellar beneath Ruby Mansell's house and then somebody set fire to it.' He watched Ranford's pupils constrict as if he'd just had a hit of heroin.

'Will she be okay?' he asked.

'Why are you so bothered about Detective Gold?' Deans asked.

Ranford brushed the question aside with a pout. 'I'm not.'

'How many others are there?' Deans asked. 'Four… five? Twenty-four… twenty-five?'

'Others?'

'In your twisted cult.'

Ranford chortled and shook his head.

Deans beckoned Ranford closer with a double-twitch of his index finger. Ranford looked at Jackson and partially complied.

'I'm not gunna stop,' Deans whispered. 'You fucked with the wrong person this time.'

Ranford stared back with a steely abstinence that told Deans all he needed to know.

'Are you willing to tell us who else is involved?' Jackson asked.

Ranford peered at Jackson and frowned.

'We found the shallow grave,' Deans said.

Ranford didn't react.

'At Bone Hill.'

Ranford blinked twice at half-speed.

'Tell us exactly who we are going to find there?' Deans said.

Ranford flashed his eyes wide and pinched his lips tightly together with his fingers.

'You're looking at mass murder,' Jackson said. 'It'll be entirely on you if you decide not to speak. *Everything* will be on your shoulders.'

Is he passing Ranford a message?

'We found camouflaged netting concealing the grave – just the same kind you used on your boat,' Deans said.

Ranford bobbed his shoulders.

'Explain how that got there,' Deans asked.

'That doesn't mean a thing,' Ranford said. 'You can get that netting anywhere.'

'We also recovered a shovel,' Jackson said.

Deans noticed Ranford baulk slightly. 'That's right, Paul. It's not a shovel, it's a spade. There's a subtle difference with its usage.'

'Same thing,' Jackson mumbled.

'Tell us what we're going to find when we examine the spade?' Deans asked. In his peripheral vision, Jackson wiggled in his seat. Deans was taking it all in. 'Your prints, DNA?' Deans asked.

Ranford sniffed and rolled his shoulders.

'Somebody else's?'

'Maybe,' Ranford said.

Deans allowed ten seconds of silence to frame his question.

'My wife. Archie Rowland and now Annie Rowland...'

Ranford's left eye half-closed. He didn't know about Annie.

'Who else are we going to find down there?' Deans asked.

Ranford appeared to drift off. Was he imagining their faces? 'Who else is in this with you?' Deans asked, making a point of looking sideways at Jackson.

'This is a waste of time,' Jackson said.

'Was my wife sacrificed as an act of war?' Deans said through clenched teeth.

Ranford peered at Deans beneath heavy eyes.

'If it's a war you want, a war you'll have.'

Ranford looked over to Mansfield and twirled his index finger beside his temple. 'Is he alright?' He looked back at Deans. 'I think you left something at that train crash... your marbles, perhaps?'

'Sadly for you and your little band of Pagan worshipers, I *found* myself at that crash site.'

'Alright,' Jackson said leaning across the table and stopping the recording equipment. 'I think that'll just about do us for now.' He glared at Deans and then at Ranford. 'You'll be staying here for a while yet,' he said to Ranford. 'So I suggest you think long and hard about talking, or not.'

Jackson, Deans and Mansfield remained in the room as Ranford was escorted away by two detention officers.

'You mind explaining what that was all about?' Jackson asked.

Deans heaved a deep breath and peered up at the sound-proofed ceiling. 'I'm figuring out my enemy.' He interlocked his hands behind his head, exposing his throat. *Show yourself for what you are, Jackson.*

'What is that supposed to mean?' Jackson said.

'Exactly how it sounds.'

Deans lowered his arms and faced Jackson. 'What now, *Sarge*?'

'Well, that was a total waste of time. You need to rein in your personal feelings, son.'

Deans scoffed and sniffed loudly. *They are the only things keeping me alive.*

CHAPTER FORTY-FOUR

The DCI had sent Jackson a voicemail while they were inter-
viewing. They were to return to the station immediately, and
she was waiting for them as soon as they came in from the
outside.

'We've got a fingerprint hit on the spade,' she said. She was
looking at Jackson the entire time. 'I am told you handled the
spade without protection from cross contamination.' The DCI
glared at Jackson. 'Why did you feel the need to remove the
exhibit in the first place?'

'I was intrigued.'

'By a fucking spade? Have you lost your mind? You have
compromised a vital piece of evidence.'

Deans' head slumped. This was what he feared would
happen.

The DCI noticed Deans. 'In fact,' she said. 'We have three
separate hits. Two are confirmed and one is still being
processed.'

Deans looked up. 'Who is the other one, Ma'am?'

'Paul Ranford.'

That meant Ranford did play more than a proprietary role

in the death of Deans' wife. He was at the site where her head was buried. Perhaps he *was* the main man after all.

Deans' mind tracked to his early days in training school when he and his induction were trained in fingerprint and DNA taking. They were instructed on how to take wet prints and were let loose to practise on one another. Same with DNA mouth swabs. It was a lot of fun, but the police weren't stupid and there is no doubt the 'practice' prints and swabs were shipped off to a lab and added to the database. After all, how embarrassing would it be for the force to a have a serial criminal in their ranks? *Ironic!*

'When are we expecting the results of the third?' Deans asked.

'It's a partial lift. They're not convinced enough at present to give a positive result, but they are re-examining the spade...' she looked at her watch. 'Andrew, can I have a quiet word, please?'

'Of course, Ma'am.'

Jackson ogled them as they walked away and into a separate room.

The DCI invited Deans to take a seat, but remained standing. She observed him for a moment. 'How did you know about the Bone Hill?' she asked.

Deans folded his arms. 'I was told about it.'

'By?'

'Denise Moon.'

'Ah, Denise Moon.'

'Hold on, Denise isn't—'

'Don't worry, I'm not apportioning any involvement to your friend.'

'Denise told me about the local history – the Viking invasion in the ninth century.'

'Yes,' the DCI said drawing the word out to emphasise her

thoughts on the matter. 'The Vikings. I've heard a lot about the Vikings recently.' She continued staring at him and began to pace slowly, as was becoming her trait. 'What I mean is, how did you find the burial ground? It was off the beaten track and hidden beneath camouflaged netting.'

Deans smoothed his fingers along the side of his face, towards his scar.

'It's okay – try me, but I'm not swallowing that "instinct" line of yours again.'

Deans glanced away and pondered his next move. His eyes darted left and right. She was taking on Jackson, so had to be an ally, didn't she? He moistened his lips and peered up at the boss.

'Detective Gold has told me some things about you,' the DCI said.

Oh, shit! Deans plunged his head into his hands.

'It's okay. I have an open mind about these things. I knew there was something *special* about you after that search at Babbage's house, and how you *discovered* that evidence…'

Deans nodded, but his hands still masked his face.

'Tell me,' the DCI pressed.

Deans peeled his head from his hands. 'I didn't want any of this,' he said.

'I understand that,' the DCI said.

'I'd rather have my family back.'

'But that can never happen. Not anymore.'

'No.' He looked away. 'Not anymore.'

'But you've got talents – talents that can be very useful to a detective – to a police force.'

'Yes,' Deans breathed.

'And I want you to use them.'

Deans looked her square in the eye.

'I want you to go to police headquarters with Detective

Gold, this evening. There, you will meet a colleague of mine who is expecting you. He is going to show you some photographs of outstanding missing persons from this district. Look at them. Do whatever it is you do. It's time to unleash your talent.'

'Why are you helping me?'

The DCI pulled out a chair and sat down. 'My mother went missing when I was eight years of age. They suspected my father for a time. And then put it down to her own decision to leave when they found no evidence of her disappearance. Hmm, that's not at all what happened. She was murdered; at least, that is what I believe. But her body has never been found.' She made a point of looking at Deans. 'I suppose that's what drives me to be the best officer I can be.' The DCI paused in her thoughts. 'And so, you can see why I find you quite intriguing… and your abilities frankly exciting. Harness your misfortune to become the most potent investigator the world has ever seen.'

'What about Jackson?' Deans asked.

'Jackson is in my sights, don't worry.'

'You know he handled that spade deliberately to mask any of his fingerprints that were already on there?' Deans said.

The DCI smiled. 'You'd better get going, or it's going to be a long night for you.'

Deans shut his eyes. 'Every night is long for me, since…'

It was nudging seven-thirty by the time Deans and Sarah arrived at police HQ. This was where Sarah was normally based so she knew exactly where to go. She used her proximity card to allow them through two secure corridors and into a sizeable open-plan office with only four work desks and a very large flat white table in the centre of the room.

Two *suits* were stood facing them behind the table, and spread neatly before them were seven columns of case file data headed by a photograph of each individual victim.

'Hello, Sarah,' the male officer said.

'Hi, Jeff,' Sarah replied. 'Hi, Angie,' she said to the female.

'You must be Detective Deans,' Jeff said striding across and shaking Deans' hand with vigorous enthusiasm.

'Yes,' Deans said, trying to wrestle his hand back. 'I am.'

'Hello,' Angie said, waiting her turn to shake his hand also. 'Thanks for coming over. How was the traffic?'

'You know the North Devon link road,' Sarah replied sarcastically. The three of them groaned together and rolled their eyes. It must have been a *Devon* thing.

'Can I fix anyone a drink? Jeff asked.

'Please,' Deans said almost before Jeff had chance to finish what he was saying. 'Coffee would be great, thanks.' He looked around the bright white office. He hadn't seen his own Cold Case Unit, but imagined it would look something similar.

'The DCI has told us all about you,' Angie said to Deans. 'I have to say, it's a privilege to meet you in person. I mean, I've obviously seen you on TV,' she qualified.

Deans gave a quick glance. *'Obviously.'*

'How do you take it?' Jeff asked from the back of the room.

'Hot and black, please.'

'Sarah... usual?'

'Yes, please, Jeff.'

Deans peered at the large white table. 'What *exactly* has the boss said about me?'

'That you have some sort of "celestial insight" with crime scenes.'

Deans scowled and rubbed the back of his neck. 'I think you may be in for a disappointment then.'

Angie noticed him studying the upside down documents.

'Go on and take a look,' she said. 'We've set this up for you to see.'

'What is it?'

'Seven unsolved missing person cases since nineteen eighty-four.'

Deans and Sarah walked behind the table at a respectful distance. Deans leaned over and looked at each of the pictures. The first three columns were clearly older investigations, given the quality of the photographs and going by the hairstyles and clothing worn by the victims.

'What about before eighty-four?' Deans asked.

'That data is archived on microfiche. We can get it, but the DCI wanted to concentrate on these for starters.'

'For starters?' Deans said. 'How many others are there?'

Angie broke away from the table. 'Sixteen missing person enquiries where there is no trace of the individual.'

'Including these seven?' Deans said.

'Twenty-three, if you include these missing persons.'

'Over what time period?' Sarah asked.

'The earliest report we can find dates back to the fifties, but the likelihood is there are more.'

Deans creased his brow. 'That's roughly one every few years.'

'Yes,' Angie replied. 'But it's not consistent. There are multiple cases in close succession and there are other long gaps between reported cases, so either we are missing data on further victims, or for some reason there were periods of time when nobody went missing.'

Deans stepped closer to the table. He reached down and picked up the file closest to him Sarah Stockdale, reported missing October 18th, 1992. He put the file down and lifted the next. Angelique Montgomery, reported missing October 24th, 1987.

The others watched him as he hesitated before taking the next file. He looked for the date before anything else: October 15th, 2001.

'Are all of these reported missing during October?' he asked.

'All but one,' Angie nodded. She walked to the file at the end of the row and read from the cover. 'Mellissa Derry – reported missing November the fifth, two thousand and six.'

Deans turned to Sarah. 'Amy Poole.' And together they said, 'October the fourth.'

Deans ran his fingers along the contours of his chin. 'What have you established about these dates?' he asked.

'Just that they are within a tight time frame of one another,' Jeff said returning to the room with a tray of drinks.

'The significance of which is?' Deans questioned.

'We were hoping you might be able to tell us that? We've discounted term times, the possibility of an errant lecturer, you name it.'

'Hold on,' Deans said, removing the day-book from his bag. He quickly tracked back several pages at a time. He slowed to look closer at each page and then stopped. He looked up from his book and turned the page towards Sarah, showing her a date that he'd circled several weeks before.

'What is it?' Sarah asked.

'The date that the *Herald* reported the sudden death of Ruby Mansell.'

Sarah leaned in closer and read aloud. 'Eighteenth of October two thousand and seven.'

Deans curled his lip and bobbed his head. 'Jackson was the officer in the case.'

'What?' Sarah said.

'Jackson was quoted in the article as expressing his sorrow at her passing.' Deans absorbed the details of the other missing persons spread out before him. 'What's the significance,' he said beneath his breath.

'Do you have a computer I can use?' he asked

'Sure, use mine,' Angie said. 'I'll log you in. What do you need?'

'Google.'

Angie tapped the keyboard and the familiar search bar popped up on the screen, which has to be said, was much larger and of a higher quality than his own monitor back in Bath.

Deans typed *significant months of the Viking age* into the search engine and a page of results came up on the screen. He leaned in close and read out loud from the results.

'The Vikings only had two seasons: winter and summer,' he said. 'Winter started on the fourteenth of October.' He paused and faced the others before reading on silently for a moment.

He pushed himself back from the desk and gaped into space.

'What is it?' Sarah asked.

'According to this article, the first month of the winter was given a name that modern-day translation calls *Slaughter Month*. He turned to face the others. 'It ran from the fourteenth of October to November the thirteenth.'

Jeff and Angie screwed up their faces and stared inquisitively at each other. Jeff asked the obvious question. 'What has this got to do with the Vikings? We are talking about *the Vikings* aren't we?'

'It's a long story,' Sarah said as Deans rushed back to the table and quickly scanned the dates.

'They are all within *Slaughter Month*,' he said eagerly and then hesitated. 'And so was Ruby Mansell… and Maria.'

'What about Amy Poole? She was taken just before that date,' Sarah said.

Deans peered into space.

'She wasn't meant to die,' he said. 'Not when she did. She was taken when they knew she was going to be in North Devon rather than Bath. They were going to keep her somewhere until the time of her sacrifice.'

'That means she was chosen,' Sarah said.

'Yes.'

'Where did they keep her?' Jeff asked.

'My guess would be, the cellar at Ruby Mansell's house, but for some reason, they messed it up.' Deans looked deeply into Sarah's eyes. 'And that's why Ash Babbage was killed.'

Jeff looked closer at the computer. 'It says here that *Slaughter Month* was a period of harvest – a time to bring food in for winter storage.'

'And what about Archie and Annie Rowland?' Sarah asked. 'They were outside of this period too.'

'They weren't sacrificed,' Deans said. 'They were executed.'

'I'm really sorry,' Jeff said. 'I... I... I'm struggling with all of this Viking stuff.'

Deans returned to the computer and typed, *Odins' Raven Banner* into the search bar. 'Here,' he said tapping the screen. 'This links everyone to the Vikings.'

Jeff sat down at the desk and took his time to read the information on the screen, while Deans retuned to the table of missing girls.

His eyes kept on returning to the same one: Tammy O'Shea, missing October 30th, 1985. He felt for the ridged scar behind his ear. *What is it with you, Tammy?*

He peeked up at the others gathered around the computer. He leaned forward and picked up the A4 image of the girl and a pulse of energy shot through his hand, up his forearm and rushed to his head. He rocked on his heels as his breath was knocked out his lungs, as if he had just received a blow to the stomach.

'Andy?' Sarah said.

Deans blinked down at the picture. She was an eighteen-year-old brunette, with an early *Madonna-style* haircut – all crimped, finished off with an oversized black bow and heavy eye makeup. He picked up the file, read the details and noted that if she were still alive, they would be the same age. He continued reading the summary: Tammy went missing on her way home from college. She lived with her parents in a small village eight miles out from Torworthy and had an older brother, Shane. She usually got a ride home with her father who worked in a butcher's shop, but not this day. Unfortunately, for Tammy, she never made it to the shop and her father reported her missing at the police station three hours later.

Deans was "tuned-in", Maria was with him and the rest of the room faded to a smudge. *Tell me your story, Tammy.*

A mound of damp amber brown leaves flashed into his head. He saw a pavement and a small grassy embankment. He had a sensation of falling backwards, but he was standing firm. He looked up at the others. Sarah was watching him judiciously. She touched the arm of Angie who turned and then nudged Jeff.

Deans could see them all looking at him, but he didn't know why. Vivid images raced into his mind. He was moving backwards, swiftly now. He saw his feet, only, they weren't his, and the heels where digging into the soft ground as they were being dragged, creating little furrows in the heaped leaves. He tried to speak to Sarah, but it was like a hand was across his mouth. His eyes widened as realisation of what was happening dawned upon him. He tossed the file onto the table scattering other paper documents into the air and stood perfectly still as the others hurried across to his side.

'Andy, what just happened?' Sarah said taking him by the waist and sitting him in a swivel chair.

'I don't know,' he breathed.

'You looked like you were about to pass out,' she said.

'Well done, you've mixed all these up now,' Jeff said fussing with the case papers on the table.

'Tammy,' Deans said. 'She was snatched from the street.'

Jeff stopped fretting and looked back over his shoulder at Deans.

'She was grabbed, dragged back away from the pavement. There were trees... fallen leaves.'

Angie took the file from the table and spent a moment looking through the reports.

'Did you read this?' she asked Deans.

He shook his head.

'What does it say?' Sarah asked.

Angie read from the file. 'An elderly resident close to Torworthy College reported seeing a struggle involving a girl at the copse, just off Newton Road around the day Tammy went missing. The witness couldn't describe anyone, couldn't be sure of the date, and so, the police at the time put it down to playful banter between college mates and didn't follow it up any further.'

'She was wearing black ankle boots, with a kind of... studded design around the top,' Deans said into his hands.

Angie turned back a couple of pages, she stopped and gawped over at Deans. She glanced at Jeff and brought the file back over to Deans.

'That's incredible. Are you sure you didn't read this?

'I...' Deans shook his head. 'I just held it and read out the summary on the first page.'

'Can you do it again?' Angie asked.

'I don't know what just happened, but I know what I was seeing and feeling.'

Jeff puffed out his cheeks. 'What else did you see?'

Deans shook his head. 'I… um, I… I don't know. The shoes. Jeans I suppose. No, wait – I could see her shins. She must have been wearing three-quarter length trousers or shorts or something?'

Deans shrugged.

Jeff peered at Angie for the answer. She ran a finger over the report, stopped after a second or two and read aloud, 'Black three-quarter-length leggings.'

'Jesus Christ!' Jeff said loudly. 'Is this for real?'

Deans scratched behind his head and peeked at Jeff. 'It is real,' he whispered. 'I wish it wasn't. But it's real.'

'Can you see where they went? Can you see who abducted her? Can you describe the attacker?'

Deans held up his hands. 'I saw what I saw. Nothing more.'

'Get it back,' Jeff said snatching the file from Angie's hand and thrusting it towards Deans. 'Try again,' he demanded.

'Hey,' Sarah said. 'Take it easy. He's said everything he knows.'

Deans passed Sarah *thank you* with his eyes. Now he appreciated how Denise must have felt in those earlier days of the investigation when he was pushing so hard.

'I'll take the file with me, if that's okay?' Deans suggested. 'I can't make any promises, but maybe I can get more information in a less pressured environment.'

Jeff and Angie looked at one another.

'Of course,' Angie said. 'You're one of us.' She took the file back from Jeff and handed it to Deans. 'Have it for as long as you need. Just keep it safe.' She stared at Deans with the wonder of a child on their first outing to Santa's Grotto. 'Will you come back?' she asked.

Deans raised the file. 'Obviously.'

'No, I mean... would you be willing to come and look at some of the other cases we've got?'

Deans noticed Sarah beaming, apparently with a degree of pride.

'Who knows?' he answered. 'Who knows?'

CHAPTER FORTY-FIVE

Sarah woke Deans from one of the deepest sleeps he had enjoyed for a long while. He was curled up in the passenger seat of the car.

'Where are we?' he asked.

'Torworthy.'

'What?' He sat upright with a start and looked out of the window in disbelief. She was right.

'I'm sorry,' he said rubbing his eyes. 'I feel absolutely shattered.'

'That's okay. I'm surprised my awful *Adele* singing didn't wake you up.'

Deans looked through the gap to the back seat. The file was still there.

'Do you fancy a drink, or do you need to get home?' Sarah asked.

'What time is it?'

Sarah looked at the dash. 'Ten fifteen.'

'Have you heard from the DCI?'

'I got a text from Sergeant Jackson. We have a briefing at eight a.m.'

Deans rubbed his face. 'I think I'm going to pass,' he said.

'Okay. Just thought I'd ask.'

Deans watched Sarah for a moment. 'I'm really sorry,' he said.

'Stop. You're entitled to sleep.'

'No. I mean for not trusting you – for hurting you.'

Sarah didn't say anything and looked directly ahead through the windscreen.

'It's not how I feel now. I just want you to know that.'

'Well, you could say sorry with a large glass of wine,' she grinned.

Deans thought about it for a moment and scratched a sudden, intense itch on the side of his nose, but instead of wine, he was thinking about devouring the Tammy O'Shea case file.

'Not tonight,' he said. 'But I'll definitely get you one soon. I promise.'

'Fine. I don't feel offended,' she joked. 'Do you want me to drop you home with Denise?'

'Yeah. That'll be good. Thanks.'

'You really can do that stuff, can't you?' Sarah said.

Deans lowered his head and nodded.

'How?'

'I really don't know.'

'Have you always had it… the ability, I mean?'

'No,' he whispered. 'I don't think so.'

'When did it start?'

Deans clenched his jaw. 'I'm not sure. Since the train crash, maybe before. Uh, I don't know?'

'How does it work?'

Deans furled his brow. 'Beats me.'

'Okay, how did you receive that information about Tammy?'

'I picked up the papers and saw it in my head, like daydreaming, I suppose. It just happened. He stopped himself and covered his mouth with a hand. That wasn't how it happened.

'Right, shall we get you back then? I need a drink even if you don't.' Sarah chuckled. 'I still can't believe I'm working with *The Angel Detective*.'

Deans let himself inside with the spare key hidden beneath a stone at the front of the house. It was a wise move for Denise to allow him to come and go, now that the investigation was at full tilt. Denise was in bed and although Deans had promised not to disturb her during his late returns, he found himself tapping on her bedroom door.

She opened the door a crack and glowered at him.

'Denise, I'm sorry,' he said looking at his watch. 'It's only eleven-thirty.'

'I know what time it is.' She wrapped her fluffy white dressing gown around her body and pulled it tight with a bow at the side. She didn't come out of the room, but waited for Deans to speak.

'Something has happened to me,' he said uneasily.

'*Something?*'

'Another connection. To a different person… a dead person.'

'How did it happen?'

'I asked it to happen. I welcomed it.'

Denise widened the gap in the door and stepped out into the hallway. She gave a tut and looked up at Deans. 'I think you'd better tell me what happened.' She walked through to the kitchen and put on the kettle.

She noticed the case file on the dinner table. 'What's that?'

'It's a cold case file on the girl I connected with.'

Denise went across, but kept her distance from the thick buff coloured file.

'They had others, but this one kept drawing me in.'

'She's ready to be found,' Denise said looking at the name on the front cover.

'I think she could be one of the Bone Hill victims,' Deans said.

Denise nodded agreement. 'Tell me about the connection?'

'I asked something like "what's your story?", as I held the file in my hands. Next thing, it was like seeing through Tammy's eyes even though I could see everything else around me in the room.'

Denise cocked her head. 'And?'

'I saw her abduction.'

'In how much detail?'

'I could see her feet. The pavement she was taken from. The grass she was dragged over. I could see the silver studs in her boots.'

'What about sounds?'

'I don't know. There was noise around me in the office.'

'Smells?'

Deans shrugged. 'Only Maria's... like there always is, when...'

The boiling kettle clicked-off and simmered away to silence.

'Do you want to try again?' Denise asked.

Deans glanced at the file. He did, but he was also scared of what he was going to see.

'It's okay, I'll be with you, in case.'

'In case what?'

'She's come to you for a reason. The time is right. Don't worry.'

'Where should we do it?'

'Right here,' Denise said, pulling a chair out from the table and taking a seat.

Deans came alongside without taking his eyes away from the file. 'Should I sit down or stand up?'

'It doesn't matter. If she wants to reconnect with you it won't make a difference where you are – you just have to be ready.'

'For what?'

Denise blinked slowly. 'Everything.'

Deans moistened his lips and opened the file cover.

'Is there a photo?' Denise asked.

'Yes.'

'Use that.'

Deans took the A4 printed photograph in his hand and stared at Tammy's face.

'Now ask yourself what you want to know from Tammy,' Denise said. 'You just need to ask the right questions.'

Deans looked between the file and Denise. 'Just like that?'

'Just like that.'

He scratched an itch over his eye and hesitated.

'She probably won't tell you exactly what you ask, but she will show you all you need to know. The rest will be up to you to interpret.'

Deans held the page firmly between his fingers. His hands were shaking. He glanced one more time at Denise and then concentrated on the photograph.

Tammy, I want to help you. Were you murdered? A taste of bubblegum came into his mouth. He rolled his tongue around his teeth and swallowed the fruit flavoured saliva. He looked at Denise. 'I think I've got her.'

Denise flashed her eyes and gestured with her hand for him to continue.

Tammy, do you know who killed you? Deans waited, but nothing happened. *Tammy, was the person who killed you known to you?*

He looked up at the blackened sky. He was lying on his back and large drops of cold rain were falling onto his face. He tried to shield his eyes from the splashes, but could not move his arms, which were wide out to the sides. He was no longer in the room with Denise. He was at this other place and the connection was far more intense than the first time around. He tugged with all his might to release his hands and could feel blood pulsing in his neck as his heart pounded with terror. He heard noises coming from behind. The sound of footsteps on snapping twigs forced his eyes to pop wide open. He tried to tilt his head backwards but the soggy ground beneath the back of his head restricted his movement. He looked quickly left and then right and a lump of dread built in his throat. He could see trees above and around him, lots of them – familiar and horrifying. And then he heard it, a voice he recognised as several black masked faces loomed into view.

He came to with Denise crouching before him. The photograph of Tammy was face down on the table. Denise held both of his hands in hers and she was soothing him with calming words.

Deans blew long and slow controlled breaths until he was feeling less light-headed.

Denise handed him a tall glass of water and Deans took it with a quivering hand.

'Just take it easy,' she said. 'It looks like you had another strong connection.'

Deans nodded and took several gulps of water.

'Did you get what you needed?' she asked him.

Deans clamped his jaw and narrowed his eyes. 'Yes,' he said. 'I've seen everything I need.'

CHAPTER FORTY-SIX

The DCI had an energy about her that was different than before. The room gradually filled as the team took their seats. Deans was seated alongside Sarah on the front row, where they had been sitting patiently for the last eleven minutes. Jackson came in with one of the uniformed inspectors and gave Deans a once over as he passed and took a seat somewhere behind.

'Right, are we all here?' the DCI asked.

Deans had always found that a strange question at this type of meeting. How could you answer if you weren't there?

'Good morning, everyone,' the DCI said. 'Today is going to be full on. I warn you now so that you can inform loved ones that you may not be home tonight.'

Sarah nudged Deans in the arm with her elbow.

'I can confirm that we have a third fingerprint hit on the spade seized from Bone Hill. It belongs to Scott Parsons.'

Scotty? I knew it!

'This morning a team from support group will be executing a raid on the last known property occupied by Parsons. He will be arrested on suspicion of conspiracy to commit murder on Archie Rowland, Annie Rowland, and Maria Deans.'

Deans rubbed the side of his nose. He felt the room bearing down upon him.

'Support Group are already prepped and awaiting a team to join them after this briefing.' The DCI raised a hand and lowered it slowly, like she was dampening somebody's attempt to interrupt. 'I have already decided who that team will be, and Detective Gold and Detective Deans will attend the address to oversee the arrest and subsequent search of the property.'

'I've said it before, Ma'am—' a voice came from the back of the room.

'And I've made my decision,' she glowered back.

Deans raised his hand.

'Yes, Detective Deans' the DCI said.

'Ma'am, I think Parsons should also be arrested in relation to the Amy Poole murder.'

'How so?'

'He was the last person to see her alive. He plied her with drink and took away her inhibitions so that Ash Babbage could abduct her.'

'Do we have evidence to this effect?'

'We would have, Ma'am, if the statement had been taken. I have a PDA entry taken at the time I spoke to Scotty. It's unsigned, but it is a contemporaneous note.'

'Fine. What's done is done. We have reasonable grounds to suspect involvement, so yes; we will also arrest Parsons for the murder of Amy Poole. The custody unit is already on standby and will be cleared out for our prisoners only.'

'Prisoners?' a voice asked from the back of the room.

'Yes, prisoners.' The DCI caught Deans' eye. 'We must keep our options open and our wits about us. Right, Gold and

Deans see me afterwards and I'll brief you about the Section Eighteen. Any other questions?'

The room was muffled in sound, but drenched in thought.

'Sergeant Jackson, see me afterwards as well please.'

'Let's go through here,' the DCI said, taking Deans and Sarah into the small interview room, having already instructed Jackson to wait for her in the CID office.

They all remained standing and the DCI closed the door and spoke with dampened tones.

'I had a call from Jeff Underhill this morning. Sounds like you had an eventful evening.'

'Yes, Ma'am,' Sarah said.

'We are fast-tracking the DNA of Tammy O'Shea against the skulls we've recovered. If she is there, then...' She looked at Deans. 'This has to stay between us, okay. Nobody else is to know at this stage. Andrew, I don't want you being treated like a side show.'

Deans nodded. 'I appreciate that, Ma'am.'

'That's why you must search Parsons' property. You can do things nobody else can.'

Deans pinched his bottom lip between his teeth.

'You want to say something?'

Deans stroked his forehead with a fingertip.

'It's okay. Just come out with it,' the boss said.

'I think we should arrest Sergeant Jackson.'

The DCI narrowed her eyes and slid them towards Gold. 'And if the media finds out?' she said. 'This is a circus as it is.'

'Then the public will know we are being transparent with our investigation. After all, it's the public who need protecting.'

Deans could see the conflict in the boss's face.

'He was texting somebody at the end of the briefing,' the DCI said.

Deans suddenly felt sick to his stomach. 'Where are the support group?' he quickly asked.

'They are on standby about a mile from the property waiting for you and Gold to join them.'

'Tell them to go in now. It has to be now. Jackson was tipping Parsons off about the raid.'

The DCI didn't need further encouragement and immediately phoned the support group skipper.

'Right, you'd better get going,' she said. 'It's happening.'

'What about Jackson?' Deans asked.

'Don't worry about Jackson. Leave him to me.'

CHAPTER FORTY-SEVEN

The police radio was full of chatter as they drove towards Parsons' address. They were on a secure channel for the operation, but talk had been non-stop since the support group went in. Parsons had already been arrested, which hadn't gone down well with his housemate who tried to fight the remaining police officers off with a machete. Fifty thousand volts from a Taser gun had done the trick and, thankfully, none of the officers had been badly injured.

As Deans and Sarah arrived, a prisoner transport unit was in the process of taking the angry housemate away. Scott Parsons was staying, as was the way with an arrest and search of a property in these circumstances. Something like this would also be video recorded, along with recordings from the officer's own body-cams, to prove that nothing had been 'planted'.

Deans and Sarah met the skipper in the living room. Scotty was sitting on the sofa with a large officer sat on either side and his hands cuffed half way up his back.

'Any significant statements?' Deans asked.

'No. He's not said a word.'

'Where have you been so far?' Deans asked the support group sergeant.

'Just this room and the hallway, when matey-boy wanted to play.'

Deans looked Scotty up and down with a snarl that he simply couldn't contain. 'Alright, Scotty, remember me? Of course you do.'

Scotty caught Deans' eye and then quickly looked away.

'Understand what's going on, do you?' Deans said. 'You've been arrested in connection with the murder of three persons – for the time being.'

Scotty remained hunched forwards and still didn't speak.

'Has he been searched?' Deans asked the support group skipper.

'Of course.'

'Mobile phone?'

'One of my team is bagging and tagging it now.'

'Tell them to stop. I want to see it.'

The skipper lingered on Deans' face and then left the room.

Deans paced in front of Scotty who was now staring at the leg boot.

'Looking at something, son?'

A smile eased from Scotty's lips.

The skipper returned to the living room and handed Deans a phone. 'It's password protected,' he said.

'That's alright,' Deans said taking the phone. He brought it up to his face and could see a partial text message displayed on the screen. *Did you get my message?*

Deans shot Scotty a knowing smile. *Oh, don't worry. He got it.*

'Right,' Deans said. 'Where was he when he was arrested?'

'Running up the stairs.'

'Okay. That's where we begin.' He looked at Scotty. 'We are taking a little walk up to your bedroom. I think that'll be a great place to begin.'

One of the burly officers encouraged Scotty from his seat with a large hand wrapped around his bicep.

'Me first,' the skipper said. 'Then the escorted prisoner, then the video behind, please.'

They took this order and walked up the stairs with Deans at the rear behind the other officers.

'Where's the weed, son?' the skipper asked turning to Scotty. The smell of cannabis was just as pungent as the last time Deans was at the house. Not an unusual occurrence in itself, but another offence to stick to Parsons if all else failed.

Scotty pointed with his head to a bedside cabinet. 'Bottom drawer,' he said.

The skipper gestured to one of his team who went across and found a large zip lock freezer bag stuffed full of the pungent green leaves. He placed it onto the top of the bed along with a small blue grinder.

'I'm further arresting you on suspicion of possessing cannabis, being a controlled substance,' the skipper said. 'Anymore?'

Scotty shook his head.

Standing behind the man-mountain of an officer still attached to Scotty, Deans could see a thick tattoo weaving up Scotty's arm, continuing towards his armpit. He had noticed it several weeks before when he first saw Scotty, but thought it was a tribal tattoo. Now he was seeing it through different eyes.

The skipper told four of his team to search the remaining upstairs rooms along with Sarah Gold, leaving himself, Scotty, the 'Bluto' officer, Deans and the drug-seizing officer in the bedroom. This was Deans' first opportunity to look around and he immediately clocked a large poster on the wall. He went across for a closer look. A piece of text at the bottom said it was the cast of *Vikings Seasons 1–5*.

Bingo!

Deans looked at two other posters on the walls – both *REEF* surfing posters. The rest of the room was much what Deans anticipated: piles of dirty clothing, a smelly sports bag and gym kit. Run of the mill stuff.

'Start with the bed,' the skipper said. 'So the prisoner can sit down once we're finished, and then work a clockwise sweep from the doorframe.'

The spare officer started on the bed clothes; removing the pillows from their casing, the cover from the duvet and working his way methodically downwards to floor level.

'What are you looking for?' Scotty asked. 'You've got the drugs. I ain't got nuffin else.'

'I'll know when I see it,' Deans said and moved around to the far side of the bed behind Scotty's back.

The searching officer came up from beneath the bed with a shoebox. Deans immediately felt a prickle through his scalp. 'Get the video on this,' he said. 'Don't open it yet.'

The skipper hollered outside of the room and the videoing officer duly attended.

'Okay,' the officer with the camcorder said and the searching officer unhooked the side flaps and lifted the lid. He peered inside the box and pulled a nonplussed face.

'Let me see,' Deans said dragging the box to his side of the bed. It was full of folded notes and letters and a pendant on a thin leather lace. Deans looked over at Parsons and gave him a hard stare. 'Seize this,' he said to the officer. He walked to the head of the bed. An Apple laptop was charging on the bedside cabinet. *Take it*, his inner voice said.

'Seize any computer equipment,' Deans told the search team.

'You're not taking that,' Scotty said.

Deans stopped and faced him. 'And why would that be?'

Scotty grumbled incoherently and turned away.

'Who is this?' one of the officers asked, lifting a photo from within the bedside drawer. He looked at the other officers with excitement and turned the photo to show them. It was a picture of Amy Poole and she was wearing nothing more than a seductive smile.

'Put that down,' Deans barked.

The officer scowled and looked at Deans like he was some kind of freak.

'I said, put it down.'

'Alright! Jesus! You need to take a chill-pill or something, dude.'

Deans walked to the other side of the bed. Scotty watched his every step. He got to within inches of the support group officer's face. 'Look at me,' Deans said.

The officer searched for his sergeant.

'Look at me,' Deans repeated.

The officer huffed and faced Deans with a self-assured smile.

Deans looked down at the picture and flipped it face-side down.

'This is not a game. We're not here to satisfy your fucked-up pleasures.'

'I was only trying to lighten—'

'Well, don't.'

'Come on you two,' the skipper said. 'John, just do your bloody job, okay?'

The officer bobbed his head and laughed at Deans.

'We're on the same team,' the skipper continued. 'Let's not have this in front of the prisoner.'

Scotty was looking over his shoulder, fixated with Deans.

Two and half hours later, and the property had been completely turned over. The only other evidence they discovered was a dozen smaller baggies of cannabis, scales and another cannabis grinder from the housemate's room. It looked like the pair were running a small dealing operation, but it certainly didn't appear that Scotty had sanitised the house in such a short space of time from Jackson contacting him.

Deans and Sarah sat on the sofa in the living room. They were the final two officers to leave. He rested his head in his hands and his elbows upon his knees.

'Shall we go?' Sarah asked.

Deans didn't answer.

'Andy?'

'Hmm, what?' Deans replied, looking up at Sarah.

'What's wrong?'

Deans shook his head. 'I don't think Scotty is involved.'

'What do you mean?'

Deans stared at a space on the floor in front of him. 'I don't think he wanted Amy to die. He still loves her.'

'But what about the poster and the pendant?'

'You can have those things without being a killer. There's something else to all of this.'

'But there's nothing else here.'

'Exactly.'

Sarah let out an exasperated sigh.

'We'll find something on the computer, something that will make sense of this.'

'Like what?'

'I don't know.'

'What about his fingerprints on the spade?'

Deans shrugged.

'I'm sorry, I don't agree with you,' Sarah said. 'All the evidence is stacking up against Scotty Parsons.'

'I know. It is. Isn't it?'

CHAPTER FORTY-EIGHT

They met the DCI in the custody reception area. Scotty Parsons had long since been booked in and was still festering in the cell. The county lock up was large enough to house Ranford in one section and Parsons in another, and neither would be any the wiser to the other's presence.

'I want to go in alone,' Deans said.

'Don't you think you should have Detective Gold with you?' the DCI replied.

'No. I'll get more out of him on my own.'

'How long do you need to prepare?'

Deans wiped his nose. 'I don't need to prepare.'

The DCI gave Deans a considered look. 'Okay,' she said. 'I'll go to the satellite room with Detective Gold. If you get into difficulty make sure you hit the panic bar.'

'I won't need to.'

'You seem very confident about that.'

Deans glanced at Sarah. 'I'll be alright. Let's just get this done.'

He could feel eyes upon him from the small CCTV camera

above the door and he wondered what conversation they were having about him.

Parsons arrived in the room with his escort.

'Take a seat, Scotty,' Deans said.

Scotty did as he was told and sat down.

'I got you a coffee,' Deans said. 'Instant mix, but it's better than nothing.'

Scotty took the paper cup and murmured his thanks.

Deans watched and waited until Scotty caught his eye.

'Why are you here, son?'

Scotty's contorted face looked towards the door and the camera.

'It's just you and me,' Deans said.

'The weed?' Scotty spluttered and sipped from his drink.

'Anything else?'

'You lot said something about murders, but I ain't done nothing like that.'

Deans observed silently as Scotty rubbed both of his wrists.

'Were the cuffs a bit tight for you?'

'Yeah, fucking kills, man.'

'I'm sorry. It'll pass.'

Scotty glanced at Deans.

'Why didn't you come when I asked you to give me a statement about the night Amy disappeared?'

'I didn't need to.'

'What do you mean, you didn't need to?'

'Because that copper came to my house, didn't he?'

Deans narrowed his eyes. 'Which copper?'

'I don't know. He was like you, but had a baldy-head and a breath like shite.'

Deans peered up at the video camera.

'Tell me what this copper did when he came to see you.'

Scotty slurped another mouthful of coffee. 'He said I didn't have to give a statement if I told him where the weed was.'

'And did you?'

'Yeah, of course. But he said he wanted to check the other rooms out too, so I let him, or he said he was gunna nick me.'

Deans waited a few seconds. 'And?' he said.

'The bastard nicked some of my tools from the shed instead.'

Deans leaned forwards. 'Tools?'

'Yeah. I know for a fact they were there before he came.'

The corner of Deans' eye twitched.

'Tell me about these tools?'

'What's the point, you lot all stick together anyhow.'

'Tell me.'

Scotty groaned and twisted the paper cup in his hands. 'Alright... a saw, a lump hammer, two chisels and a spade.'

'Your spade?'

'Yeah, my spade. And two fucking chisels, a lump hammer and a saw.'

'Did you see him leave with them?'

'No.'

'Then how do you know he took them?'

'I didn't see him leave. He was out back and I didn't see him again.'

Deans stared down at the table and didn't speak. The longer he sat motionless, the more Scotty became uncomfortable in his seat and began to fidget.

'What are you going to do about my weed?' he asked after another thirty seconds of silence.

Deans didn't answer.

'Mate, am I in trouble about my weed?'

'You're not here about your weed, Scotty. How soon after I saw you did the baldy-head copper come over to see you?'

'I dunno? Probably about an hour.'

'The same day?'

'Yeah, the same day.'

'Okay Scotty. I'm going to have to return you to the cell for a bit while I speak to my boss.'

'Has the interview finished?'

Deans stood up. 'The interview hasn't even begun.'

'Am I gunna be in here all night?'

Deans looked him in the eye. 'No, mate. You're not.'

The DCI was already waiting beside the custody desk. She gave Deans a look that didn't need interpreting.

'Follow me,' she said and took Deans to a sound-proofed consultation room, normally used by the solicitors and their 'clients'.

'Where's Sarah?' Deans asked.

'She's making a phone call to Exeter. I'm getting another support group.'

Deans nodded. 'Heard enough?'

The DCI huffed. 'More than enough.'

'How are we going to play it?' Deans asked.

'I'm going to send Jackson to headquarters, catch him off guard. We'll arrest him there and I'll give authority to enter his property.'

'Properties, Ma'am. He has one here and one there.'

Sarah bounded through to the custody unit and joined them.

'Done?' the DCI asked.

'Done,' Sarah replied.

'Good.'

The DCI took out her mobile phone and dialled a number. She waited ten seconds or so and then spoke. 'Stephen, this is

Heather. I need you to go to HQ right away. Forensics have come up with something interesting from one of the unknown skulls. We're going to be tied up here for the immediate future, so I need you to go instead.'

Deans watched her eyes dart left and right and then twinkle as Jackson took the bait.

'Good,' the DCI said. 'I'll contact them and let them know you are en-route. What ETA should I give them?' She waited.

'Ninety minutes, that's great. Keep me updated with the findings and I'll see you later.' She ended the call and her eyes lit up. 'Let's get to work.'

CHAPTER FORTY-NINE

'We keep this between us,' the DCI said. 'Let's wait for the support group to secure Jackson and then we'll go in.'

'All due respect, Ma'am,' Deans said. 'We simply don't know if there are others. He could tip them off. We could lose our element of surprise – even after his arrest.'

'You're right, but we're restricted by our powers of search. We can act on this as soon as he is arrested. Sarah, do we have Jackson's local address?'

'I could get it.'

'Not if it involves the help of any other officers.'

'No, I'm sure I wrote it in my diary ages ago when he once asked me to pick him up.'

'You've been there?' Deans asked.

'Only outside. I wasn't invited in.'

Sarah flicked through the pages and stopped with a prod of the page. 'Got it. Six Orchard Square, Hemingsford.'

'Hemingsford?' Deans repeated. 'Figures!'

'You know how to get there?' the DCI asked.

Sarah nodded. 'Yes. It's not far from the address he was sending me to when I was taken.'

Deans looked at the DCI and together they said, 'Figures!'

'Okay. I'll follow in my car. You two take an unmarked transporter in case we need to fill it with exhibits.'

They spent the next ten minutes preparing raid-boxes with everything they would need to keep forensically secure. And of course, the big red key: the door ram. It wouldn't be a "textbook" entry, but in these extreme circumstances, needs must.

'Does anyone else live there?' the DCI asked.

'I shouldn't think so,' Sarah said. 'It's his bachelor pad when he's not in Exeter.'

'Dogs?'

'Doubt it,' Sarah said. 'Given the amount of time he's been spending in this office recently.'

'Ranford told me he was in a relationship with a PC. It's possible she may be there.'

'I'm going to need to inform someone that we're going in, just in case?' the DCI said.

'How well do you know the FIM?' Deans asked.

'The Force Incident Manager? Not at all – they'll be based at comms.'

'Do you think Jackson will know them?'

'Can't see why?' the DCI said. She thought about it for a second or two. 'Okay. It's probably a safe bet and no better person to muster the troops if things don't go according to plan.'

'Wait until we have the property in sight before telling anyone,' Deans said.

'Yes, you're probably right.'

As prepared as they were likely to be, they made their way towards Jackson's Hemingsford address and stopped short, using a house on the corner of the junction to offer them a degree of shelter from any prying eyes. It was now dusk and the sporadically spaced streetlights in this small residential area were buzzing amber above their heads.

'The lights are off,' Sarah said sneaking a glance around the wall line.

'Any update from support group?' Deans asked the DCI.

She looked at her mobile phone and shook her head.

'Should we wait until we know he's definitely gone?' Sarah asked anxiously.

'We can't afford to,' Deans said.

'We can't afford to do it any other way. This has to be by the book – especially as this is Jackson we're talking about. As soon as I have confirmation that he's contained, we'll go in.'

'Let's at least take a closer look,' Deans said. 'Make sure the place is empty.'

'Good idea,' the DCI said. She looked at her watch. 'Can't be much longer.'

They crossed the road and attempted to look as innocuous as possible. Sarah was first to the door. The DCI gestured for her to try the handle. It was locked.

Number six was one in from the end terrace, but with no obvious access to the rear and limited time, they had to force the issue and hope for the best.

Deans' breath spiralled slowly into the sub-zero night sky. He blew on his hands and rubbed them together. 'What do you think?' he said to the boss.

She looked at each of the darkened windows and then around at desolate streets.

'Get the van as close as you can to the front,' she said.

Sarah brought the rattling diesel to within several feet of the terraced front.

Romeo Charlie Hotel Two-zero, the radio said breaking the silence.

'Two-zero, go ahead,' the DCI said.

As per liaison with the FIM – we can confirm affirmative contact. I repeat we confirm affirmative contact.

'Received.' The DCI looked at Deans. 'Do it.' She stood back with Sarah Gold as Deans used the heavy steel door ram to smash his way through with relative ease.

Deans turned to the others. 'If he didn't know we were coming, he does now.' He kicked his way through the splintered doorframe and entered the low-ceiling cottage. His heart raced, more than it usually would in these scenarios and his head prickled with electricity. *This is it.*

He heard Sarah behind telling somebody that they were the police and not to be alarmed. The DCI drew up alongside Deans.

'Where do you think we should start?' she asked.

'Let me go alone. I've already got a feeling. It's calling me on.'

'Have you got your spray?'

'Yes,' Deans said.

'Get it out. We don't know what to expect here.'

The three of them stood in silence and strained to listen for noises.

'Okay. Go,' the DCI whispered.

Deans held his spray in one hand and a pen-torch in the other. He stepped forwards and peered through the narrow beam of light. The front door opened directly into an open-plan living room area with a small kitchenette looking out into the estuary. The walls were whitewashed and large irregular-shaped flag stoned flooring gave the impression the cottage was old, and going by a noticeable bow in the wall, it probably was. The hard plastic base of his leg boot slapped against the hard floor despite his attempts to make stealthy progress.

Upstairs, his head said, but not in his voice. It was Maria.

An open wooden stairwell kinked upstairs from the living

room. Deans caught the DCI's eye and pointed upwards. She nodded and he slowly clunked his way up the awkwardly narrow walkway.

At the top, he was faced with only two doors – one to the left and one to the right. Both were closed. The hairs on his arms felt like they were being brushed by an invisible hand. His body shuddered. *Maria?*

He saw his hand moving for the door handle on the left, even though it wasn't a conscious decision. He pulled down on the handle and pushed the door inwards.

The room was dark. The drapes were pulled. Deans felt for a switch and illuminated the room.

He stood rooted to the spot and took it all in.

'Um,' his crackling voice said, 'I think I've found what we're looking for.'

The DCI and Sarah hurried up the stairs and joined him in the centre of the room. They all took a minute to look around the four walls. Nobody spoke.

Finally, it was Sarah who asked the overriding question. 'What is this?'

Deans shook his head. He'd never seen anything like it.

'Are we forensically sound?' the DCI asked.

Deans and Sarah nodded. They were all wearing blue vinyl gloves.

'Don't touch anything. We leave it exactly as is. Sarah, grab a camera from the raid box. Evidence the room as is. I need to get the crime scene manager here ASAP.'

CHAPTER FIFTY

Crime Scene Manager, Mike Riley arrived with a team of three officers, as interest in the raid was gathering momentum with the locals. 'What have we got, Heather?' he asked.

'It's hard to explain. Just come up and see for yourself.'

The CSM entered the room and gawped at the walls and ceiling just as the others had done. He dipped the DCI a puzzled gape. 'This is Stephen Jackson's home?'

'His second home,' the DCI said.

The CSM scratched his head and puffed out his cheeks. 'What is it?' he asked.

'My guess is the words are Runic texts,' Deans said. 'Don't ask me what they mean – I haven't got a clue, but I know someone who will.'

'The museum proprietor,' Sarah said.

'Yep. We should get him over.'

'Make it happen,' the DCI said to Gold. 'Get him here. I need to know what this says.'

CSM Riley was in front of the wall behind the bed. 'This looks like—'

'A family tree,' Deans interrupted, coming alongside the

CSM. The walls were intricately painted with hundreds, if not thousands of ineligible Runic texts.

'It's extraordinary!' the CSM exclaimed. 'This must have taken years to complete.'

'Who is that?' Sarah asked looking up at a massive portrait taking up the entire ceiling.

Deans looked at each wall and approached the one where the lineage appeared to start. 'My guess would be this guy.' He pointed to the name at the top of the tree. 'Hubba.'

'Hubba,' the DCI repeated.

Deans nodded and stared at the maze of names in front of him.

The DCI looked at Deans for a long minute.

'It appears from this that Jackson believes he is a descendant,' Deans said following the lengthy tendrils to the name at the bottom of the tree.'

'Oh my God!' the DCI inhaled. Her eyes grew wider as she scanned the room. 'He has been giving his ancestor some sort of *offering*.'

'That would give us a motive,' Deans said.

'What about Ranford, Babbage and Annie Rowland?' Sarah asked.

'He probably needed recruits. Ranford was a local cop, the perfect foil. Babbage had access to vulnerable people – individuals who may not have had family, people who were looking for help, reassurance or just plain interested in psychics – that is how he met Amy Poole. And Annie Rowland had the tools and know how to dissect and dispose.'

'It's a bit far-fetched isn't it?' the CSM interjected. 'I mean… really?'

'My pregnant wife's uterus was cut open and my unborn child removed decapitated and stitched back into my dead wife's beheaded body. How far-fetched do you need?'

'Okay,' the DCI said attempting to placate the building tension. 'Let's not lose *our* heads.' She gave CSM Riley a stern glare. 'Mike, I want you to do the works with this room. Budget is no issue. Just do it. Leave me to deal with your purse-holding superiors.'

CSM Riley grimaced.

'What?' the DCI asked.

'We'll need more staff, more equipment.'

'Then get it.'

Deans glowered as Riley made his way to leave the room. 'Wait,' Deans said. Riley stopped. Deans recalled the enthusiasm Riley had shown at the pebble ridge scene of Amy Poole's murder. He was different now.

'I want another crime scene manager,' Deans said.

Riley placed his hands upon his hips and stared Deans down. 'I don't think that's your shout. Just remember who you are.'

'Trust me,' Deans glared. 'I do.'

The DCI came over and stood between them. She faced Riley, then turned to Deans and they shared a *moment*.

'Hold on,' Riley shouted angrily. 'This is outrageous. Don't tell me you are considering his whim?'

'Just bear with me,' the DCI said and left the room. Deans held Riley's antagonistic stare and could hear the DCI talking on her phone outside in the hallway.

She returned in less than a minute. 'Alright,' she said. 'We'll get a new forensic team.'

'Do you think *this* has something to do with me?' Riley shouted.

DCI Fowler gave Deans a silent question mark with her eyes so that Riley couldn't see.

Deans did just enough to show her a shake of his head.

'No, Mike, I don't. But you have been overseeing the Bone

Hill excavation and I don't want a future defence barrister in court suggesting that your presence at both scenes is the reason for any forensic comparisons.'

The DCI had come up with a plumb reason not to use him that he couldn't refute.

'I want a fresh forensic team at this scene. Thank you, Mike.'

Riley grumbled beneath his breath and left the room.

'What do we do until then?' Sarah asked.

'We sit tight and wait for the troops to arrive. I suggest we all grab a brew and something to eat. This is going to be a long night.'

CHAPTER FIFTY-ONE

It was now nine fifty p.m. Jackson was in the cells and police activity in Hemingsford was high. The road leading to Jackson's property was shut down. Police cordons kept the public and assembled media at arm's length and a mobile Major Incident Control Unit parked blocking the view to the entrance of the cottage. Social media speculation was rife and somebody had already posted that a serving police officer lived at the address. Some questioned if he had been killed inside the property, some suggested terrorist activity, and others came to conclusions a little closer to the truth. Either way, there was unrest and alarm permeating through the community.

The DCI briefed the new team of supervisors inside the fully equipped major incident truck. Deans was the only non-supervisor privy to the conversations. The DCI gave them unconditional access to the house; turn over everything, lift floorboards, search every nook and cranny, swab, dust, photograph, video and seize anything that would help convict Jackson. This was as big as it got. People were dead and one of their own was responsible. There was an air of unsettling anticipation. Anticipation, because cops loved this sort of job –

get her source out of her – I don't care if it's done here or at the station.'

'Yes, Ma'am,' he said. 'Leave that to me.' The inspector scooped his flat cap from the desk and exited the van.

'Who do they think they are? If she's got information, then we must have it.' The DCI's phone rang in her pocket and she answered it with an irritated tone. 'DCI Fowler.'

As she listened to the caller, Deans watched anger in her face turn to dismay.

'What is it?' he asked.

The DCI held her hand up and nodded across to Deans. She closed her eyes and leaned her body weight against the desk.

'Ma'am?' Deans said louder.

'Okay,' she said. 'Treat it as a crime scene. I need to be the first to know of any updates. Do you understand me?'

She sucked a deep breath through her nose and slowly lowered the phone to her side.

Deans looked on.

The DCI took several controlled breaths and turned her head to face him. 'That was custody.'

Deans grabbed for the back a chair. He knew what was coming.

'Jackson...' her eyes broke away for a second or two.

'Ma'am?'

'Jackson ingested something.'

Deans' lips parted.

'They found him on the floor... convulsing.' She sniffed and shook her head. 'They were too late. He's dead.'

CHAPTER FIFTY-TWO

Neither of them spoke. Deans slumped back in a swivel chair, his hands locked behind his head, his eyes searching for answers.

'I'm sorry,' the DCI said.

Deans laughed ironically, but didn't look at the boss.

The voice of the news reporter filled the silence as she interviewed local residents and drew out the drama for the viewing public to wallow in.

'They are reviewing the cell CCTV,' the DCI said.

'Uh ha.'

'They're going to email me the file so we can see...'

Deans dropped his chair forwards with a loud clunk and looked at the boss. 'Why wasn't he put on constant obs?'

'He was in a camera cell. Just like any other high risk prisoner.'

'Was he given something?'

'They say he was fiddling with a ring, just before he... They think he had a poison concealed somehow.'

Deans sniggered. 'Of course he did.'

The DCI walked over and stood in front of Deans so that he

had no choice but to look up at her.

'There's something he said to the cell camera just before… it was some sort of message. For you.'

'What message?'

'I don't know yet.'

'When are they sending the footage?'

'As soon as it downloads.'

Deans sniffed and looked around the truck. He didn't know whether to laugh or cry. He felt bereft all over again. 'What now?' he shrugged.

'We've still got Ranford.'

'Huh,' Deans chuckled. 'Jackson was the core. Ranford is a follower.'

'But he may give us more information.'

Deans sank his head and flopped forwards. A ping on the DCI's laptop made him look up. She clicked in to her email and a file downloaded on the screen.

'Here we go,' she said.

Deans stood up and went across to the desk. He was looking at a familiar scene; a corner-sighted camera looking down at Jackson seated on the thin blue mattress of his cell. Jackson stood up and came to the corner of the wall. His face appeared large in the screen, distorted by the wide-angled lens. He was smiling, almost joyous.

You probably think you had me, he said. *You almost did.* He began to laugh. *You've been good value, Deans. I've enjoyed jousting with you. You will probably come to conclusions about me, but they'll be wrong. I gave you the chance to walk away, but you wouldn't. You did this to yourself. Think of it like Newton's law: For every action, there is an equal and opposing reaction.* His eye grew large on the screen. *For every good, there has to be a bad.* Jackson turned his head away from the camera, elongating his nose. He turned quickly back. *I've got a message for you, Deans.* His face got closer to the camera and he whispered. *You know what I am, and I know what you are. This... is just an inconvenience. It's not over... for you.* A large smile beamed from his face. He winked and made a *click click* noise inside his mouth. Jackson went back to the mattress, picked at a ring on his finger and emptied something small into his hand. He looked up at the camera, smiled one last time and stuffed it into his mouth.

Less than a minute later, Jackson was lying in his own vomit, convulsing on the floor.

Deans and the DCI watched silently as a further minute went by before officers rushed into the cell.

'What was that?' the DCI asked.

'I don't know.'

'What did he mean?'

Deans didn't answer.

The rear door to the truck swung open and the replacement crime scene manager climbed inside. He handed an exhibit bag to the DCI.

'What is this?' she asked.

'A mask. One of five we found in the second bedroom.'

'Let me see,' Deans said.

The DCI handed Deans the clear plastic bag. It was a black mask – like a bird, long hooked beak and all. *Just as Sarah described.*

'Does this mean anything?' the CSM asked.

The DCI looked at Deans who nodded.

'How many, you say?' Deans asked.

'Five, so far.'

Deans counted them in his head *Jackson, Babbage, Ranford and Annie Rowland.* That left one over. *Parsons? No.* He didn't believe so.

'We need to speak to Ranford again,' Deans said.

The DCI agreed. 'I'll come with you.'

CHAPTER FIFTY-THREE

Ranford was already seated in the interview room when Deans and the DCI entered.

'Jackson is dead,' Deans said remaining on his feet.

Ranford laughed, 'You're going to have to find a different tactic to that one, Andy.' He grinned. 'Give me some credit.'

'Sergeant Jackson is dead,' the DCI repeated.

Ranford's smile waned.

'He was arrested,' the DCI continued. 'We raided his properties and he poisoned himself in custody.'

Ranford looked at Deans who tossed the facemask onto the table.

'Five masks,' Deans said. 'Three dead and you – who's the fifth?'

Ranford peered down at the mask.

'The fifth,' Deans repeated.

Ranford scratched the side of his nose. 'I don't know,' he said quietly.

Deans went over and grabbed Ranford by the neck of his sweatshirt and twisted it tightly. 'The fifth.'

Ranford leaned back and wildly shook his head. 'I don't know of a fifth. Really. I don't.'

Deans let go of the material and shoved Ranford backwards. The DCI didn't attempt to stop him.

Deans paced and took long juddering breaths. He glared at Ranford who was slowly resting his weight onto his forearms. 'Why did you do it?'

'Is he really dead?' Ranford asked the DCI.

'He's left you,' Deans replied. 'Whatever promises he made to you, they're gone.'

'Then it's just me,' Ranford muttered.

Deans continued to track back and forth in front of his prisoner. 'Why did you follow him?' he asked.

Ranford clutched his head in his hands. Deans could see he was crying.

'He can't die,' Ranford sobbed.

Deans sat down and jerked Ranford's arm away from his face. 'He's dead.'

Ranford looked at Deans. He was a pathetic sight.

'Look around you,' Deans said. 'Nobody cares about you now.'

'How did he—'

'He killed himself,' the DCI said taking the seat next to Deans.

'No,' Ranford breathed.

'Why did you kill those people?' the DCI asked.

Ranford's lips moved as he said something quietly to himself.

'Who did Jackson say he was?' Deans asked.

Ranford's eyes flickered and he peered at Deans. 'He was a God.'

Deans leaned back in the chair. 'Figuratively… or in reality?'

'You already know the answer to that to be asking me.'

'How many did you sacrifice?'

Ranford tugged at his ear shook his head. 'Don't know.'

'Who else was with you?'

Ranford dropped his eyes to the table.

'Scotty Parsons?'

A frown told Deans the answer. 'Riley?'

Ranford flicked Deans a look, but then shook his head.

'Okay,' Deans said. 'Who killed my wife? I know you were protecting Jackson by admitting to the murder before.'

Ranford looked at the DCI. 'He's really dead?'

'He's really dead,' she repeated.

'I um… I only killed Babbage. He was going to break. I was following—' He stopped talking and looked to the ceiling.

'Maria,' Deans said.

Ranford rubbed beneath his nose and looked Deans in the eye. 'I wasn't there. I took her from Bath, but I wasn't with her when… she was taken to Annie.' He looked down to the side. 'You angered the Gods and had to pay.'

'When did you find your *God*?' the DCI asked.

'Jackson found me. I didn't find him.'

'How?' Deans said.

Ranford tilted his head and gazed into space. He was having a cognitive moment. Neither Deans nor the DCI interrupted.

Deans suddenly saw visions in his mind: children and laughter – clambering through fences. A train track.

'You met Jackson when you were fostered.'

Ranford looked up at Deans.

'He was older. You looked up to him and he stood up to Babbage.'

Ranford broke eye contact for a second before restoring his gaze.

'How did you both end up in the police?'

'He interviewed me,' Ranford whispered. 'Made things happen.'

'Jackson took vulnerable people and made them strong,' Deans said. 'But what about Annie Rowland?'

Ranford shook his head. 'She was pure evil. Would do anything Jackson told her. She loved death.'

'And she was in the perfect job,' the DCI said. 'Who killed her father?'

Ranford shrugged. 'Jackson? Annie? She hated him. She was never good enough, but Jackson made her feel like a Goddess.'

'Who killed Annie?' Deans asked.

'I don't know.'

'Why are there five masks?' the DCI asked.

'I don't know. Jackson told us what to do and when to do it.' Ranford stopped talking.

'What about the old cases, the missing girls from the fifties and sixties?'

Ranford smiled. 'He's only gone in this life. He'll be back.'

'Jackson?' Deans asked.

Ranford nodded. 'He doesn't die. He evolves.'

Deans squinted.

'You're not safe. He will come back for you, but you won't know it until it's too late.'

Deans covered his mouth with the back of his hand. How could Ranford know about Jackson's message from the cell?

'I'm dead too,' Ranford said blankly. 'He'll come for me; as a prisoner, as a cell guard or even the dinner lady.' He smiled and whispered. 'I'm already dead.'

'Okay,' the DCI said. 'I need to talk to Deans, so you're going back to your cell.'

Ranford nodded and slowly rose from his seat. The DCI called out for a detention officer and Ranford was taken away.

'What do you think?' the DCI asked.

Deans pouted. 'He believes it. All of it.'

'What about you?'

Deans rocked his head. 'There's nothing to prove otherwise. He may be right.'

The DCI scratched behind her head and blew a long slow breath. 'I think I need a drink.'

CHAPTER FIFTY-FOUR

The DCI watched Deans hugging his coffee mug. 'You look tired,' she said.

'I am.'

'When did you last get a full night?'

Deans twitched his eyebrows and shook his head. 'I don't know. Not for a long time.'

'When are they expecting you back at the office in Bath?'

Deans glazed over for a moment and then took a sip from his drink.

'Have you ever considered transferring?'

He flicked his eyes to the DCI and shook his head.

'I want you on my team.'

Deans sucked a lung full of air and scratched his ear.

'You would be an incredible asset. Do they know back in Bath, what you have?'

'No.'

'You haven't told anyone?'

Deans pulled a face. 'Not exactly.'

'I suppose that was until the media got hold of your story. I can't imagine there's a police force in the world who hasn't heard of you by now.'

Deans blinked and coughed behind closed lips.

'Do you think we've missed anyone?'

'No.'

'Ranford was being truthful?'

Deans nodded. 'I don't think there's a fifth person. This ends with Ranford.'

'He's going to stand trial for all of the murders. He has to. If the jury believe what he says about Jackson, Babbage and Annie Rowland, then he may get away with only one of the murders. He certainly wasn't responsible for the older ones, that's for sure.'

The DCI watched Deans for a quiet minute. 'He's going to come back for you, isn't he?'

Deans ran a hand over his head.

'What are you going to do?'

'Jackson didn't want me around because of my abilities, but he had ample opportunity to kill me if he really wanted. I think he was testing me. Seeing just how far I could go.'

'And how far can you go?'

'I don't know. New things are happening to me every day.'

'What will you do, just go back to a normal CID life in Bath?'

Deans looked away. 'Life can never be normal again.'

'Will you stay in the job?'

He heaved in deeply. 'I don't know. I haven't been thinking about a future without Maria.' He rubbed his face and looked at the boss. 'Maybe I'll take the opportunity to go to Australia, or the States.'

'They'd have you like a flash. I can see you cracking complex cases and having your own TV show.'

Deans allowed himself a partial smile. His eyes tracked to the door. 'Do you know what? I think I want to go home.'

'To Denise?'

'To Bath. I'm ready to go back.'

'I'm sorry, but I don't want to lose you.'

He bit his top lip. 'I'm already lost.'

'And that is what gives you your quality... okay... you can go. We've got everything covered here, thanks to you.'

'I don't want thanks. I wanted justice...' He shook his head. 'And Jackson made sure I couldn't have it. That was all he wanted – to make sure I was punished. Well, he succeeded.'

'Someone here is going to miss you.'

Deans nodded. 'Where is she?'

'Back at the station. You want a lift over?'

Deans rolled his wedding ring around his finger. He waited for the scent to come to his nose. It didn't.

'Okay.'

Sarah finished speaking with the DCI and came over to Deans who was gathering up his belongings.

'Is it true – you're going home?' she said.

He looked into her welling eyes. 'Yes. It's the right time.'

Sarah glanced away. Her mouth was open and she appeared lost for words.

Deans took her hand. 'I don't want to come over as presumptuous, but...'

'Yes,' she said quickly.

'If you like me...'

'Yes.' She squeezed his hand.

'I'll need time.' He shook his head. 'I don't know if I'll ever...'

'Don't say anything else,' she said touching a finger on his lips. 'Leave me with *something*.'

He dropped his head and squeezed her hand back. Sarah pulled him towards her and they embraced.

CHAPTER FIFTY-FIVE

Denise pulled up outside of Deans' house. It was almost eleven a.m. She turned off the engine and faced him. Deans stared ahead.

'Do you want me to come in with you?'

'No,' Deans muttered. 'I need to do this myself.' He tugged at the door handle and cool air whipped into the footwell.

'This is just the beginning, for you,' Denise said.

Deans hesitated. 'I don't want to say goodbye to you, so I won't. I hope you understand.'

Denise smiled. 'I'll look forward to the next time you phone me then.'

Deans looked back at her and he smiled for the first time that day. He grabbed his bag of damaged clothes from the back seat and closed the front passenger door. The window came down and Deans leaned in.

'Don't forget who you really are,' Denise said. 'And call me whenever you like.'

'Thank you,' Deans said and turned towards his home. He walked down the pathway, aware that Denise was still watching him and let himself into the front door. He gave one last look up to the road and saw Denise wave. He dropped his bags onto the floor and closed the door.

The hallway was cold and the air was damp. He sucked in the mood and made his way slowly upstairs. He entered the bedroom and found Maria's favourite teddy bear, *Bob* waiting for him on the pillow.

'Hey, Bob. Dad's home.' Deans sat down on the edge of the bed, whisked Bob into his arms and broke down.

A noise at the front door woke him. He unravelled his body and placed Bob back onto Maria's pillow. He rubbed and blinked the starchiness from his puffy eyes and stepped slowly down the stairs. He had only been home for a matter of hours and already the well-wishers were pissing him off. He shuffled through to the front hallway, checked his dishevelled appearance in the mirror, prepared a smile and opened the door.

Nobody was there.

He rubbed his eyes again and turned back into the hall, and then he heard snivelling coming from outside.

He stopped, drew a slow breath, leaned out through the opening of the door and peered along the front of the house. Hunkered down, with her back to the wall, he saw a woman with her knees around her ears and her head in her hands. She stopped sobbing and looked directly at him. Mascara streaked around her eyes and down her cheeks.

'Are you okay?' he asked.

'You're... Detective Deans,' she garbled between sniffles.

Deans looked away and groaned beneath his breath. He rubbed the back of his neck and shook his head. 'No,' he said and moved to go back inside.

'I need you to help me,' the woman said with more urgency.

Deans grunted, interlocked his hands at the back of his head and looked up to the skies.

'Please,' the woman said. 'I'm desperate. I really need your help.'

Deans closed his eyes and sucked air in through his nostrils. He turned around and re-entered the house.

'It's you,' the woman shouted. 'I know it is.'

Deans was aware that she was now standing at the entrance to the door. He turned back and saw her waving a tabloid newspaper cutting in her hands.

Oh God, he thought, and walked back towards the kitchen.

'I'm desperate,' she said stepping into the hallway as he walked out of sight.

'Close the door as you leave, please,' Deans said opening the wall cupboard and removing his trusted bottle of Jameson's, which he plonked down on the work top with a determined thud. He listened for the slam of the door; it didn't come. He unscrewed the top from the whiskey and dragged a thick glass towards the bottle.

'Look, I'm tired and need to rest. Whatever your problem is – take it up with the cops where you live.'

'But you're the one,' the voice came.

Deans dipped his head, closed his eyes and brought the opened neck of the bottle beneath his nose. The smell of the strong liquor was inviting him to jump right in.

'You are *The Angel Detective.*'

Deans opened his eyes and stared at the bottle.

'I need you. Nobody else can help me. Only *The Angel Detective.*'

Maria's perfume wafted in front of his face. His eyes searched left and right and he slowly screwed the cap back onto the bottle without pouring a drop.

Maria's smell enticed him back to the hallway. He stood at

the entrance to the kitchen. The woman was now just a silhouette in the doorway to the outside. He slowly stepped towards her. She lifted the paper cutting and tapped the full-length picture.

'It *is* you,' she said.

As Deans closed the gap between them, Maria's smell grew stronger. He inhaled and held her deep inside. He stood motionless for a moment and then gave the woman a quick once over. Apart from her streaking makeup, she appeared perfectly presentable. Deans reached up and grabbed the edge of the front door. The woman instinctively stepped back outside – nobody wants a door slammed in his or her face.

He hesitated with the door half-closed, and lowered his head. The woman stepped closer.

'Please?' she quietly pleaded. 'I know you really want to help me, because of *what* you are – *The Angel Detective.*'

Deans pushed the door, but stopped himself, leaving a small opened crack. A teardrop escaped from his eye and flowed in slow motion down his cheek. He wiped it away with a fingertip and counted to five in his head. He opened the door to the woman again and looked deeply into her eyes.

'Yes,' he said. 'I suppose I am.'

He dropped his eyes and paused. Maria was with him. She was now *part* of him. He opened the door wide and stared at the woman.

'Well,' he said softly. 'I guess you'd better come inside.'

The End

ENJOYED THE BONE HILL?

Tweet James **@JamesDMortain**

Follow on Facebook **@jamesdmortain**

Keep up to date with the latest news and get closer to the action by joining James' mailing list and receive *The Real Story Behind Detective Deans* as a FREE welcome gift!

Visit **www.jamesdmortain** to sign-up today!

Thank you!

HAVE YOU DISCOVERED CHILCOTT YET?

DEAD RINGER

A DI CHILCOTT MYSTERY
(Book One)

———

CHAPTER ONE

Friday 21st February

5:45 p.m.

'Are you doing much this weekend, Sammie?' Jeremy Singleton asked as Samantha Chamberlain raced through her last-minute Friday afternoon office duties.

Re-assembling the stationery on her desk that was clear for the first time that week, she placed the customised *Singleton's Accountancy* embossed pens, correcting fluid and stray treasury tags inside a small metal mesh pot beside her computer terminal. She acknowledged the question from her boss with a nod and smile, but didn't answer.

Samantha had been with the company for only a few months, having moved back to Bristol following university to be closer to her family, but especially closer to her father who she missed through her formative years when he was always away. At first, she found the attention from Mr Singleton quite flattering – he may have been about the same age as her father, but it was nice to be noticed and welcomed so enthusiastically into a new job. Soon though, it became blatantly clear that he was nothing but a lecherous old sleazeball of a boss and she was his latest *"play-thing"*. The other girls in the office knew it too. Oddly, they all looked remarkably similar to her: long dark hair, slim athletic builds and well spoken in an educated way. There were times, several times in fact, when she wanted to mention in passing what her dad used to do. You know, just throw it out there and watch Singleton's face change. She already knew how it would play out; it would be the same reaction as every other male who strayed a little too far over the line, but he was her boss and she needed this job. She'd just have to stomach the flirting, for now. Singleton was married of course and by all accounts had three children aged between three and seven.

'I'm actually meeting an old school friend and we're having a good old-fashioned boogie in town,' she finally answered, placing a Post-It pad onto the top of a stack of three other sealed packs of the sticky yellow labels.

Jeremy perched the butt of his Italian cloth suit onto the edge of Samantha's desk, managing to trap the tips of her fingers beneath the material and the desktop. She tugged her hand away and placed it into her lap with a short measured smile. He returned the smile with interest and shuffled himself into a more comfortable seated position so that his right thigh was only inches away from her.

Samantha coughed behind closed lips and wheeled her chair back by an inch or two.

'Oh, I'm in town tomorrow night,' Jeremy crooned, widening his legs in a deliberate show of confident masculinity.

Samantha's eyes darted towards his now open groin area and she inwardly flinched. *Was that an erection beneath his trousers?* She blinked nervously and swiftly turned away, her cheeks flushing.

'Where will you be going?' he asked with his affected velvety tone.

Samantha smiled falsely. 'We haven't decided.'

'Is it...' he leaned towards her conspiratorially. 'Just... the two of you?'

Samantha caught Michelle's eyes staring wide at her from across the room. Michelle flashed an urgent look of caution, wobbling her head from side to side and then ducked low when Jeremy quickly turned in her direction.

'I may bring my boyfriend... and his rugby friends,' Samantha replied. 'I haven't decided yet.'

'Well,' Jeremy drooled, now leaning his weight through a hand placed directly in front of her. 'You've got my number.' He looked over at Michelle's desk just as her head disappeared behind the computer monitor once again. 'We could get together separately, if you like. I could...' he hesitated and then parted his lips looking intentionally down at her mouth with doe-eyes. '...I could thank you properly for all of your hard work since Deborah left.'

Samantha glanced again over at Michelle, who again ducked behind her screen as Jeremy followed Samantha's line of sight. He stood up from the desk and put a gentle hand on

Samantha's shoulder. 'I'll wait to hear from you,' he whispered. 'It'll be fun. I promise.'

As he walked away from the desk he glared over at Michelle who stayed low until he had left the room.

'Bloody hell, Sammie! Stay well away. Do not meet up with him under any circumstances.'

'Don't stress, I'm not going to. He's totally gross.'

'Is your boyfriend really going out with you?'

'No – at least, he wasn't. I might ask him along now though.' She laughed and turned to the door. Singleton was standing on the other side of the half-frosted glass looking directly back at her.

Samantha blushed and lowered her head.

'Right, that's me done,' Michelle said pushing her chair tight up to the desk. 'Thank God it's Friday! Do you want me to wait for you? We can walk to the station together.'

'No, it's alright. I need to pop to the shops, but thanks.'

'Okay, hun. Well have a lovely time tomorrow, sounds like it could be *interesting*.' She flashed her mascara-painted eyelids and they both sniggered.

'Thanks, Miche. And you. Take care and see you on Monday.'

Michelle wrapped a vibrant coloured silk scarf around her neck, pulled on her rain jacket and left the room with a breezy wave. Samantha took her iPhone out of her clutch bag and typed a quick message to her boyfriend before leaving the office.

Just leaving. I'll pick up some Choo Choo. Home in about an hour xxxxxx

Corkers wine shop was just a five-minute walk from the office along Cotham Hill and a further thirty-minute walk downhill to Temple Meads train station where she caught a sprinter to her flat, which she shared with her boyfriend, Dan. Samantha could have used any of the dozen convenience stores on a more direct route to the station, but none of them stocked her favourite brand of wine: Bacchus Rosso Piceno Ciu Ciu, or *Choo Choo* as it was pronounced and more easily referred to. She first tasted the moorish red at her favourite Italian restaurant and it had become a staple favourite since.

Bottle in hand, she turned into St Michaels Road and began the long descent towards Bristol city centre. The cool fine drizzle that had clung to her face like a second skin just moments before, was turning into something more persistent and overtly annoying. She pulled the hood of her canary yellow mac up over her head and pulled the belt a little tighter around her waist as the rain began to bite. She enjoyed the changing seasons, but couldn't wait for the first hints of spring to arrive. It had been a long drawn-out winter. Samantha loved photography and would often visit the Downs with her digital SLR camera, or her swanky new iPhone 11, taking photos that she would share with the rest of the world on social media. Hashtag *naturepic* and hashtag *ourplanet* being her two personal favourites to tag to her images.

Although this route took longer to walk than the more direct pavements of Whiteladies Road, Samantha much preferred the solace this offered as opposed to the throng of pedestrians escaping their weekly office routines. Of course, a few people still attempted the steep incline of St Michael's Hill, but today with the penetrating rain, they were clearly only here if they had to be. As she approached the lower end of the road, she looked back over her shoulder. She was alone, but an inner voice was telling her to move a little quicker between strides. She didn't get easily spooked, but began to quicken her pace. Nearing the disused church on the high section of raised pavement, she became aware of a dark figure hovering near to a row of trees in her path. She knew the area well, walking it most days. A hot spot for the local graffiti artists trying their luck at becoming the next *Banksy*, but even they would be lying low in this weather.

She reached the corner of the abandoned church building and the first evergreen tree, from which she'd spied the lurking figure. Now walking briskly, she removed her mobile phone and put it to her ear.

'Yeah, that's right,' she said loudly. 'That's me by the church…' She paused to get the effect of someone talking back to her on the phone. 'You can see me? Great!' She waved high in the air as if acknowledging someone ahead on the lower, far side of the road. 'I'll be with you in a second.' She put the phone down to her side, but kept the screen active. The dark hooded figure stepped out into her path looking down to the opposite pavement below them – the way she'd just waved. She tightened her grip around the white recycled paper wrapping the neck of the wine bottle and hugged the metal railings at the side of the tall pavement as she passed the trees. The figure countered the movement and the gap between them swiftly closed. Samantha was now upon him, but he was still facing away. Seven feet, six, five… her breath became shallow and she took a deep gulp of air. Simultaneously and with one smooth, fluid motion, the stranger swivelled to face Samantha and with a sudden sharp thrust of a hand, grabbed her throat forcing what little air she had out of her mouth as her feet were literally swept up off the floor and she found herself 'floating' backwards at speed through the trees and towards the church building. She clawed at the hand gripping her throat. She wanted to scream but the force of pressure around her windpipe was preventing any noise from escaping. A second hand joined the first and the pain and fear intensified. She became aware of her feet bouncing and bumping off rubble and debris left by years of damage to the old church, before being slammed down backwards onto a hard stone surface, forcing the remaining capacity of her lungs to escape in one massive surge. Her mobile phone spilled to the ground. The wine bottle was no longer in her grasp. She looked up desperately at the kneeling attacker, unable to see anything of his face other than two intense cold eyes peering down upon her through the narrow slits of a balaclava. He said no words. There was no heavy breathing. No sound of exertion whatsoever. The hands around her neck were pressing tighter and tighter, the thumbs pushing down like crushing vices on her windpipe. The pain was unbearable, but the shock and fear cast that far into the shadows. Samantha's eyes rolled backwards and she noticed the high fractured and open roof of the derelict church. Rain dribbled down and patted gently onto the stone floor around her. She couldn't call out. Couldn't scream. Couldn't fight back. Darkness filled the periphery of her vision, until slowly, uncontrollably the darkness closed in like an old TV set shutting down to a final, faint, hazy circle of vanishing light. And then everything went black.

He stood astride his victim and assessed his work. It was a shame: she was a fine looking young woman, but a job was a job. The day he saw it as anything other than that would be the day he'd get sloppy and make mistakes. And he didn't make mistakes.

He had watched her every Friday for the last three weeks, waiting for the conditions to be just right. He almost had to abort again today, but the weather app on his mobile phone hadn't let him down. He needed the rain and it had come just in time. He lifted his right foot over the body, paying attention to the watery footprint disappearing away on the stone floor leaving no trace. A quick glance back outside satisfied him that nobody had noticed and even if they had, he'd be out of here long before any police could arrive. His escape route was well planned. Twenty-three seconds and he'd be back on his motorcycle and soon after that he'd be in amongst the heavy commuter traffic and able to take one of four different directions away from the scene. No one would be any the wiser. No one would bat an eyelid. This was what he was trained to do. Blend. Execute. Blend. He leant down and felt for a pulse through latex-sleeved fingers. She was dead. The job was done.

To be continued…

Buy *DEAD RINGER* today!

BOOKS BY JAMES D MORTAIN

DETECTIVE DEANS

Book One

STORM LOG-0505

Could his best lead be a voice from beyond the grave...?

DETECTIVE DEANS

Book Two
DEAD BY DESIGN

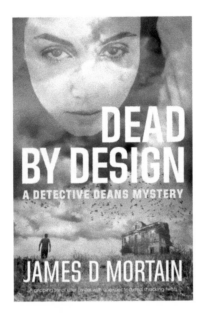

How far would you go to save the lives you love most?

DETECTIVE DEANS

Book Three
THE BONE HILL

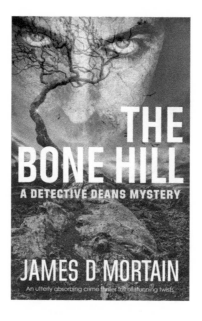

A killer at large. A gift obscured by tragedy. One last chance
for justice…

DI CHILCOTT

Book One
DEAD RINGER

Two Dead. No Witnesses. One Hope…

Book Two *COMING 2021*
Book Three *COMING 2021*

ACKNOWLEDGMENTS

Being a writer isn't a glamorous existence. Many sacrifices have to be made, especially when you are trying to write aside a 'normal' day job. Unfortunately, the nearest and dearest endure the brunt of these sacrifices. It is not always easy. My writing priorities don't necessarily correlate with family priorities and there is a fine balance that has to be tread, and so I owe my family a great debt of gratitude.

I must send a huge thank you to many other people who have helped to create this book. To my superb editor, Debbie Hobbs-Wyatt who makes the editing process so painless and to my brilliant cover designer, Jessica Bell. Not forgetting, my fantastic background team of advisers: Terry Galbraith, Phil Croll, Varun Sharma and Barbara Olive. I now have a team behind me that I can truly rely upon to help me make the best books possible.

Thank you to my team of Advance Readers, many of whom have become friends. You give me the encouragement to keep going through the gloomiest of days. Your support means everything to me. Once again, the support of my local community in North Devon has been unbelievable. You are a very special bunch of people and I am lucky to know many of you and call you my friends.

Finally, a sincere thank you to all of the readers who take the time to review my books and contact me. You give me the hope that writing can one day be my full-time occupation. Your kind words and encouragement truly mean the world to me.

Thank you all.

ALSO BY JAMES D MORTAIN

Photograph Copyright of Mick Kavanagh Photography.

Former British CID Detective, turned crime fiction writer, James brings compelling action and gritty authenticity to his writing through years of police experience. Originally from Bath, England, James now lives in North Devon with his family and is happiest when creating fictional mystery and mayhem.

Don't miss the latest releases by following James on Amazon, Bookbub and Goodreads.

Visit www.jamesdmortain.com to get your free copy of *The Real Story Behind Detective Deans*.

Please email jdm@manverspublishing.com to contact James.

facebook.com/jamesdmortain
twitter.com/@jamesdmortain
instagram.com/jamesmortain

9 780993 568787